Sweet Jessamine

WANDA MILLER

Sweet Jessamine

ISBN 978-0-692-29950-0

Acknowledgements

Thank you to my father in heaven for his favor, grace and mercy; to my wonderful husband, Kasiem, for being my rock. I love you baby; to my parents, William and Hanna for your teachings and patience that brought out the voice of an introvert daughter; to my sisters, Wendy and Kim, for all the love and support and for being the greatest siblings anyone could ask. I love you both so very much: to my brothers, Anthony and Ryan you guys are the best, I love you dearly; and to the rest of my awesome family, I love you all.

Contents

Chapter 1

Virginia 1940

"Come with me baby, I'll do you real good like you ain't ever been done before."

Evelyn Harris's voice sent lustful vibrations through his body. The look she gave him suggested there was more raunchy talk to come as her hands rubbed the inner part of his thigh. She aimed to get Abraham Davis excited and judging by the expanding bulge in his pants she knew she was succeeding.

He was extremely handsome with coal black hair that curled slightly at the nape of his neck, a trim mustache, massive barrel-like chest and heavily muscled arms. His chocolate eyes were rather nice as well and especially popular with the women around town. He wasn't excessively tall like his brothers but at five eleven his body was intimidating, and made even the brawniest of men think twice before challenging him to a fight. At thirty-four he was of stocky build and in excellent condition. No one wanted a taste of his huge fists, the short jab being favorite ways to knock his opponents clean to their knees.

Abraham tossed back his fifth glass of Kentucky bourbon. Closing his eyes to allow its potency to overtake him, he signaled the man behind the bar to pour him another, the warm liquid slowly coursing through his body. It was a great way to forget the stress of his job, depression of being poor, and the fact his wife's vagina was no longer what he desired. Her younger sister, on the other hand, was definitely his flavor, for now.

Dancehall Sugar Baby's had everything a man could need: music, liquor, dancing, and big breasted women. He pulled Evelyn onto his lap and watched as she drank the contents of his glass while looking over the rim with lust in her eyes.

Bringing her breasts up against his chest so he could see right into her big thick bosoms; she licked his ear while whispering heated words meant to entice. Abraham grabbed a handful of her luscious derriere and pushed her forward. He always wondered how she did it. Being a school teacher by day and a whore by night couldn't be an easy task. She was the bread winner for the house, raising two boys, one stayed in Virginia with the father and the other in Maryland with her. Her sorry ass husband, lazy and out of work, stayed home most days, preferring to be in his own miserable state of mind. A man like that wasn't respected and always had jabs thrown at him by others in the small working class town.

Abraham could take better care of her than her husband could, and he knew it. He also knew the moment they laid eyes on one another he was going to have her. The temptation was far too great to pass up, going from once a- month bedding to almost four times a month. He had become obsessed with wanting her. Her body was like eating a hot apple pie straight from the oven, sure to burn the hell out of you but so delicious when you tasted it.

He wanted at least a couple more hours with her until she went back to Maryland; knowing he may not see her again for weeks, he wanted to make every minute count. His wife was constantly pregnant, year after year, a fact she never ceased to let him forget when he was home. Mary was always nagging, demanding he take out the trash, or vomiting upon occasion, sending him straight to Sugar Baby's to get away from her. He loved his six kids, especially the oldest girl Christina, who had just turned nine years old, but sometimes they required too much of his attention. Evelyn, on the other hand, could get all the attention she wanted. She was his breath of fresh air, the peace he got away from home. He just wished he could have it all the time as his face buried itself again in her sweet bosom. And with every minute that ticked by he knew the time was drawing closer for his manhood to be in between the best pair of legs this side of the Mason Dixon line.

Abraham was trying to focus his attention on the beautiful woman in front of him, but the commotion across the dimly lit club was distracting him from Evelyn's lustful advances. He pulled Evelyn towards his inner thigh, spanking her bottom to keep it still while he tried to focus on one worker's voice that drew the most attention.

Butch Curtis was a senior track worker for the C & 6 Railroad Company with over forty years of service. Everyone respected him, not just because he was older but because he taught Abraham as well as others section hand work and bridge repair. There weren't many older workers who survived the harsh conditions the railroad offered, so for someone like Butch Curtis to be present to teach the younger generation was not only a blessing but a miracle. If you wanted to know anything involving the railroad, including who to ask for steady work, you asked Butch Curtis.

"Whatcha sayin', Curtis? Them bosses got something planned out there?" One of the men spoke up from the group.

"I'm sayin' somethin ain't right when a man is fired without notice or just cause."

"How you know that, Curtis?"

"Two weeks ago Curly Thomas got fired for nothing. Then just yesterday, Boss man got a new Ford!"

"So maybe he saved up or somethin'."

Curtis shook his head with an exhausted look on his face. Trying to convince these men was taking more time then he cared to admit, and his patience was wearing thin.

"You kiddin? They make money off us then they dump us. You boys got to pay attention. Stuff ain't right out here and it's time we do somethin' about it."

"Aw, Curtis, them bosses can do whatever they want. We can't cause we ain't got a union like they do up north in Cheecago."

Butch looked him directly in the eye. "We need to stand up for what's right."

"What you 'spec tin' us to do, Curtis?"

He took seconds to answer. "We got to strike."

The room's silence quickly rumbled to life as everyone started talking, voicing their opinions. Some thought the idea was crazy and that Curtis had truly lost his mind. Others were all for it, betting that size in numbers could intimidate the employers to meet their demands. It was hard for Abraham to figure out who thought what because each man shouted louder than the next, trying to be heard. Finally Curtis hushed the crowd.

"We have to doin' somethin', else they'll think they can just walk all over us without as much as a warning."

There were a few grumbles of objection as some men shook their heads and ordered more shots from the bar. Abraham watched a few accept Curtis invitation and listened as he tried to further convince these men how the hourly wages and working conditions needed to be addressed. He agreed the wages weren't at all what they could've been. His cousin's wages in DC were much higher at one-hundred dollars a month while his were a meager seventy-seven dollars. This would be all right if it was just him by himself but he had a wife and children to support. Seventy-seven dollars wasn't shit and was downright pathetic when you asked around. He was in his prime, after all, and the railroad provided high status on a significant level just below the military, which, for a black man in the nineteen forty's, was a great accomplishment. Nervous tension began to build in his body like a pressure valve. If something were to happen, who would be there to get them out of this mess? Most of these men had never thought of a strike in their town, let alone being a part of one.

They would need more than five men if they wanted the bosses to listen. Abraham wondered why Curtis wanted the strike so soon. What was in it for him if this thing went all the way through? One thing was definitely certain; if they stirred in this shit long enough it would stink. A true saying especially now since this stink was going to spread across Henry County. Curtis made his way around the club looking for men to champion his cause. And despite his longing to retire upstairs with Evelyn, fear held Abraham in his place. He felt pressure to go along with the strike, as five more men joined the group.

What was a hard-working man to do in a situation like this? How was he to support his cheating if worked stopped for him? He showed all his whores a good time paying them well, even accommodating a drink or two. Now, he had to hear of a strike and whether his job would be in jeopardy. It wasn't an option to go without work nowadays, especially with his wife pregnant again for the sixth time.

Curtis's voice rang out in anger. "Look here, fellas. Besides the money the bosses ain't doin' enough to keep us from getting killed on the job. We dyin' every month while they sit behind a desk collectin' on our insurance."

There were additional murmurs of agreement but no one budged. Abraham wondered if they were just as tired of hearing Curtis talk as they were with the poor working conditions.

"They can afford better work areas and paying us more money if they wanted to," Curtis replied.

Abraham knew this to be true. On more than one occasion there were rumors when men started asking questions about the working conditions and their wages they were either fired or had their work station ruined. Just three days ago, he overheard Gilroy, the head boss, talking to someone about firing a couple of workers. He followed Gilroy back to the office to discuss concerns he'd had about workers' safety. They were perched against the desk talking about their plans of firing workers to meet their own needs. It was enough to make Abraham's blood boil, but it also caused enough discomfort for him to keep quiet around the other workers, only telling his wife when he went home.

Now it was a different story, as there were men willing to confront them for the same reason he heard not too long ago. This could be the time to take action and be known for something greater in life other than a kicking ball for rich folks.

Pride made Abraham pay attention to Curtis's words, despite his longing to retire upstairs with big tits Evelyn. Soon five more men joined Butch's cause. This group now numbered ten men, middle aged and fit, who had been on the job a total of more than twenty years of service to the company. Long enough to know how things were done and to never question the head boss or the people working above them. What was a hard-working man to do in a situation like this?

Two more men affirmed they'd go with Curtis and the ten rail workers he already had with him. One of the men said he had two brothers outside of town that might be willing to help with the strike, and he left the club to go look for them. With twelve men set to go and others waiting to jump on the bandwagon, Butch Curtis turned his crinkled brown eyes on Abraham, who had been listening the whole time.

"What do you say, Davis? You coming with us or not?" he asked.

Abraham thrust Evelyn off his lap but kept hold of her arm as he approached Curtis. "Shouldn't you be telling the boss man about this? Maybe he can talk some sense into the head man."

The old rail worker chuckled for a second. "You think boss man gonna listen to a lowly Negro worker such as yourself or any of us? They don't care about our black asses, just their own."

"So how are we supposed to get them to listen?"

"The only way to get this thing done is to meet them head on with a united front. As long as we're of one accord can't no one or anything touch us."

"I don't know, Curtis. We're just workers needing to feed our families."

"Listen, son, them bosses been cheatin' everyone since I was a young-un and they ain't stopped yet. They greedy, and greed begets greed. They've cheated me for the last time and I won't stand for it." He eyeballed Abraham. "You coming with us?"

Abraham had settled on the word "no" when Curtis started his rambling, but that quickly changed when he realized his job could be on the chopping block any day now, and he knew their plan hadn't come to a final decision yet. If those bosses decided to get rid of him he was gonna be in some real deep shit. Abraham set his eyes tightly on Butch Curtis and finally revealed what he'd heard.

"I overheard them bosses talking about firing some workers a couple days ago. They've got it in their head they want to reap the benefits of workers they let go so they can have more money for themselves. It's supposed to happen sometime this month. They have to fire enough workers before the head man notices. They'll be at the rail tracks tomorrow about forty minutes north of here for another meeting."

"Well hell, boy, why didn't you say somethin' in the first place?" Curtis cried. "That's just the salt we need to shake things up and get started on this thing here."

"Do you really think they would fire hard workin' men over somethin' like that?" Abraham asked. "It seems stupid to fire good workers that could make you more money than if you were by yourself."

"It's what they call easy money son. If you fire your help without anyone knowing, what happens to the money that's owed to them?"

Abraham was poised to answer but Curtis beat him to it. "Well, I'll tell you what happens to it. The head man keeps it. If no one is there to collect money and the workers are still on the books in name only, them bosses gonna reap the benefit."

He nodded his understanding. This was the first time he had heard such a thing happening in the area before, as there had been no reason to doubt his employers when it came to paying him his well-deserved wage. So long as the bosses were filling in the time where these men normally work they could pocket the money without anyone knowing. This whole thing started to make sense to Abraham as Curtis kept up his ranting.

"Same thing here. They want to get rid of perfectly good workers for the hell of it. Those assholes got another thing coming if they think they gonna take old Curtis out. They can plot, plan all they want to, but we'll see who gets the last laugh. Were they local bosses or state?"

"They were local. The big bosses up state wear suits and ties to supervise everyone else underneath them. Local bosses try to fit in with everyone, wearing what we wear."

Butch grimaced. "One boss would be okay. Three is pushing it. We need all the hands we can get."

"My car can hold at least five men."

"I got a horse and wagon with me. It can hold two if no one minds the bumpy ride. I don't have a car or truck like you young fellas."

"You can ride with me, Curtis," Abraham offered.

"What about my horse?"

"You can come by my house tonight after everyone is asleep and leave it there. My wife can watch after it until we come back. There's a couch near the fireplace where you can sleep if you want."

Butch slapped Abraham between the shoulder blades. "Sounds good, son when are we leaving?"

"First shift starts at seven in the morning. If we all meet here around six, we can go together to confront them as a group. Then they'll have no choice but to listen."

Abraham looked at Evelyn, who winked and smiled. As long as Curtis didn't want to leave right this minute, he was going to stay where his body wanted to be the most, and he wasn't about to turn a sweet temptation like Evelyn down. Tomorrow would be a different story altogether. He took her by the hand and led her up the stairway. "I've got some things to take care of," he said, looking at Evelyn. "Be sure to tell my wife I'll see her tomorrow."

"Make sure you don't oversleep, Davis," Abraham heard Curtis say as he and the other men laughed while leaving the dancehall.

The only thing he was thinking of was the succulent goodness between the sweetest pair of legs in Mills-town, Virginia.

Fog had settled in the next morning, making it difficult to see. Abraham quickly dressed, leaving his sleeping mistress to pick up

Curtis and meet the men back at the dancehall. There were fifteen men altogether on their way to the rail yards. Seven were from Richmond, and the rest were from Henry County. Abraham's best friend Charles Stewart decided to join in on the strike even though he didn't work at the railroad. The other's had everything at stake. William and Robert Jenkins were cousins and first generation rail workers. Ali Crable was a senior bridge worker much like Butch Curtis, who was looking to cash in at his retirement. They picked up the remaining four men driving past Caroline County: Terry Henderson, John Pickney, Joe Morris, and Henry Pleasant. All men intended to stand together to iron out differences they had with the bosses and to hopefully save their jobs. They reached the rail yards early before anyone else. Abraham was so nervous he had to relieve himself before joining the men. His bladder didn't seem to want to hold this day like it did any other time.

The men were silent as they looked around at the stillness of their surroundings. The marshaling yards were scattered with old rails, piles of coal, water tanks, and railway sheds. Bits of grass peeked out from between the old rails and hardware strewn about the area. The bleakness of the site would make some cringe to step foot there, yet to the men this area was like a second home. They spent most of their time at the rail yards, well over six days a week, operating every piece of machinery from the locomotives to the rail corridor where trains came to rest from their long travels. They also helped assemble goods to be loaded onto the rail cars headed for destinations unknown, and took pride in their work.

They made their way to the office door and stood there watching the road for familiar cars or trucks, the clanking of irons could be heard miles away. The fog didn't seem like it wanted to leave as the sun slowly crept over the horizon to mark the start of the morning. It was hard to imagine all of this could be taken away from them with one nod of the head or flip of the tongue by some pencil-pushing punks who thought it best to fire hardworking men for their own gain. Why, the sheer thought of not being able to work made Abraham's anger rise, and what was even worse, they didn't give a damn.

"Are we too early?" asked Joe. "Maybe they decided to take the day off."

"Bosses come to work any time they feel like it. That's somethin' we'll never be able to do and they know it. Good thing we're here before they are," Curtis replied.

"Seems to me we got good time and representation on our side boys," Terry said.

"If the bosses all come here at once—"

"That will never happen."

"How do you know, Pleasant? They could make it a point to all be here just for the hell of it."

"Bosses don't make plans, they create them," John pointed out.

"It's too early, plus they might be at the whore house down the road. Davis can tell you a little something 'bout that."

"Shut up, Pickney. What the hell do you know about it?" Abraham asked.

"I know if I had a pretty pregnant wife at home, no woman whore or otherwise could make me leave. I see you at the hall sometimes, but I don't say nothing thinkin' you'll learn sooner or later."

"Well, good you don't say nothing. Just mind your own damn business."

"I don't think they're at the whore house, Big John," Curtis interjected.

"How do you know that?"

"Just a feelin I got. Davis, you sure they was gonna be here this morning? Or did you get the days mixed up?" Curtis asked.

Abraham looked annoyed. If it's one thing he hated the most it was answering the same question he had already answered before. "Yes, dammit, they said they'd be here today, right here in the office. All we have to do is wait so we can talk to them."

"I'm sick of waiting already. I might go to that whore house after all," Johnny said, rubbing the center of his pants.

"You couldn't get it up if someone spit on it, Johnny Boy," Abraham replied.

All the men laughed at this statement. Johnny Boy's reputation as a quick draw went through the gossip rounds fairly quickly as each woman had to see if what the other said was true. On more than one occasion the whores from Sugar Baby's mentioned Johnny Boy sails went down just as quickly as they went up. He was known to be in the room one minute and down at the bar the next ordering more whiskey shots before he took another woman upstairs. Quick draw was putting it nicely when the working girls referred to Johnny.

"My dick is a tree trunk, Davis. What the hell do you know about it?" Johnny asked, gesturing to his crotch and clearly proud of his physicality.

"You'd have to fold it up in the women for them to feel it Johnny."

The men lowered their faces, and covered their mouths to keep from laughing out loud.

"It better than yours Davis, ask around."

Abraham looked at him and laughed. "My Johnson is well known around Mills-town. Just ask your wife."

"Why you no good son of a bitch!"

"Good God, you two sound like old women," Curtis said. "We're not getting anywhere standing around here doing nothing. Let's pack it up and go home. We'll try this another time when the bosses will sure enough be here."

"Easy, Curtis. They're late is all. Maybe they decided not to come in this morning. If that's the case then I'll find out their whereabouts," Abraham said.

"Alright, we'll give it a good fifteen minutes and then we're going."

"Hey, who's in the brown car coming up here? Maybe it's not a lost cause after all."

"There's another one not too far behind," Johnny replied, sounding nervous.

The men braced themselves for what was about to happen. They hadn't prepared for what they were going to tell the bosses, just that they weren't going to stand for being fired for no apparent reason, especially when they worked their asses off for the railroad on a daily basis.

11

They needed guarantees, but some feared their questions wouldn't get answered even if they did outnumber their superiors five to one.

"Just be sure you ask them if our jobs are at stake, then we can maybe negotiate some things." Joe Morris spoke for the first time since pulling into the yard.

"We need to make our demands known so they take us seriously."

They all nodded their agreement as the first car came into view. "Abraham, you didn't give me a proper kiss goodbye," Evelyn yelled from the brown Chevrolet.

They all let out curses, some kicking the ground and others throwing their hands in the air at the woman they had seen Abraham with the other night.

"And just how did you think you were supposed to leave me, huh? High, horny, and dry?"

Abraham smiled. Evelyn did have a flair for the dramatic. He waited while she got out of the car, watching her hips sashay towards him before saying, "I thought you were headed back to Maryland."

"I couldn't leave without giving you a goodbye kiss, baby. I really needed to see you."

They were wrapped in each other's arms again. Abraham didn't think he'd ever get enough of this woman. Warm and supple, she molded to him like cooking lard to a hot skillet. Three minutes later a black Ford woody style station wagon turned into the rail yard and came to a complete stop in front of the men.

Abraham didn't notice the woman getting out and greeting the men as she looked for her husband. She was very pregnant and carrying a lunch pail in her right hand. It was Abraham's wife. Some of the men groaned inwardly and others chuckled, knowing that any minute they were about to witness what was going to be a huge blow-up for the day. They may not have gotten any action out of speaking to the bosses yet, but by God they were going to get some right now with this little show that was about to take place.

Evelyn reveled in Abraham's arms, pressing herself against his hard chest. Her back was turned from the rest of the men as she was concentrating solely on her beau. "You gonna give me a kiss before you go, sugar?"

Abraham smiled. "You know it, baby."

They kissed each other passionately, oblivious to the woman who was making her way through the crowd of nervous men.

"Abraham, you left your lunch and…"

Switching positions so quickly that he almost knocked his kissing partner over, Abraham was a bit surprised to find his wife standing in front of him.

"Mary, what are you doing here?" Abraham blocked Evelyn, almost shielding her so his wife couldn't see her face.

"I came here to give you your lunch that I left on the table, seeing as you didn't come home last night. But I can clearly see you've already started lunch."

"Thanks, baby."

He kissed his wife on the cheek and took the lunch from her. She waited for his explanation but he stood in front of her as if he hadn't just been sticking his tongue down the tramp's throat a couple seconds ago. She finally decided to confront him on his obvious indiscretion.

"So who is this?" she asked, gesturing to the woman behind him.

"Who is this? This is just a friend of mine coming to see me before she leaves."

"She got a name? Cause anyone caught kissing my husband must have some kind of name." Her hands were lightly stroking her protruding belly. "I'm sure I can think of a few names right now."

Evelyn stepped up beside Abraham to face her older sister. "That won't be necessary, Mary."

The slap was heard amongst everyone in the group as all eyes were now directed at the two sisters. Mary had closed the gap between her and her sister upon that bit of news. Evelyn placed a hand on the cheek that was now red and stinging from the powerful slap her sister had just given her.

"It was never my intention to hurt you, Mary, but I'm in love with Abraham. I was the moment we met."

Shock and dismay covered the older sister's face "He has six children, Evelyn, six and a wife who loves him dearly. You think you can just take that away?"

"We didn't plan this, Mary. It just happened. What do you want me to say?"

"I don't want you to say anything, Evelyn. I want you to be able to look at our kids and tell them their auntie will be taking their daddy away for good." She shook her head and fought back tears. "Do you really think you're the only pussy he's with at the moment?"

Evelyn observed at Abraham with a questioning look. He simply shrugged his shoulders as the men chuckled behind him. Their knowledge of his indiscretions was already known; hers it seemed was just catching up. Mary realized her sister had no clue as to the whore Abraham really was. "Don't tell me you thought you were the only one he's had in our marriage."

Evelyn's face registered hurt and confusion. Since the moment they met she and Abraham were inseparable. She came down as often as possible to make sure he was the only man she was going to bed with, besides her husband. Mary, reading her sister's face, quickly jumped at the opportunity to clue her in.

"Let me give you some information. For over a year Abraham has been screwing not only you but women down the street and every other whore nasty enough to open her legs to him."

Evelyn looked at her lover for confirmation, but he only had a smirk plastered on his lips. She took that to mean he thought his wife was lying.

"I don't believe you. How do I know you're telling the truth?"

"This question is coming from the sister that's been telling lies to her entire family? I bet you've been planning this the whole time."

"No! I didn't want any of this to happen, it just did. I swear I wasn't thinking about you when we first got together."

"Of course you weren't thinking. If you did you'd know that my heart would be breaking right now knowing that my little sister is screwing my husband behind my back."

Mary fought back tears that threatened to appear. Of all the people in her life, she didn't think her sister Evelyn would betray her so easily. They were only two years apart and the closest out of thirteen children. She even considered her a best friend and was more hurt than surprised at what she saw when she walked up on them. She knew Abraham was seeing someone else because he hadn't touched her in months. His pattern with screwing around was consistent and she knew when it happened with the little to no sex going on at home. Her feelings changed from sad to angry just above boiling level as she looked her sister in the eyes.

"You are dead to me. From now on you will stay the hell away from my family."

"What about my nieces and nephews? Are you going to keep them away from me too? How are they supposed to get to know one another as a family?"

"You don't care about your nieces and nephews. You can barely keep up with your own kids, being up north with Lewis and down here with Roger. Lewis doesn't even know half his family because his mother would rather fuck her brother-in-law than her own husband."

"Lewis has learning issues so I have to keep him with me. I'm the only one that can teach him correctly."

"Well now, isn't that funny. He'll be learning how to be a whore from a professional."

"That's not fair, Mary. You don't know what it's like to have a husband that doesn't want to work cause he's been fired from every job there is."

"So you try to steal mine? What kind of sense does that make?"

Evelyn knew she was losing this battle. Her sister could barely look at her. She tried to salvage what little relationship she had left. "Listen, Mary, I know you're upset with me, but these kids need one another just like you and me need each other."

Mary pointed just inches from her face. "You weren't thinking about my kids or yours when you had your legs in the air now were you? Screwing my husband means more to you than the love you have for your family."

Evelyn didn't know what to say. She knew one day she and Abraham's relationship would be discovered, but she couldn't have predicted this horrible outcome would hurt as much as it did as tears made their way down her face.

"Please don't say that, Mary. I love my children, my nieces and nephews. Don't hold what I've done with Abraham against me."

Mary looked at her as if she didn't see her. The betrayal had come full circle and it was now time to face the consequences.

"You'll never see your nieces and nephews again. You made your bed, Evelyn. Now sleep in it like the dog you are."

"Mary! No, Mary!" Evelyn shouted, but to no avail. Her sister didn't even acknowledge her voice as she turned around and left.

Abraham watched the scene unfold before him: His pregnant wife walking back to the family car supporting her lower back, his mistress calling after her in distress. It was almost comical. He made no move to console either one. Mary sped off down the road like a bat out of hell. She would cool off before he got home, he was sure of it. He really wished she hadn't caught him in the act like that, but now since it happened he didn't need to hide his feelings for Evelyn anymore. She would eventually understand and everything would go back to normal as it had been.

He would still have a mistress on the side taking care of his needs when his wife wouldn't. Figuring out where he wanted to live would have to wait until later. His kids needed him, so Mary would have to understand his need to keep his kids close while he figured out what to do next. He heard Evelyn sobbing and groaned inwardly. Did she have to make a scene in front of the guys? He knew this sister would need more time to figure this all out. He didn't know how to comfort her either and decided this was as good a time as any to talk to the guys about their plans. The day's events weren't turning out as well as he'd planned. Hopefully that would change with what they were about to do. This was just a little setback. Abraham adjusted his shirt and went to join the men.

"I guess you lost both women, eh, Davis?" Crable said with a slight smirk.

"Hell no I'll be back home in the bed before you can say shuckin' corn," Abraham said arrogantly.

"Will you listen to that, boys? He thinks he's John Wayne, except the only thing he's slangin' is his dick," Pleasant added.

"Women are too much of a distraction. It's time to get serious, fellas, if we want to do this right," Curtis said.

"What the hell are we doing, fellas?" Johnny demanded. "We come all the way out here and there ain't no bosses to voice our problems to. What we gonna do? Just leave without sayin' anything?"

"Cool it, Johnny Boy. We gotta be careful 'bout this. If we rush it we stand to lose more than our jobs. Ain't that right, Curtis?"

"That's right," Curtis said angrily. "We gotta get this right if we're going to see our demands met."

Evelyn closed her eyes for a moment. This wasn't what she had envisioned when telling her sister she was in love with her husband. She shouldn't have been shocked by what just happened, but she was, and it hurt that much more to know they both were the cause of her sister's pain. The black station wagon had disappeared down the road, and she was staring at the place where her sister not too long ago disowned her. Evelyn spotted Abraham surrounded by the men, laughing and being patted on the back. She walked towards the car and waited for him to notice her. Abraham didn't make a move. He continued his conversation as though his wife hadn't just shown up and caught them groping and kissing each other. What nerve! Was he that conceited and self-absorbed? She felt a sinking feeling in her stomach and wanted to sit on the hard gravel beneath her feet. What had she gotten herself into? Was this the man she wanted to be with, someone who had no sense of feeling or emotion? Someone who could hurt people and not care one way or another? Her husband was nothing like this. In fact he was the exact opposite: a homebody, yes, but he loved and respected her. He was nothing like this man, and after a couple of minutes of him ignoring her she was more than emotionally upset, she was pissed.

"Abraham, I need to talk to you," Evelyn shouted across the rail yard. Her voice resonated with such abruptness it made the men, including Abraham, look in her direction.

He didn't answer, but his expletive suggested he was annoyed with her pulling him away from the raucous group. He dragged Evelyn by the arm just out of earshot from the men, and held both sides of her face. His arrogance was beyond her comprehension. A self-serving asshole meant to destroy, and he did. He was the devil and she his slave, and certainly he knew how to mesmerize, didn't he? She'd risked everything for him, her entire family, and her job. Dear God, she'd let him touch her in places her husband never knew existed; yes, she'd given him everything and it would make it that much harder for her to try and move on.

He devoured her with his eyes, this broad chest handsome man, and wore an obsessive expression that more than matched his demeanor. She felt her body gravitate, trembling from the dominance radiating from him. As tempting and enticing as his touch was, she tried to hold fast to her decision not to be swayed. He misunderstood her reaction and stroked the side of her face. "Why did you lie to me, Abraham? How many women have there been?" There was no response except a hunch of the shoulders and a wicked grin from the man that once claimed he loved her. He's not even remorseful, Evelyn thought, and that realization finalized her decision.

Evelyn continued to press him for an answer. Abraham was playing a game and she intended to stop it. "Please, Abraham, if you ever loved me, tell me." She tried to look for some semblance of remorse from this man but there was none. "Or, you can leave me alone."

His eyes seemed to change from charming to cold, and the hand that was stroked the side of her cheek dropped to his side. "Go home, Evelyn. The rail yards are no place for a woman. Let me take care of things here and I'll be in between those sweet thighs as soon as I'm finished." He swatted her on the backside and rejoined the men, leaving her eyeing him with a shocked expression on her face.

Evelyn started the car and pushed hard on the gas. The farther she got away from the rail yards the better. She traveled down the road, vowing to stay away from Abraham Davis forever.

"What do we do now, fellas?" Abraham asked, rejoining the group.

"Seems to me we need to wait," Curtis said. "No sense in leaving when we been waiting this long."

Abraham watched at the group of guys and couldn't help but be annoyed. The wait was becoming unbearable. He usually could clock the bosses by the minute they would come in and start raising cane. For some reason today was different. He couldn't shake the feeling that something wasn't right with this whole scene. They all had waited long enough for the bosses to make an appearance, so why wasn't there anyone here yet?

Five minutes later the crack of pistols and rifles broke into the air, as men scattered to get behind piles of steel and hills of wooden planks. Some bullets claimed their targets, while others went flying in all directions around them, inserting themselves in office buildings and surrounding trailers. The roar of the truck engines racing into the yard alerted the rest of the living to the approaching threat as gunmen scattered to find the remaining men. They were trapped like rats in a cage as the murderers surrounded them, torrential noise of gunfire and screams were heard mixed with shouts of triumph.

The eerie silence that followed was nothing like Abraham had ever experienced, as he'd sought shelter behind one of the rail cars parked in the yard, and waited until these men appetite for killing was satisfied. His heart pounded with extreme fierceness. With men now on the ground, one of them spotted Abraham crouched behind the rail car and headed for him. Abraham realized that the man meant to kill him. There wasn't any escape other than running to the nearest empty rail car, which was twenty feet away. He'd never make it with the amount of gunfire out there. Abraham squared his shoulders. If he was going to die he'd die fighting the sorry bastards. His children flashed before his eyes. I didn't have enough time with them, he thought as he stood his ground and waited for the gunman to find him. His mind registered his last day on earth as the gunman finally reached Abraham's hiding place. He drew back a little once he saw Abraham's size, quickly drew his gun and fired two shots into his chest. The pain was consuming; the burning sensation never ended as he dropped to his knees. And then an undeniable numbness overcame him as he watched his killer walk away, shouting to the others just before his eyes closed a final time.

When the last shot was fired there were no workers left alive, save for one elder employee who had previously made a deal with the supervisors. In return for revealing what he knew of Davis's ease dropping he would be promoted to a management position receiving additional money on top of decent severance package. It was a business proposition too pretty to pass up. The strike was a definite ploy to get the young rail hand attention, however Curtis didn't know others would be willing to jump on the band wagon and so looked at them as nothing more than collateral damage when they volunteered. They were a good diversion to the real plan at play.

Early that afternoon, fourteen bodies were removed and tossed on the back of a pick-up truck to be carried away. The heavy whistles of trains drowned the roar of truck engines as new cars were being ushered into the rail yards. There would be no one to hear the boss's conversation to get rid of these workers, nor anyone to do an investigation into the deaths of fourteen black men in the rail yards. The only people to mourn these men were their families, the children most of all, for they would grow up without one of the most important beings in their lives, a father.

Chapter 2

Henry County, Virginia, 1950

The walk home seemed to take forever. Evening had turned to night in Mills-town, and with it a cool wind spiraled its way down the street. Its usual serenade was lost, falling on deaf ears as the evening's event played over and over in her mind. When she finally saw Lewis that evening, he stood at the beginning of the gravel road of their meeting place, a white cotton shirt covering his young nubile chest, the only thing visible against the darkening sky.

He greeted her with a simple kiss on the cheek but avoided any other touch or eye contact. She thought that strange since before yesterday it seemed he couldn't keep his hands off her. His potent kisses had left her breathless and wanting more, which was one of the reasons she quickly left the house to meet him. Now his emotionless demeanor and lack of affection couldn't be missed, and everything had gone downhill from there. He hadn't offered any reassurance to their relationship, only allowing the news of their incestuous behavior to permeate her mind. It was unbelievable at first, which is what she told him. How could their relationship be forbidden when they were clearly in love with one another? He ended the meeting with an apology and stated they couldn't be together. She stood stone still; her feet wouldn't allow her to move. He then had the nerve to ask for a reply.

She couldn't say anything and did the only thing she was capable of at that moment; she turned around and walked away, leaving him standing there calling her name. Now during the walk home she felt stuck somewhere between confusion and rage, her heart in pieces, and at this point she didn't know which to concentrate on first. The brown wool coat felt like heavy burlap next to her skin. The tears, now dry against her face, formed two paths on both sides of her cheeks. She didn't hear her shoes hitting the gravel or the cars driving by swerving not to hit her.

Earlier that day Christina had looked forward to seeing Lewis and telling him the wonderful news of her pregnancy. The previous baby had been terminated by the town doctor, and she needed to tell him before this one was taken in the same way. Thankfully she didn't have morning sickness, which would have alerted both her and her mother sooner. The only person she had confided in was her grandmother, who immediately took her to the doctor for the second termination. This one however, was more developed and she quietly rejoiced in the knowledge that she and Lewis would become parents. The need for discretion was important, as Christina was still a teenager living at home and the relationship with her mother was somewhat rocky. Christina was like every other teenager going to the occasional dance, having fun with her friends, and driving without permission every now and again. All of this was against her mother's wishes, as indicated by the many slaps received. She would sneak out of the house for those parties and come back to find the door locked. Sleeping in the back seat of the car was a ritual for her on various occasions, as her mother was against coming in after eight o'clock at night.

Their arguing increased from time to time making communication difficult, and recently, they'd given up daily conversation unless it was about her job at Mrs. Evan's house. The silent treatment was more of what she got from her nowadays, both of them tiptoeing around one another to avoid confrontation. They never really talked.

Her Grandmother, on the other hand, was the only person she could confide in other than Lewis. Christina knew she had to tell him she was pregnant right away before anyone else learned of her secret. She had practiced every line down to the moment where she would tell him about the baby. They would then make preparations for their marriage, each informing their families of the up and coming wedding. The fall season in the small Virginia town was the perfect background setting for conveying the good news, as leaves had turned vibrant colors of yellow, red, and orange. It seemed to be the perfect romantic scene.

But was she in for a huge surprise. As Christina observed the night sky she shook her head in disgust at the whimsical immature notion, and buried her face in her hands. There was no romance now, no love. She should've paid attention to the expression on his face when she arrived at their meeting place. He couldn't quite look her in the eyes and was distant, like he wanted to be somewhere else. She couldn't have imagined what she was asking for was impossible, inconceivable. In addition to being three and half months pregnant, she was alone, unmarried and had mistakenly fallen in love with her cousin. This was going to be the talk of the town. Her cousin! The knowledge of her indiscretion hit her like a ton of bricks, almost causing her to vomit several times on the way home. She had to stop and suck in deep breaths of air to keep the nausea from overtaking her. She couldn't believe her ill-fated luck.

They had met at the County Fair in Fredericksburg, a small town with old colonial estates that sat on the Rappahannock River. It was an annual event at the end of each summer that drew people from everywhere in the state of Virginia. The excitement was palpable that day as she drove the forty-five minutes with her friends to their destination. Mama didn't want Christina going anywhere that wasn't within reach of Mills-town, which meant she didn't have permission unless her mother or uncles were with her. But there were ways around her rules, and Christina made sure she was two steps ahead when it came to breaking them.

This time she enlisted the help of her friends and their parents, who were more than willing to back her story, seeing as how she was a "good" influence on their daughters. There were a number of people from all over enjoying the festivities when she and her friends finally got there. They were so thirsty from their long ride they immediately paid for their tickets and searched for a lemonade stand. That's when she saw him. He and his friends were hanging out by a bench right beside the lemonade stand and talking about which girl they'd take to the swing dance contest.

When Christina walked up they immediately locked eyes with one another. It was love at first sight and they began their whirlwind romance from there. She would meet him in Fredericksburg at local spots and at dance halls, his touch sending electric shockwaves throughout her body. She couldn't get enough of him. Soon their meeting places graduated to more expensive locations such as hotels and motels that catered to their growing lust for one another.

The rendezvous kept going until he came to her house in Henry County. That's when everything changed, and no one had the decency to tell her that day that they were kinfolk. Not once looking back at the place she left him, Christina knew there was no turning back now as she walked the last mile to her house. And the one person she would need support from was the one she knew would be the most disappointed, her mother.

Christina Danielle Davis was nineteen with a slender frame, sepia skin and chocolate brown hair with eyes to match. A pert nose and full lips were the envy of many women in town, young and old. Her beauty was well known in Henry County, which is why her mother and father tried to shield her at an early age from possible suitors. From age five to thirteen she went to stay periodically with relatives in the Northern Neck of Virginia to attend Howland Grade School in Northumberland County, a one-room schoolhouse. Her family kept Christina busy around the house after she returned home, running errands for her mother's friends in the Autumn Horizons group, and cleaning houses for the rich folks in downtown Richmond. But distance didn't stop the rumors of her beauty, only enhancing the mystery of her appearance once she returned home for good.

Christina's father kept the suitors at bay for a while, even threatening them when they got a bit too close and wanted to see what she looked like. After his death, Christina's uncles protected her as best they could, putting a gate at the front entrance of her mother's house so no one would come on the property unannounced, and escorting her to the market when Mama needed vegetables that weren't available in the garden. Christina had been sheltered most of her life up until this point. Now she wished her father were here to protect her from the mess she was in. Her Dad was her hero, her shoulder to cry on. She drifted back to the day she had scraped her leg against a rusted nail while playing with her brother in the barn. The blood had made a smooth path down her leg, staining the only play pants her mama had made.

"Chrissy, you bleedin'. Mama gonna get you." Russell's sing song voice was followed by laughter and skipping. He came up beside her and pointed to the red river making its way down the side of her leg, staining the only play clothes she had.

She shoved her brother in the shoulder. "Shut up, Russ. Help me get back in the house before Mama sees it."

"Nuh uh. Gonna stay out here and play." He kept skipping around her while she stood still, oblivious to her panicked expression until she let out a little moan. Finally he stopped. "Why? Are you scared?"

"No, I'm not." She wasn't scared because she knew she hadn't done anything wrong, plus Daddy would understand she was just playing around. He wasn't like Mama, who fussed at everything she did whether good or bad.

"Christina, come here now."

Her father's voice was heard clear across the yard. He'd been hoeing the garden to plant crops. The sweat from his brow ran down to the collar of his blue cotton shirt, which he wiped away with an off-white handkerchief. He must've heard Russ's big mouth as he was taunting her.

"You gonna get it now, Chrissy."

She gave her brother a nasty stare, sticking her tongue out before walking towards her father. Christina dropped her head until told otherwise. She'd been playing with Russell the better half of the day until her little accident, and didn't want to go in until supper was ready. She knew she'd have to clean up soon but was having too much fun besting Russ at his little game. She peeked up to see if her father showed any signs of being mad, but she couldn't tell. The sun was directly in her line of sight.

"Christina, keep still and look at me."

Shielding her eyes with her forearm, she glanced up at her father, whose eyes were like cold steel. She always thought he looked angry whenever he was working outside, like he wanted to get all of his stress out at once. This time was no exception, as the chopped wood went flying in opposite directions with one giant downward swing of his ax. She looked towards the house to see if anyone was watching, but really she was trying to avoid his icy stare. He was a big man with a temper to match. It was once said her father became so angry with Jackson, the mule he used to tend the garden that he chopped its head off because it wouldn't move when it was told. Her uncles were the first to reveal that story, telling of the horrendous act to anyone who would listen. They didn't tell him at the time, but they didn't think killing the mule was necessary. They would never tell him that to his face. They weren't that crazy.

The only person who ever stood up to her father was Mama. And even she chose her battles carefully. Christina never asked him if what he did was true, choosing to think of her father more as a protector than someone with an anger problem who took it out on defenseless animals. She hated when her father was upset with her. Christina would rather anyone be angry at her than her father. She hesitantly waited for his voice to explode over her.

"Go to your big ma's house and have her sew that leg up," he said in a gruff voice. "Don't let your mama see it or she'll have a fit."

"Yes, Papa," she exhaled, suddenly realizing she was holding her breath while waiting for her Father to yell at her, but he never did. She turned around and ran to her grandmother's house.

That was one of the last times she spoke with her father. Abraham Davis was just thirty-four years old when he was found dead alongside the railroad tracks just a couple miles from where he worked. The police came to the house and asked Mama to come down to the station to identify the body. She fainted instantly. It took smelling salts and several additional minutes for her to wake up and get the full story. One of her father's co-workers, Butch Curtis, was standing beside the officer, hat in hand, claiming to have witnessed what happened. He told of arriving at the yards earlier that morning to find a group of men working on the rails when a train heading in their direction suddenly jumped its tracks, pinning the men underneath it. He was sure the men couldn't have leaped out of the way in time and apologized for their family's loss.

When Christina and the rest of the family heard the news it was like a dark cloud had suddenly formed around them without notice. She immediately ran to her uncles and aunts' houses down the road and knocked frantically on the door until someone answered. Between the tears and catching her breath she managed to tell them what happened. They rushed to the house to comfort their sister. Christina couldn't have asked for a better support system than what they provided that day, and all the days after that. They were her mother's rock, never leaving her side, and choosing to stay at the house several days until she felt better. After the funeral the family pitched in around the house, helping with the cooking, cleaning, and gardening until they felt the older kids could handle things on their own. Questions occasionally arose about how such an accident could've occurred when workers were given scheduled times of trains and where they were stopping. Clearly no one who worked there was willing to provide an explanation as to what happened, and the police considered it an open and shut case. But the family knew better. Something didn't sound right and Christina vowed along with her oldest brother Russell to figure out what happened to their father no matter how long it took.

That first year without him was very hard. She missed his presence terribly. When her father was alive they didn't have to worry about who was going to tend the garden or fix the barn door, gather the pigs in when they tried to escape, or start a fire to get the house warm from the frigid cold air in the winter time. After he died there was a huge void felt by everyone in the house. Christina's younger siblings turned to Russell, the eldest son, and her uncles for a substitute father figure, while her mama handled the finances and putting food on the table. Christina and Russell helped as best they could with money coming from their jobs, which helped pay for milk and clothing. But Mama cared for the majority of the house. She knew her mama missed her father, especially now during this time when she felt she needed his support most of all. He would know what to do in this situation, because at this moment she had no idea.

Now walking closer to the front porch, Christina brushed a strand of hair away from her face and looked at the front window to the house. She saw a figure pacing back and forth. Mama must be worried about something. The porch screen door swung open as Christina made her way up the steps. From the way her mother looked at her, she knew her secret was out.

"Mama, not now," she started.

"Yes now, young lady, we need to talk. Go to the kitchen and sit down."

Christina couldn't believe this night could get any worse than it already had. Her mother's voice sounded angry. She closed her eyes, made her way to the kitchen, and sat on the chair closest to the door, just in case she needed to exit in a hurry. The house was dead silent except for the crackling of the wood burning in the fireplace. She looked around and noticed that her brothers and sisters weren't there. Christina wondered how long she'd been gone. Her mother entered the kitchen behind her and propped herself against the stove. Dinner must've been over hours ago or else Mama couldn't simply stand beside the wood stove with the amount of heat that could come from it.

Mary Davis stood a mere five-foot three, yet you would've thought she was six feet tall the way she commanded attention. Her salt and pepper hair was pulled back in a tight bun away from her face. She worked from sunup to sundown as a housekeeper, a job that she and Christina shared in common, and then came home to feed all six children. If anyone was built to withstand the news that Christina was about to share, it was her mama.

"I know you and Lewis have been seeing each other and I should've told you sooner that your Aunt Evelyn would be moving back to Virginia with him. I thought things would settle down and that you'd finally realize who he was, but you didn't." Her gaze left Christina's wide-eyed expression briefly to place two cups on the table.

"What I'm trying to tell you is that you two are related, so your attraction will have to end, now. I'm sorry, but we just can't have that in the family."

She sat down across from her, poured lemonade into a cup and waited for her to answer. Christina's expression never faltered. Her breathing had slowed as her head finally caught up to what her mother was saying. Seconds ticked by. She was speechless. Did Mama know this whole time?

She leaned forward, her voice trembling with anger. "You knew? All this time I've been seeing him and you knew?"

Mary sighed in frustration. "No, I didn't know. I didn't even know you two had met until last week. I should've told you about him when I saw you both together yesterday."

"Yes, that would've made a huge difference," Christina said, shaking her head.

"Don't sass me, little girl. That smart mouth won't be tolerated in this house."

"Yes Ma'am."

"I should've paid attention to the looks you gave one another in the beginning, and maybe this wouldn't have happened. Luckily your Aunt Evelyn got wind of it before something more serious happened."

Christina watched as she placed a hand on her forehead. It might've been cool outside, but it felt like someone just lit five fires inside the house. She stared at her mother trying to calm her shaking voice.

"Mama, you could've told me something."

"If I knew I would have. How could I have known you two had met before all this happened?"

She was fanning herself with an old newspaper, too fatigued to look at the expression on her daughter's face.

"But it's fine now. We can put this whole mess behind us. I'm glad I told you in time before it got too far."

Christina watched her turn, opening the cabinet to take out a plate.

"You want something to eat? I fixed some chicken and dumplings with buttermilk biscuits. I know it's your favorite." The clatter of dishes and drawer door opening were the only noise heard in the kitchen.

Christina's silence caught her attention.

"What's wrong is there something you're not telling me?"

She took a deep breath and closed her eyes. "Mama, I'm pregnant." A pin could've dropped to the floor just then and it would've been the loudest sound in the room. Christina watched her as she turned away and clutched the stove. She braced herself for another slap. This one would probably hurt worse than the others. "No, Christina."

It was almost a whisper. She shook her head in disbelief and covered her mouth to keep from crying out loud. The same hand moved slowly to her chest. Christina couldn't say anything. She dropped her head and waited for the shock to wear off. It didn't take her mother's voice long to change from quiet and reserved to angry and frustrated. It had been a common transformation when they argued before, but this time Christina felt she was more at fault.

"You don't pay attention to anything I tell you, and that's a fact. Even when you were younger I could tell you not to do something and you would do it anyway."

Christina kept her head down. The embarrassment and shame felt like a knife cutting through her heart. Should she have waited to give her the news? Anything was better than the lecture she was getting right now. She listened as her mother kept up her rant.

"You were trouble then and you're more trouble now than all your brothers and sisters put together."

She sat still, having heard this several times before. It was always the same. Things weren't at all different; they were just lying dormant, waiting. She wanted to run out of the house, but stayed glued to the seat. This was her punishment and she wasn't going to run from it, not now.

"I'm warning you, Christina, this house will not be a whore house. I didn't raise you this way and it surely will not be an ongoing thing of opening your legs to every swinging dick that comes around. Do you hear me?"

"Yes, Ma'am."

"Oh lord, what will the family say?"

"What about me, Mama?"

"I think you've done enough, young lady. If you had told me earlier we could've gotten rid of it, but you wanted to be sneaky. I have to make this right for all of us."

"What do you mean?" she cried, watching with a worried expression on her face.

Mary was moving back and forth with her arms folded in deep thought. The gossip about her family was rearing its ugly head once again, and she didn't think she could go through the ridicule, and constant stares like she did ten years ago when Abraham died. There was only one thing to do.

Her mother didn't look her way, leaving a distraught Christina in the room only to come back carrying a pencil and paper in hand.

"You'll have to write to your Aunt Bessie in Charleston and ask her if you can stay with her for a while." She handed her the pencil and paper.

"With any luck we'll have you down there in no time, well before the baby is born."

Christina shook her head. This was going entirely too fast to wrap her head around. Charleston? What had been going through her mother's mind for the past five minutes? There was nothing for her in Charleston. She had never even been to Charleston.

"Mama, I can't go to Charleston. My home is here."

"I don't think you understand your condition, girl." Her stare was penetrating and stern. "You are pregnant, by your cousin, and without a husband."

She pointed her finger at Christina. "You will not disgrace this family any further. I will not be known as the mother of a bed wench. Do you hear me?"

Christina could hear raw emotion in her voice. And although she'd never really seen her mother cry she thought she might this time, and it was all her fault.

She watched as her mother adjusted her pleated skirt and tried to keep her voice calm. "You are going to Charleston even if I have to drag you there myself. If your father were here he would do the same." Christina doubted that very seriously. Her father's image suddenly appeared in her mind. Christina missed seeing him, and just knowing his presence would have comforted what she was going through right now made her want to cry all the more. Just as she did the day he died.

"Daddy would never send me away."

"Oh really? You think your father would approve of you sleeping around with a boy right under his nose? Play in fire and you will get burned."

"Daddy would love me despite what I did with anyone." Her emotions were getting the best of her again, and her voice was elevating itself to a familiar level.

"Your father only loved himself," she said quickly averting her eyes from Christina's horrified face.

"What?"

"Nothing. I've said too much." She adjusted her skirt and patted her cheeks. Mama was flustered but also something else; she was bitter.

Christina didn't know whether to pursue the conversation or let it go. She was waiting, almost hoping for her to explain her meaning, but she didn't. Her conservative stance remained intact, as did her demeanor. Whatever it was that wanted to come out and be exposed decided to stay inside for the time being. One thing was for certain. Mama was hiding something from her, and she didn't know if now was a good time to delve deeper into questioning her. She let it go. Quiet minutes ticked by while she gathered her thoughts together before speaking again.

"Mama, please don't make me go away. I want to raise my baby here. It's not our fault. We didn't know we were kin to one another." My God, did she actually think sending her somewhere else would solve anything?

"Mama?" She tried sounding calm. Her hands began to tremble as if she were bracing for impact when really it was the final say from her mother that she was bracing for. It had been a mistake to reveal her pregnancy. It had been an even bigger mistake to try and hide her relationship with Lewis from her mother. She put herself in this predicament, and knew she would be the only one responsible for what was to come. If only her mother could see she was willing to make the effort.

"You are going to Charleston, Christina. Understood? I have spoken my piece, and I don't want to hear another word about it."

That settled it. Mary Davis's expression said it all; it was stubborn and unyielding. She knew this battle was over. Her appeals had fallen on deaf ears. When her mother made her mind up there was no changing it.

"Yes, Ma'am."

She could only stare blank-faced at the tabletop in front of her, knowing there was no more arguing at this point. Every plea fell through, and her opinion didn't matter to the person standing in front of her with a singular definitive agenda.

"Write good now and make sure you don't sound too eager, else she might think something's wrong."

Everything was wrong Christina thought to herself as she put her head down and tried to keep her hand steady.

Dear Aunt Bessie,

It's been a while since we've last spoke. I'm nineteen now and a lot has changed on the family farm. Papa has been gone for some time and Mama is working twice as hard to take care of us all. I'd like to come down and spend some time with you if that's alright. It would make Mama's life a little easier without her having another mouth to feed. And I have a lot of news to share with you.

Love, Your niece
Christina

Christina sat in the chair watching her mother fold her letter of deceit and place it in an envelope.

"Good. Now all we have to do is wait the sooner she takes you the better."

Christina felt like hurtling herself at her mother's feet and holding on until she gave up the idea of sending her away. But she thought better of it. Mary Davis' body language read cold and indifferent. She should've just told Christina to get rid of the baby for all the coldness she was giving at this moment. Just skip all pretenses and hit her where it would truly hurt the most.

"I'm going to bed. Make sure you turn that lamp off before you turn in for the night."

"Yes, ma'am."

Christina didn't move from that spot for a while. She heard the crackling of the wood in the fireplace and the wind outside as it hit the shutters of the house in rhythmic progression. She was sure her body was glued to the chair, which was the reason she didn't move. Her limbs felt numb, like an animal bitten by a venomous creature meant to devour it for a later time. The only thing she did feel was her heart beating hard against her chest. She hadn't spoken to her Aunt Bessie since Daddy died. It was a very brief conversation that lasted all of three minutes before the funeral. From there her aunt spoke with Mama, and stayed near her throughout the day before traveling back to South Carolina.

How would her aunt feel now about her staying with her after all these years? She doubted she would allow it, given her current condition and the fact that she would be an added burden to an already single household where children were absent.

As she twisted the kerosene lamp, dimming its lighted visibility in the kitchen, she thought about Aunt Bessie's life in South Carolina. Aunt Bessie chose not to have children a long time ago, saying her body wouldn't allow for it. In Henry County this type of thinking was unheard of. You went to church, school, and when you were old enough women got married and had children. That was the plan from the time you were born, if you were a girl. If people found out you didn't want children, you might as well tell them Virginia didn't have four seasons. It was unheard of.

Auntie wouldn't have made it in this town. She would have been ostracized, gossiped about, and made to live as a recluse. Mama always thought she preferred to be alone, focusing on her job and maintaining her everyday life. Preparing for bed, Christina wondered how her aunt managed that type of independence in South Carolina. She took off her day dress and stared at her naked frame in the full-length mirror. The little pouch protruding from her stomach looked strange on her slender frame as she felt and held the under curve of her belly. Was Auntie looked down upon for choosing a life that was different from everyone else? She wondered. More importantly, would people treat her differently once they found out she was pregnant? The cotton nightgown felt cool against her skin as it settled near her ankles. She reached to turn the last kerosene lamp off in the house and prayed that sleep would calm her mind and nerves. At least for the next eight hours, with her head nestled against the pillow, Christina could pretend she hadn't ruined her entire life.

Chapter 3

The next morning Christina stretched her limbs and sat on the edge of the bed. She tried to think happy thoughts as the sun's rays shown its lighted presence through the wood framed window. She remembered when she had made her first homemade pound cake; how the accomplishment made her feel and how thrilled she was to discover that she could do something without Mama looking over her shoulder. The time Russell taught her how to ride a horse. The first time she'd realized she was pregnant; the expression on her grandmother's face.

It wasn't working. She could still see her mother's expression of shock and disappointment from the night before, and she suddenly felt depressed. The same troubled thoughts and feelings were deeply ingrained in her mind as Charlie the rooster made his early morning calling. She had one hour to get dressed and ready for her final day of work at the Evans house in Richmond. Now that she was waiting to move to Charleston, Christina knew her house serving days were over, and she didn't want to prolong the inevitable with long drawn out goodbyes. She quickly took a sponge bath and dressed in her uniform. Grabbing a corn muffin and glass of warm milk before leaving the house, she made sure not to wake the rest of her brothers and sisters.

While driving the twenty-five minutes to Ginter Park, Christina felt nervous about revealing the details of her pregnancy. She didn't want to seem too defensive, which could potentially ruin her working relationship and any future job opportunities in Richmond. Mrs. Evans was a well-known socialite from old money, who came into her own when her husband died of natural causes and left her with a substantial inheritance. She was in her mid-sixties and a role model to many women in her community when it came to integrity, manners, and charity. She was also a conservative woman, very opinionated, and always willing to share her lifetime experiences, which influenced Christina greatly about what she wanted to accomplish. Mrs. Evans understood that many people didn't associate blacks with intelligence or higher education other than grade school. She was quick to encourage Christina's ambition for wanting to become something other than a nurse or housemaid, which was the standard for many African American women in the community.

As the car pulled in front of the house, she wondered how to explain to Mrs. Evans that this was her last day working for her. Christina sighed. Her eyes gradually focused again on the house. The picture that began in her mind of the impending conversation made her walk slowly toward the servant entrance. Richmond was a mid-size city; however, the small community of house servants made gossip fodder for the masses as each quietly listened to the daily conversations in their employers' homes. Christina knew that if Mrs. Evans ever were to discuss her pregnancy elsewhere she would be humiliated, not only in the white community but in her own as well.

The home was immaculate. White pillars graced the two-story brick mansion with rose bushes and lilies adorning the front yard. Red pattern bricks decorated the driveway from the entrance, while a light grey stone pathway led guests to the porch steps, just before they knocked on the massive oak door. Christina was expected to walk through the service entrance, which was a side door leading to the kitchen, her favorite part of the house. She always liked to feel the countertops underneath her fingertips, a smooth grainy like material that never seemed to scratch when pots and pans were placed against it. Beside the refrigerator were two huge ovens, each one receiving different entrées needed for Mrs. Evans' daily luncheons with her women's society. There was always a large supply of food in the pantry, as every day she took inventory of what was needed, and then gathered all of the food and ingredients from the market.

She knocked lightly. "Mrs. Evans, it's me, Christina." Putting her ear to the door she listened for sounds of life inside before entering.

"I'm by the fireplace, Christina. Please come in here."

She put her keys and coat down and followed Mrs. Evans' voice to the living room area. "Good morning, Mrs. Evans."

"Good Morning, dear have you had breakfast yet?"

"Yes, ma'am."

"I haven't."

"Yes, ma'am. I'll get that started right away."

"We'll also need a decent menu for the early afternoon lunch. I'll need several good dishes, preferably something light and decadent."

"Yes, ma'am."

"I hear this will be your last day with me. I can't say that I'm happy about that."

"Yes, ma'am. I'm going to live with my Aunt Bessie for a while in Charleston, South Carolina."

Christina didn't want to say too much and definitely wanted to change the subject. She tied the apron around her waist, and gathered the skillet and pot from the pantry.

"Ah, Charleston, such lovely décor and charm you're very lucky to be going to such an historic and prestigious place."

"Yes, ma'am."

Christina's hands suddenly felt clammy, and she could've sworn her forehead was sweating under Mrs. Evans' inquisitive stare. She waited for the inevitable question while starting the pot of water boiling for Mrs. Evans' breakfast poached egg with grated cheese on toast.

"Christina?"

"Yes, ma'am?"

"Your mother told me everything, dear. Now you know I don't condone fornication."

"Yes, Ma'am." She tried to focus on something other than Mrs. Evans' stern look. Her throat suddenly felt like it was clogging up with mucus and she tried to find the words to best explain the situation. When Christina finally looked at her, she noticed her glasses were being held up somehow on the edge of her nose, and she was waiting for her to answer.

Christina cleared her throat. "It wouldn't be proper of me to discuss the details, Mrs. Evans, if you don't mind."

"No of course not I do understand the need for discretion indeed I do."

This was the moment she was going to get fired. Christina squared her shoulders and prepared for the news.

"I can prepare the dish and leave if you'd like me to."

Her firing would be quick, she thought. Maybe it was a good thing Mrs. Evans knew about her pregnancy rather than having to explain the story to her. Christina could only stare at the little progress she had already made, wondering if she should leave the cut tomatoes and cheese to cover the bread for someone else to do.

"Nonsense. I know something about what you're going through, and no one has the right to judge the other. We must all carry and practice our Christian upbringing so that someone else can be a witness."

Christina felt elated and quickly loosened the breath she was holding. Why couldn't people back home have said the same thing?

"Thank you, Mrs. Evans."

"Oh don't thank me, dear. Your mother was kind enough to inform me of what was going on. You young girls nowadays are so very ignorant of your bodies. I blame the music. It's blasphemous."

Christina watched her walk from the kitchen and took a deep breath, slicing the loaf of fresh bread and gently slipping the egg into the boiling water. She was thankful Mrs. Evans left her alone for that brief moment to get things going. News sure did travel fast, especially in her family, she thought. Her mother was quicker than a fox after its prey when it came to delivering news. But for once she was grateful for her mother's quick action.

Mrs. Evans' voice rang from the parlor.

"I expect you to bring that baby by here once you return." Christina smiled.

"Yes, ma'am. I sure will."

"Wonderful. Now make sure you sprinkle a little salt on that poached egg. I'll be waiting in the dining area to be served."

After breakfast, Mrs. Evans reviewed the menu choices with her just before her company arrived at the start of lunchtime. They were mostly housewives to council members and doctors in the Richmond area. Christina had prepared a light lunch, which consisted of an assortment of fruit: strawberries, red grapes, and fresh cut apples. Baked chicken salad with tomatoes, cucumbers, and radishes lined the serving dish, with buttered rolls on the side. For the finale two desserts were prepared: sweet potato pie and berry tartlets. She certainly felt much better now that she knew Mrs. Evans wasn't going to fire her or criticize her for what happened.

"Christina?" Mrs. Evans stood in the kitchen doorway dabbing at the corners of her mouth.

"Yes, ma'am?"

"Once the dishes and the kitchen are in order you're free to go home."

"Yes, ma'am."

"Tell your mother thank you for the coconut cake she left this morning."

"I will. Thank you, Mrs. Evans, for everything."

"You're welcome, dear."

She heard the ladies voice their approval of the food and asked Mrs. Evans where she acquired such a good colored cook. Christina would've enjoyed Mrs. Evans' compliments had it not been for the need to go home and start on the evening meal there. Her mother seemed to be arranging a lot lately and she couldn't help but wonder whether this would be the answer to every other problem that may come up.

Outside she took in deep breaths of air and looked around at the stately homes in Ginter Park. This rich upper class neighborhood with its white picket fences and arched doorways stood in stark contrast to the neighborhood she had lived in all her life. The wind blew a few leaves past her feet and she bent to pick up one, twisting the stem absentmindedly.

In the distance she heard a door close followed by a disturbing chuckle. The laugh made the hairs on the back of her neck stand straight up as she watched Butch Curtis slowly make his way towards her zipping his trousers, obviously ending his "services" at the house right beside Mrs. Evans. His face was like old leather dark and weathered. Those black eyes didn't seem to miss anything as he scanned her body from head to toe, missing nothing not even her nervousness. Every bone in her body wanted to run from this man. There was something about him she didn't like but couldn't quite put her finger on. His smile seemed to spread wider the closer he got to her.

"I remember you little girl. I watched while you slept in your bed the night before your father was killed." He paused for a reaction and relished in her frightened expression.

"You was a sweet thing then, even at that tender age."

"Good Afternoon Mr. Curtis, how are you today," she replied wanting to keep the conversation light but his expression and tone of voice said otherwise.

"How's your pretty Mama? You know I should've gotten real close to her that night." His laughter sent shivers down her spine and lingered even while she bid him a "Good Day" quickly leaving his presence. Her mind recalled the night before her father died as they all were unaware of the events that would change their lives forever, even to the danger that slept in their house right beside them. How could her father allow another man in the house with his wife and children unaware? That was the only time in her life when she recalled he didn't protect them like he should have. Before his death he would be eager to tell her and mama to stay in the room and kitchen when his friends would come over. Or she would go to her grandmother's house and stay there until they left.

The baby's fluttering movements stopped her trail of thoughts. Would she be able to protect her child from hurt, or harm and what about providing clothes and decent living? Would she one day be able to live in a neighborhood like Mrs. Evans? There were colored folk who had money during this day and time, though they were few and far between. Cold Harbor Farms had some of the richest black men in Henry County. Why couldn't she have that type of life? Her body felt overly exhausted, and it seemed as the baby grew, her strength was decreasing. Maybe it was better that she stop working so she could focus on her health as well as the baby. She would need all of her energy for bringing another life into the world.

Driving back home the scenery changed from multiple grand homes and buildings with brick driveways to trees and dusty gravel roads with smaller homes and log cabins. Christina noticed some women dressed in housekeeper uniforms waiting for the bus, and wondered whether they had any other expectations from what they were told. Growing up in this town, she found that women were supposed to conform to a certain way of life. They weren't supposed to have any goals or plans that surpassed that of their elders. In some cases when young women had more than others they would be considered as "uppity" or "snobbish." No one saw the hard work that many of these women did in order to get the very little they had.

The Great Depression didn't help matters as black people were forced into limited professional opportunities, with large families to support. Despite the economic crisis, blacks still contributed to the needs of their communities, addressing as many problems as possible. Her grandmother, Martha Washington, was one of them. People still went to her for health remedies to this day because of her educational background in medicine, which was how she made her money, that and selling moonshine every once in a while. It was quite an accomplishment, and yet because of her goals she was still criticized. Christina remembered being told by her grandmother that she was the only one for a time that had a brick house on their street. She was accused of being "high and mighty" because no one else had a brick house. This type of ignorant pettiness in the community was prevalent and she often referred to some people as crabs, always trying to bring someone down once they reached the top of the barrel.

Mama Washington still set the standard for education and better living. Auntie and others soon followed her example, but there was still jealousy, even amongst her own family members. Aunt Bessie was probably glad she no longer was a part of this town. Christina soon doubted her letter would have any effect on Auntie's decision allowing her to stay. Auntie had a life and a well-paying job, Christina thought. At least in Charleston she could be who she wanted to be without the ridicule. Could she have a fulfilling life, while having a child at such a young age? She was definitely sure her aunt had better things to do than take care of an unwed young woman.

Chapter 4

Christina was having second thoughts about her letter to Aunt Bessie. The letter was rushed, and in her opinion she didn't think Aunt Bessie would agree with Mama's decision in sending her down there. She and Lewis hadn't spoken for almost two weeks now, however she wasn't sure that was long enough for her mama to change her mind, if the thought had ever entered her head.

Christina felt defeated and knew that if she confronted her mother now she probably wouldn't have enough strength to defend herself in the yelling match that would undoubtedly occur, so she rolled to her side propping herself on an elbow and turned on the kerosene lamp. The white envelope caught her attention and instantly she knew what it was. For a moment, while opening the letter, she thought seriously about letting the fires burn all evidence of its existence. She had to read it twice before her aunt's words finally sunk in.

Christina,

I pray this letter finds you and the family well. I would be delighted if you came to stay with me. Charleston is a beautiful place and I know you would enjoy the many social events as well as the ocean, which is not too far from my house. My home is on James Island, one of the many lovely communities close to the downtown area. I'm sending Uncle Joseph to come and collect you in three weeks. Be sure to pack lightly and give my love to my brothers and sisters, nieces and nephews, and especially to your mother.

I look forward to seeing you. All my love,
Aunt Bessie

She had no idea where James Island was, and the more she thought about it the more she became frustrated with the whole ordeal. Her emotions were clearly causing her mind to jump back and forth in the decision-making process. One minute she enjoyed the thought of leaving; the next minute she wished things could go back to the way they were before she met the devil. Why couldn't time stop so she could breathe and collect her thoughts? Christina put the letter away, washed her face, and dressed to start her chores. She was surprised Auntie had approved her stay so soon. How long did it take for a letter to get that far anyway? Or did someone else notify her before she received her letter? Christina suddenly had the distinct impression her mother had something to do with Aunt Bessie's quick decision.

She made her way to the kitchen and noticed the dishes, cups, and utensils were all set to be put on the table. Mama had coffee already prepared, which meant she would need to get started on squeezing the lemons for lemonade. Making coffee for her parents was a morning tradition that dated back as far as Christina could remember. She used to make her father a cup when she was home from school on the weekends. He would come in, pat her on the head and take his favorite mug from her outstretched hand. His eyes would close at the first sip and off he'd go. His was always made first with a dash of sugar and goat's milk. Christina would then start on her mother's. It was always in that order. She touched her throat, recalling the memory that seemed not that long ago.

"Good morning, Mama. I didn't hear you get up this morning."

It took several seconds for her to answer. There was a steady silence except for the sizzling of pork on the stove top, and the salt fish aroma coming from black iron skillets.

"Good Morning, Chrissy."

"Did you need any help?" she asked warily, knowing full well that wasn't the question she wanted to ask.

"Dress the table, and make sure your brothers and sisters wash their faces before coming to the table."

Christina stood uncomfortably before her mother, willing the words from her mouth. She didn't want to start an argument. The constant bickering had to cease at some point and she needed some peace between them before she left.

"Have you read Aunt Bessie's letter?" Christina leaned against the countertop, studying her mother's reaction.

"Yes, I have." She gave her a pointed stare over her shoulder just before breaking eggs into the small bowl. Christina adjusted her stance, careful not to seem too eager in her quest for answers.

"It came quickly, don't you think?"

"I don't think so. I sent a separate letter before sending yours explaining the situation. The letter is right on time."

Christina wasn't surprised by this bit of news. She raised both eyebrows and let out a little sigh; it was another victory for her mother, who seemed to be on a roll when it came to tying up loose ends.

She watched her beat the eggs rapidly before setting the bowl down. "And when did you tell Mrs. Evans?"

"It was yesterday morning before you started your day hours. You didn't think you were going to still work there, did you, in your condition?"

"No, I guess not." She tried to hide the sadness in her voice. She definitely wanted a change to her employment but wanted that choice to be her own. Now that everything was slipping away at a rapid pace, Christina felt like she was losing some of the things she was accustomed to.

"What did she say?" Christina asked.

"She didn't like it very much. Mrs. Evans is a devout Christian, with a respectable name in the Richmond community."

"She told me to bring the baby by when I returned." Hoping she'd change her mind about giving her baby away, Christina waited for her answer.

"Your cousin will be taking care of the baby, so she will let Mrs. Evans see it when you return."

Christina shook her head and pressed her lips together. Starting an argument now wouldn't do her any good.

"That woman let you finish your job with as much dignity and respect as possible. You should be thanking me, not giving attitude."

Christina looked out the kitchen window towards her grandmother's house. Before the day even got started she wanted to go over there and lay her head across the woman's lap. Frustration and anger were the usual melody sung between her and Mama, and this morning was no exception.

"If it were anyone else, Christina, Mrs. Evans would've sent them on their way. She favors you, girl. You should be grateful."

"Everything seems to be going so fast," she said in a small voice.

"What do you think would've happened had anyone else got wind of you being knocked up? They would've tossed you out and soiled your reputation."

Christina wanted to end the conversation. If she didn't Mama would just keep talking, which would have her own anger at boiling level. So she did the normal thing when they argued; she apologized while placing blame on herself.

"I'm sorry, Mama. You're right. I should be grateful."

"Yes, you should. I'm only doing what's best for you, Christina."

Yes, you keep telling me that, she thought. She watched her pour the eggs into the skillet, whisking them rapidly until they took the usual fluffy shape. Christina wished she could believe those words, but part of her still had the feeling her mother was doing all of this to save the family's reputation with little regard for her daughter's wellbeing.

"We'll still need to go over a plan for your stay in Charleston and your duties for when you return."

She bent down and pulled the sausage from the oven; its aroma filled the kitchen instantly, making Christina's mouth water.

"Remember, the less people know the better. That way you don't have a whole mess of folks in your business."

Christina set the table, placing the scrambled eggs and sausage side by side in the serving bowl with the napkins and forks by each plate. She listened to her mother's elaborate plan. The idea would be to stay in Charleston a year and a half and then travel back to Virginia. Her time in Charleston would be used to focus on her life and the direction she needed to take before returning home. She was being told over and over that this was a necessary thing in order not to disgrace the family name, so much so that it was starting to be believable.

Upon her return home the child would be given over to an older cousin to look after. They would figure out later what to tell people about the child's sudden appearance into the community when she returned. Her mother was determined to set things right, which meant keeping the gossip and humiliation to a minimum. Christina wondered what she would tell people about her sudden absence from church and elsewhere.

She left the room just then to gather more bacon from the smokehouse, calling her younger brothers and sisters in for breakfast. Christina sat in the chair as tears made their way down her cheeks again; the shame and embarrassment of what happened was taking on new significance. Abigail was the first sibling to come into the kitchen before the others. Christina quickly wiped the tears away, careful not to let her sister know anything was wrong.

"Can I have some juice?"

"We have some lemonade." Christina got up and grabbed the pitcher from the cabinet.

Abigail took a seat opposite Christina's. "Chrissy, can I ask you something?"

"Sure, what is it?"

Christina poured the water into the pitcher and was just about to cut the first lemons when her little sister asked, "Am I gonna be an auntie?"

Christina paused for a minute. She had obviously overheard a conversation between her and Mama. She didn't think she was going to have to answer these questions so soon. Abigail was only ten years old. She was the youngest and most curious of all her siblings but still very young. Christina quickly cut and squeezed the lemons, placing them in the pitcher. She carried the sugar cubes along with the pitcher to the table and poured a cup for her little sister.

"Yes, you're going to be an auntie. What do you think about that?"

Abigail hunched her shoulders and grabbed a sugar cube from the holder to sweeten her lemonade. She was about to take her first sip when she looked at Christina. "You're gonna be a good mommy, Chrissy."

"You think so?"

"You take care of Mama and the rest of us real good."

"Thanks, Abby. That means a lot."

They sat in the kitchen afterwards, talking about baby names and whether it was going to be a boy or a girl. Christina was touched by her younger sister's support. Abigail didn't blame her for getting pregnant and showed genuine interest in the baby. She watched her younger sister make her plate, while the rest of her brothers and sisters took their seats at the table.

Ever since Christina could remember, Mama and Papa wanted every meal at the kitchen table. That was their family time to discuss work on the farm and other issues that may have come up during the week. The children were never allowed to speak during conversation because it was disrespectful to talk while adults were talking. Now that Papa was gone, the two oldest were allowed to talk to Mama about their plans and goals for the week.

Russell was always the first to start the conversation. "Mama, you're gonna be real proud of me. Boss said I was the best cook he ever had."

"Work going that well, eh, baby?"

Russell stuck out his chest like a proud peacock. "Yes, ma'am in the next couple years I could work my way up to something different. I wanna drive one of those big machines one day."

"You'll get there, son, you will."

Christina was glad for her older brother's rambling at this time because she didn't have much to say. She sat at the table listening to him go on and on about joining the army at Fort Lee. She kept her eyes focused on her plate until breakfast was over and then began cleaning the dishes. When everyone had left to resume their activities outside, the air in the kitchen returned to the tense atmosphere it was before.

"I see you didn't have much conversation at the table, Chrissy."

"I'm sorry, Mama, but I have a lot on my mind," Christina replied.

"Listen, I know this move is going to be difficult for you. But think about your family. Do you want your younger sisters to think it's okay to open their legs at such an early age?"

Christina lowered her head. "No, ma'am." That statement made her feel horrible. She didn't want her sisters to think she was that kind of girl.

"And what about your younger brothers?" her mother continued.

"They'll see that it's Okay to get a woman pregnant without marrying them first. Is that the kind of behavior you want them to see?"

"No, ma'am."

Christina wondered if her mother was going to tell her she was a bad influence on everyone in the family, including the elders.

She grabbed her hand and squeezed. "Good. Remember you're the oldest girl and all your sisters and brothers look up to you. The family needs you to be strong. This move is really the best thing for you."

She remained silent, refusing to look at her mother as she finished washing the remaining dishes. She wanted to ask, What about me? Don't you give a damn about what I'm going through? But she thought better of it. It was as if her mother valued the reputation of the family more than the feelings and wellbeing of her own daughter. She felt like she was rubbing the silver off of the silverware, trying to ignore her mother's condescending tone. She patted her on the shoulder and left Christina standing there staring at the sink with an emotionless expression on her face.

The kitchen suddenly felt stifling as if there was no air inside and she needed to get out. Taking a pitcher of lemonade, Christina walked to the porch and watched Abigail and the rest of her brothers and sisters playing in the yard. The glass of lemonade made a small water puddle on the step as the warm sun melted its icy contents inside. She watched them until the sun dipped behind the trees signaling the evening hours. It wouldn't be long before dinner started. Her aunts and uncles usually came by once a week for dinner, a ritual they all shared ever since her daddy died. The smell of ham and homemade biscuits soon made its way outside, making her mouth water. The baby made its feelings known as well, as she felt movements within her stomach.

ℰᗩ

That evening laughter from the end of the road drew closer as she greeted her aunts and uncles making their way to the house. She kissed all of them on the cheek before ushering them into the house.

They sat around the table as Mama was putting the finishing touches on the dishes. There was ham, turkey smothered with gravy and onions, buttermilk biscuits, macaroni and cheese, corn on the cob, greens, and for dessert, blackberry roll all of them being Christina's favorites.

"Mary, what is going on these days down at the church?" Uncle Carl asked.

"Why don't you come by the church sometime?"

"No, thank you. Somethin' ain't right wit dem peoples."

"What do you mean? They're people just like everyone else," Mama said, placing fresh mats on the table.

"They say one thing and do anotha. Half those folks done messed up so many times and got da nerve talkin bout other folk."

"They're still church people, Carl, so show some respect."

"I'll start respectin dem when dey starts respectin others."

"Christina, make sure your brothers and sisters wash their hands before they come to the table."

"Yes, ma'am."

She hurried to gather her siblings from the front yard, being careful to listen to the conversation going on inside the house. Thank God the windows were open so she could hear their conversation.

Uncle Carl kept up his rant. "Mean spirited is what they is might as well stay home wit yo bible if you ask me."

"Well, no one asked you, Carl," Mama said with an exasperated look on her face. "Where's Bill?"

"Aw, you know him. He got some gossip early on this afternoon says he'll see you tomorrow."

"Bill better stop that mess. A man liking gossip that much ain't natural."

"You see Vera today, Mary?"

"No, we haven't seen Vera all day today. She normally stops by before heading on over to her sister's house."

"I think she cheatin', Mary."

"Vera loves you, Carl," Mama said reassuringly.

Christina noticed a wobbly silhouette swinging open the door, creating a loud sound. She immediately knew who it was before everyone else. Her aunt was disheveled, clearly intoxicated, with her hair half braided and wearing a floral printed house dress that seemed slanted to one side. The top two buttons were undone.

"Hey, who wants some gray haired pussy?"

"Well, look whose comin in da house," she heard Aunt Harriet say in between laughs.

"Vera, I done told you to stop that nasty talk. There's chiren around," Uncle Carl cried.

"Vera, where have you been?" Mama asked. She reached down and grabbed the bottle out of her hand.

"I see."

Christina noticed her mother helping Aunt Vera to her seat as she ushered her brothers and sisters back into the house to wash their hands.

"Car, you lefs me at da housh," Vera said, plopping down in the chair Mama had given her.

"I did no sucha thing. I left you over yo mama's house, Vera. Don't you member?"

"No."

Mama handed her a cup of water. "Drink this."

"Tank you, Mary."

Uncle Carl shook his head.

"Oh shtop lookin like dat, Car. I give you a lil piece once we leave here." Vera pulled her dress up a little to show her leg.

Carl shoved her dress down. "Oh hell naw you won't, I'm takin yo drunk ass home."

"Good." She pointed a bony finger at him. "I betta get some when I gets there or Ima cut yo pecka off and use it on myself."

"Then you jus gonna have a dead pecka in you cuz I aint givin you shit!"

"Hush, you two. Ya'll gone raise the dead with all that cursing," Mama said, shaking her head.

"I hope its Georgia May who comes back."

"Your old girlfriend. I never see her look mo happy den when she was in dat casket, away from you," Vera spat.

"She a lot betta than yo drunk ass."

"Naw suh, she aint got dis sweet goodness here," she said, pointing down at her crotch.

"That ain't nothin there."

"It what all da fellas want."

"Yo pussy ain't got no face, jus a smell and a taste."

The kids started laughing, which quickly got Mama upset. She never liked that kind of talk around her children.

"Vera, Carl, hush now. Vera, sip some more water to calm yourself," Mama said, clearly annoyed with their crass bickering.

Christina knew Uncle Carl was tough enough to handle by himself, but when he and Vera got together that was a different beast entirely.

She often saw Mama anoint herself with oil after being in their presence more than a couple of hours. Tonight would be no exception.

She shook her head. They argued like that for another five minutes until Mama broke it up. She wondered if they ever had a conversation where they weren't fussing or cussing each other out. As she made her way to the kitchen to make plates for her brothers and sisters, she recalled one time Mama had to pull Uncle Carl off Aunt Vera while they were at the liquor store. They were arguing because he'd caught her trying to get into another man's car and she was too drunk to understand the trouble she was in. Uncle Carl got so mad at her he picked up an empty barrel and threw it square at her head which knocked her out cold. She laid on the ground until Mama and Uncle Bill put her in the wagon to take her back to the house. She only suffered a knot on her head, but it was enough for the elders to have a serious talk with Uncle Carl and Aunt Vera about their behavior as husband and wife. They were the strangest couple in Mills-town, and yet by divine grace they had managed to stay together for over seventeen years.

The dinner resumed as usual with an additional person added to the table. Christina enjoyed the company of her aunts and uncles but she couldn't help but wonder about Uncle Bill's absence. It wasn't like him to stay away from the house, especially at dinner time. He usually was the first one there, way before the others showed up. He was always talking about the latest gossip he'd heard down the road. She pushed the thought aside and concentrated on the evening's conversations. Aunt Harriet was giving advice on how to spice up a marriage while Uncle Jessie was trying to shut her up. Christina knew she was still inexperienced with it all and thought better of asking any questions, especially when she wasn't sure who knew her secret.

Her mother decided to join the conversation.

"Abraham and I used to argue about who was more affectionate when we first got married."

Everyone stopped their chatter to let her speak. The air in the room suddenly became heavy with emotion.

"Both of us was good in expressing how we felt. We realized it was silly to argue and never did after that."

Christina never heard her mother talk about her father that way before, nor did she miss the looks that went back and forth between her aunts and uncles. She wondered if they were hiding something, especially now that Mama had started sharing stories about her father. Was there something about their relationship that she didn't know about? Maybe they had hit a rough patch in their marriage like some of the elders talked about from time to time. Whatever it was it not only affected her mother but everyone else as well. She wanted to grab her mother's hand, but knew the affection wouldn't be returned, as she buried her hands in her lap. She watched her mother's eyes focus on the past, as if she were remembering a different time and waved her hand away, trying to get control of her emotions.

Aunt Harriet picked the conversation back up, and everyone started chatting again. Christina looked over at her mama as she patted her cheeks. The memory had clearly affected her deeply. She adjusted her house dress and listened to the rest of the conversation.

That's how it was sometimes. When Mama needed her moment, her family gave it to her.

Chapter 5

Christina sat on the edge of the bed, willing the nauseating sickness that had awakened her to go away. Last night's dinner would've made an unwelcome appearance on the cold wooden floor had it not been for the deep breaths she was taking. A timid knock sounded at the door as she tried to process how to get dressed without the room tilting. Christina answered, hoping her mama was on the other side to assist her.

Abigail walked in wearing faded overalls. Her hair was braided in pigtails, and smudges of dirt lined her young forehead. A smile spread across her face as she all but threw herself on the bed, the smudges of dirt now a permanent stain on the white cotton sheets.

"Abby, I thought I told you to stop jumping on the bed," Christina said, swatting at her sister's backside.

Her sister playfully rolled over to avoid the ineffective swat and kept up her infectious laughter as Christina caught her and tickled the sides of her neck. She would miss these moments with her younger sister. She noticed that Abigail was trying to talk, so she ended her assault long enough for her to catch her breath.

"Mama sent me in here to get you. She thought you might need some help since you was takin' so long."

"Thanks, Abby. Has Mama started breakfast yet?" Christina asked while retrieving her wardrobe for the day from the dresser drawer.

Abigail stretched and walked over to the door. She peeked out and looked back and forth down the hall before answering.

Her silence caught her oldest sister's attention. "Abigail, what is it?"

"Mama had to bad mouth a Harris this morning while you was sleepin'."

Christina felt the nausea rise again but this time for reasons entirely different than before.

"Go on, I'm listening."

"The Harris woman came down the road a-cussin' and a-fussin' so loud Mama went and got the blessin' oil before she hit the door."

"What did she say?"

"She said how you was loose and got Lewis in trouble, but that's as far as she got cause Mama told her to get the hell off the porch."

"Watch your mouth, Abby. Remember those are adult words, not for children."

"Yes, Chrissy," Abigail said, putting her head down.

It suddenly dawned on her that other people might have already known about her secret before Mama did. The community shared one telephone line also known as "the party line". Anyone could pick up the receiver and listen in on their neighbor's conversation without being discovered. She was certain this was how they knew about her and Lewis' child as she didn't tell anything to his side of the family about the baby. Christina remembered Uncle Bill receiving a terrible tongue lashing when he listened in on Mrs. Carter as she reported to the police her first husband killed himself. From then on he wasn't welcomed at her house for prayer meetings, or any other social gatherings, not that he would've gone anyway.

Abigail peeked at her sister to see if she was upset for using bad language. Christina smiled, trying to ease her sister's discomfort, though she was baffled at how she was being blamed for being pregnant. After all, the last time she checked, it took two people to create a child, not just one. She ushered Abigail out of the room and slowly made her way to the kitchen. The scent of sizzling sausage quickened her pace as she found her mother at the wooden stove wiping the sweat from her brow with a white towel.

"I think I need to talk to Lewis."

"I don't think so," her mother said emphatically as she stirred the pot of grits before adding butter. Christina could tell the comment displeased her by the frown lines that creased her forehead. She didn't look as worried as she had the past couple days, only a bit concerned. Mama's face reflected concern over her suggestion. That was a first.

"Christina, you'll be leaving in a couple days. Why would you be stirring up this mess?"

"I walked away from Lewis without really talking about the baby, Mama. He's probably wondering if I want to speak with him," Christina said. She yawned and covered her mouth; lack of sleep was becoming an issue the closer she came to going away.

"And how long ago was that?"

Christina frowned. "Couple of weeks why?"

"He's driven by this house like a bat out of hell during those weeks and not once has he stopped by to ask how you or the baby is."

Christina considered this. She took a good long look through the window to the road that crossed in front of the house and decided that her mother was half right, though she didn't tell her she thought so.

"Maybe he was scared to hear what I was going to say."

"And maybe he's already henpecked and can't speak for himself, cause he's not really a man to begin with." Mama looked annoyed and turned to continue making breakfast. The smell of food made Christina's stomach growl to the point she almost forgot the conversation. Before she walked into the kitchen that morning, her thoughts had been on the previous evening of seeing her family talking together. Why couldn't she and Lewis do the same thing? After all, they were adults and were going to have a child soon. She needed to ask him if he wanted to raise the child with her, which she should've done that fateful evening. The shock of their kinship had terminated any further conversation. It would be better for them to sit down and discuss their situation, and maybe just maybe Mama would reconsider sending her away when she saw that Lewis was just as interested in raising the child as she was.

"I just want to know if he feels the same way about this child as I do," Christina answered.

"He hasn't tried to come and see how you are, Christina, which means he doesn't care."

Christina shook her head. It was hard to face that truth, but she knew it was there. Lewis' actions would explain his skittish ways when he saw her relatives outside of the house or her mama at the store. Every time he spotted them he made a quick getaway that left smoke standing in the place where his car had been. She had to try something, and speaking to him face to face might be just what both of them needed to settle their differences and talk about raising their child. It was a chance she was willing to take.

"Do like I say, Christina. Stay away from Lewis Harris."

Mama poured the grits into bowls and called everyone to breakfast. Christina made sure fresh orange juice was on the table by the time they got there. As she said her blessings, her mind was settled on what she'd do that day. Going over to Lewis' house would only be successful if he was the only person there. She didn't need the interference of his aunts or women who frequented from the church.

❧

Before she reached the front yard Christina heard the plucking of guitar strings bouncing on the afternoon air. And then the two-story white house with black shutters came into view, a beaming vision against the glimmer of the sun. On the front porch were a group of men lounging on rocking chairs, railings, and the small stone steps leading to the front door. There was trash talking and laughter accompanying the guitar music, a familiar scene at Mama's house every week that spoke volumes about life in Mills-town. She knew once she left the house people would be around on this end of the street, just not in front of the house like they were today. Like moths to a flame, they came from everywhere, drawn not only by the music but also by the fellowship with one another. This place was where people came to raise a family and be surrounded by the people they loved.

Christina felt right at home amongst the boisterous men. Their banter and laughter was infectious to the point where even she wanted to join in the fun until they recognized who she was. The moment they saw her, the music stopped on a jarring note. Christina squared her shoulders and looked around for Lewis. He was the main priority. It was now or never. She reached the top steps before being stopped by a voice she hadn't heard in years. The sea of men had parted to reveal an elderly woman looking surly and just as surprised to see her as she was.

"Well, if it isn't li'l Chrissy Davis from down the street how you doin, sugar?"

Lewis' grandmother was sitting at the end of the porch and fanning herself with a folded up newspaper. Her burgundy colored housecoat was splattered with flour from her shoulders to her waist, indicating some cooking had been going on prior to Christina's arrival. Her chalk white hair was pulled into a neat bun, which was a stark contrast to the messy clothing she was wearing.

Christina managed a smile, and then timidly walked the couple of feet to stand in front of the stone steps. She glanced at the front door briefly, hoping to catch a glimpse of Lewis, but all she heard were the scrambling of boots against the ground and knew if she turned around she would see all those men standing in groups, some behind bushes, waiting to see what was going to happen.

"Hi, Mrs. Harris how is you this afternoon?"

"I'm just fine and prayin' my strength holds fast and true. What brings you by?"

"I'd like to talk with Lewis, ma'am."

"Lewis? He's with his fiancée, dear. Didn't your mother tell you?" She showed no anger and didn't raise her voice not even a little. Christina would have preferred rage to the cold indifference Lewis' grandmother was displaying toward her.

"No, ma'am," she said evenly. She absentmindedly began rubbing the lower half of her stomach in a circular motion, which caught the attention of the elderly woman sitting in front of her. Mrs. Harris' eyes were cold and unfeeling with only a slight twitching of her mouth that gave any indication of emotion. Christina swallowed hard. She knew this subject would come up and thought she could handle it, but the flood of emotion that washed over her at that moment almost caused her knees to buckle.

"No, she didn't. I just wanted to talk about the baby that will be coming soon."

"And whose baby is that?" she asked, folding her arms across her chest. She was daring Christina to say the name.

Christina's heart was beating at an accelerated pace. Staring into the woman's chilling eyes, she had to remind herself to get the rest of her sentence out of her mouth. "Lewis', ma'am."

"Oh no it's not!"

She stood up from her seat and planted her hands on the porch pillars. Her eyes were wide and Christina thought for sure she saw fire shooting from them. When she did stop shaking, Mrs. Harris burst into a loud torrent of words, some of which Christina couldn't understand. Perhaps her mother was right after all; this wasn't the best time to come down here.

"I heard you was tryin to get my boy leg shackled and I won't have it."

"But Mrs. Harris, Lewis is the father to my baby. I just want to talk to him for a moment." Her voice stuttered a little as she tried to keep it as even as possible while speaking to this unreasonable woman.

"You Washington women are all the same. You lay down with men like dogs in heat. Well, you won't have my grandson. I'll see to it, dammit."

Christina didn't understand any of this. She wasn't asking for Lewis' hand in marriage. The love she felt was slowly diminishing day by day. She was simply asking for him to acknowledge their baby. The rest of the family didn't have to, and she knew some wouldn't by the reaction she just witnessed.

"What do you mean by that? My Dad was my mother's first. Everyone knows that."

"I'm not talkin' 'bout yo mama, girl. Your aunt Evelyn was the one who couldn't keep her legs closed. Do you think we've forgotten what happened?"

What was she talking about? What right did she have to judge her aunt. Sure she wasn't there while Christina and her brothers and sisters were growing up, but that didn't mean much. Her aunts and uncles worked constantly, so she only saw a few of them when she was younger. There was a deeper meaning behind her scathing words. Whatever it was she was sure she'd hear about it later on. "That's not true."

"It sho nuff is, and I'm not gonna have it. You're not gonna ruin my boy's good name."

"Grandma, I'll take it from here."

Christina heard Lewis' voice and thought for sure her heart had stopped in her chest when he came through the door. He was lean and hard from head to toe, from his unmarred face to his flat, narrow waist, to the tense solid muscles of his long limbs. She could still picture her hands spanning the width of his wide shoulders as they made love time and again, an image not so endearing right now. His face was light brown, the skin lustrous for a young man, which made him quite striking. But it was his wavy black hair and hazel eyes that combined to make his face so handsome, even beautiful. The lips were full with a slight pink hue inside the bottom edge, just enough to make them look incredibly sensual. And those eyes, his most arresting feature, were brown with green flecks, and were absolutely gorgeous. Twenty-one, slender, and six feet tall, he was the embodiment of female desire and he absolutely knew it.

Being near him, Christina was more aware of her pregnancy than ever before, especially when his eyes travelled up and down her slightly protruding belly.

"You were here the whole time?"

"Yeah, I was listening," Lewis said, coming forward to lean against the railing, arms crossed over his chest.

"Please tell your grandmother that this baby is really yours." Silence followed as he looked the old woman in the eyes. His confirmation could definitely change everything, from her keeping the baby to staying in Virginia. Finally she wouldn't have to carry the stress of their forbidden relationship by herself.

"I can't do that, Christina."

"What?" Her heart stopped. She had made the effort to come down here to talk to him only to be rejected again.

Lewis looked at his grandmother and managed a half smile before patting her arm.

"I can't say I'm the only man you slept with, Christina."

Who was this person? Clearly he'd heard that from his grandmother, and who was going to go against that old bird?

"But you are. I told you." She was confused. All the talks they had together. He knew he was the first for her. Lewis stepped down towards her. His hands were stuffed in his pockets, and his face was void of emotion.

"You're upsetting my grandma, Christina, and as the man of this house I'm going to have to ask you to leave."

The breath she was holding throughout their conversation was finally let go as she turned to leave. It had taken a major effort on her part to come down here despite all of the name calling, whispering, and downright rudeness. When she finally saw him after weeks of not talking he turned around and acted like the pussy her mama and uncles told her he was all this time. Well, she wouldn't let him get away with this.

"You self-centered lowdown dirty dog."

The emotions she was holding in, knowing he had been listening the whole time, combined with the anger she was feeling toward her mother finally came out.

"Don't you talk to my grandson like that, you hussy."

Christina ignored her for the time being. The old bird looked like she wanted to fly off the porch towards her.

"Mee Ma, let me handle this."

"Lewis Harris, this is your baby and when I'm gone you'll realize the mistake you've made by not claiming this child as your own, you piece of shit."

"Get off my land before I have you thrown off," Grandma Harris yelled.

"Go to hell with you and your land and your grandson."

She didn't wait for Lewis to reply. All he did was stand beside his grandmother patting her hand like he was soothing a lion before it was to strike. Wasn't he supposed to be soothing her? Instead he just stood there saying absolutely nothing. What a pussy! She heard coughs of laughter and the clearing of throats. They were still there! Christina stomped all the way back down the dirt road. Her feet were in pain, throbbing with each step by the time she reached her grandmother's house. Mama was right. It was no use stirring in the stink that was already caused. One of these days she would learn to listen to her advice. For now she just wanted to be around people who loved and supported her. Christina walked through the door and found her grandmother reading the bible by the bed. No words were spoken as she went to the bedside, dropped to her knees, and laid her head on her lap. The tears finally poured out of her and she sobbed uncontrollably on the one person she knew would understand her pain. The elder woman's hand gently touched the top of her head.

"It's alright Chrissy. Tell Nanna all about it."

Chapter 6

The widow Morris provided some form of entertainment for the afternoon as Curtis slid his penis in and out of her pumping hard and fast. She was a thick woman with a hefty backside and firm tits to match. He liked being behind this one pulling on her long braid and reaching around to her love button, teasing it with his finger ensuring she came before reaching his second climax. Turning her over he licked her nipples down to her stomach and wondered how she'd feel knowing he was the cause of her husband being killed ten years ago. The thought of her angry with him almost got his manhood hard again as he watched her slide from underneath him, put a robe on and sit on the edge of the bed crossing her legs. He leaned over grabbing his britches from the floor and started to dress slowly.

"Tomorrow okay with you Curtis?"

"Just fine with me," he replied.

Very few words were spoken between the two which helped their situation stay as neutral as possible. He didn't need a clingy woman always questioning his whereabouts and she wasn't trying to get married again.

"Close that curtain before you go," she said lighting her first of many cigarettes for the day.

Curtis closed the left side and was just about to close the right when he saw Christina come outside her house talking with two girls. He eyed the girls for minutes before his bed partner reminded him of his exit.

He needed to be close to her. To let her know he was there, that he was watching her every move. It wasn't a coincidence he chose the house right across the street from her mother's house. The widow Morris all but dragged him in when he showed at her door offering pleasures she didn't have since her husband was dead. He could watch Christina freely, without her seeing him which he'd done ever since her father died. Now that she was of a marrying age, he needed to act quickly before one of the young men around town asked to court her for marriage. He knew she was knocked up which made it even easier for him to take her off her mother's hands. Curtis wanted her and nothing was going to stand in his way of getting her.

℀

"Hey Christina." Her friends Porsha and Roxanne walked into the yard laughing, beckoning her to put down the cleaning broom. Christina was sweeping off the porch careful to stay behind the porch pillar just in case Lewis drove by. She noticed he avoided her end of the street unless he had no other choice. Porsha and Roxanne were her only friends left, as everyone seemed to disappear when they heard she was pregnant.

"Come with us. We're going for some ice cream."

"I don't know. I'm kind of busy here."

"Doing what, counting days?"

Christina laughed a little and looked around. Her friends were right; that's exactly what she was doing. The yard didn't need any work and the house was spotless, thanks to her countless hours of cleaning and scrubbing. She could at least spend some time with her friends.

"Okay. Let me take this apron off. Are you coming to church tomorrow evening?"

"I have to help Mama with the programs for the afternoon service on Sunday."

"What about you, Roxanne?"

"I'm going to the races with Papa. Apparently he's got a bet going on a horse."

"So I'll be there by myself?" Christina tried not to sound disappointed by this. She thought at least one of her friends would keep her company while the vultures swarmed around her.

"Who's throwing the going away party?" Porsha asked.

"It's supposed to be the Autumn Horizons, but Mama is behind the whole thing."

"It'll be fine. Before you know it you'll be sipping lemonade by the Carolina Ocean and not giving a care what happens here."

"I'm going to miss you both," she said, bringing both of them in for a hug.

"We'll miss you too," they said in unison.

They walked the mile and a half down the road towards the ice cream store laughing and talking about the year-end festivals happening in the next couple of months. They arrived at the ice cream store just as it was about to close.

"I have got to go restroom. This baby is working my bladder something fierce."

As she left her friends ordering their favorite flavors, Christina could feel a pair of eyes following her. The outdoor toilet was a couple hundred yards away and there were people everywhere as this was the primary hang spot for teenagers in the neighborhood. She closed the wood door behind her and made sure critters weren't crawling as was the case most times before squatting on the wooden opening.

Christina was adjusting her clothes when two eyes peered through the cracks in the door and a voice she immediately recognized spoke through the opening.

"So that's what you look like with your draws down, and here I thought I was missing something."

"Someone help me please," she cried holding the door closed with one hand while pulling her panties up with the other.

"Why'nt you let me come in and see what all the fuss between those legs is about?"

"Go to hell Curtis," she said pushing her weight against the door opening it which sent him staggering in the opposite direction. Christina quickly half ran half walked back to where her friends were. This was the second time she'd seen Butch Curtis and both times she felt like covering herself with the nearest blanket. He sent her skin crawling for the nearest ointment.

"Marry me Christina. I could take real good care of you baby. All you need to do is tell ole Curtis whatcha need."

"I need you to leave me alone," she said over her shoulder.

"I think of you often little girl your hair your breasts. You think you too good to talk with ole Curtis? Ima ask for your hand real soon. I figure I owe it to your dead daddy seeing as I was the reason for his death."

That statement stopped her in her tracks as she turned to confront him.

"What the hell do you mean by that? What do you know about my father's death?"

"You know what your daddy's problem was he couldn't keep his dam mouth shut."

"If you're saying you had something to do with my dad's death Mr. Curtis then you're going to be in big trouble, and I'm not talking with the police."

"Trouble didn't start until your daddy came around now look where he at, six feet under."

"Hey Christina there you are." Roxanne and Porsha walked around the corner just then before Curtis tipped his hat and walked away.

"What was that all about?"

"Nothing he used to know my dad."

"That guy scares me. His eyes are small and beady like a mouse."

"Not a mouse, Roxanne, more like a rat."

Christina thought about the encounter on the way home. Curtis words cut through her like a knife and she wished she'd popped him right in the eye socket for speaking about her father that way. She was also thankful she hadn't bumped into Lewis or his friends while they were at the store. She didn't think she could stomach the sight of him while eating her ice cream. And she definitely didn't want to be questioned by her mother if someone saw her talking to him.

When it was time to go, they returned to the house, hugging Christina for the last time and from the front porch she waved goodbye as they disappeared down the road. Just then a car sped past her house and slowed as it reached the end of the street. Lewis. She stood behind the screen door so he wouldn't notice her watching, as if he was seeking her out anyway. He seemed to be in a hurry, not even glancing at the houses as he passed them.

The Chevy's black roof and cream colored slick body was always a sight to see in a town where there were still horse drawn wagons. She guessed this was his way of avoiding her too; a kind of mutual guilt on both their parts. It was just as well; she wouldn't know what to say to him anyway and she'd be leaving in the next few days. Christina rubbed her stomach. In the next couple of days, baby, you and me are going be gone from this place, and I for one cannot wait.

℘

On her last day Christina was sweeping the kitchen while Mama was sitting at the table shucking corn when the screen door swung open making a crashing sound.

"Hey, Chris, I heard that boy knocked you up." Uncle Bill burst through the screen door, his long legs making their way towards the kitchen area. Christina groaned inwardly. It didn't take long to figure out her uncle was getting viable information about her and Lewis, possibly from his family. The kind of information she guessed was none too pleasant.

Mama gasped. "Hush up, Bill."

He leaned down and kissed his sister on the cheek. "What? I'm just saying what all them Harris folks down the road there was talkin' bout."

He turned back to Christina. "Lewis did a job on you, girl. They're marrying him off to Stella Armstead. Pretty little thing with skin like butter, hair and nails all done up. What do you think about that, Chrissy?"

He grabbed an apple from the basket on the counter and took a bite, willing her to answer with a mischievous gleam in his eyes. Christina knew his motive. He wanted to see if he could make her angry. Uncle Bill was famous for starting trouble with people. All it took was for him to know your personal business and off he'd go, but not today. Today she was determined to avoid the negative talkers and naysayers that seemed to seep into her everyday existence now that word had spread to people around the neighborhood. God knows who else knew about it now that Uncle Bill got wind of it. She was sure half of Henry County had heard the news before morning breakfast, as Uncle Bill was the regular news anchorman around town.

Christina pretended she was busy cleaning the spotless table to avoid her uncle's stare.

"Good for him. I hope they make it." She kept her voice steady and void of emotion. She didn't want to give him any more ammunition than he already had. Christina turned away from him so he couldn't see the tears welling up in her eyes. She didn't notice he had inched close to whisper in her ear.

"You know what they say, closer kin deeper in."

Christina took slow deep breaths to control her temper. His disgusting attitude was getting to her and she was trying hard to not let it show.

"Stop baitin' Christina, Bill," Mama warned.

"Oh come on, girl, I'm just messin' with you. I know how you really feel."

You don't know a damn thing, she thought. Closing her eyes for a split second, she kept the circular motion of the rag going against the table. "They'll be married come this summer. Hope you pick out a pretty little dress." He said the last sentence with as much mockery in his tone as he could.

"That's enough, Bill," her Mother said, finally ending his taunts.

"Aww, I'm just teasing her, Mary."

"Come and tell me what's going on down at the mill. I heard they had another terrible accident."

He turned away from her with a smirk on his face and went to talk to his sister. Christina snorted and threw the cleaning rag down on the table. She couldn't call her uncle an ass; it would be disrespectful. But she sure wanted to at the moment. That bit of news felt like a knife had just been thrust through her gut for the second time. She sat in the chair and looked out the window, wiping away a tear that unknowingly made its way down her cheek.

The pain in her heart seemed like it was increasing every day with every bit of news about Lewis Harris. And now he had a fiancée? Charleston, South Carolina was looking better by the minute. She wouldn't have to listen to anymore sarcastic remarks from her uncles, or hear the laughter behind her back from people who had known her for years. She definitely didn't want any more embarrassment coming to her family. And most of all she would be as far away from Lewis Harris as she could possibly get.

The afternoon was creeping by at a snail's pace. After finishing the kitchen clean-up, Christina decided to sit and read anything to take her mind off Uncle Bill's traitorous ways. She was on the first chapter of the book Mice and Men when a car pulled into the yard. Christina slowly put the book down beside her on the bench as Roger, Lewis' older brother, got out with both hands in the air.

"I come in peace," he said.

She always thought Roger was a good guy even though she was well into her late teens when she finally got to know him. He was willing to help at every request and a gentleman to every woman he met, which was a stark contrast to Lewis at this point. She watched as he made his way to the porch. Roger and his wife Virginia lived in Mills town behind the church. They were married at eighteen with their first child being born soon after that. Christina knew Roger would be a good father who took care of his family. His brother Lewis obviously didn't know what that meant. Why couldn't she have met him first? *Oh shoot; he's family too.*

"Hey, Chrissy," he said, leaning forward and putting one foot on the step.

"Hey, Roger. What brings you by?"

"Lewis tells me I'm gonna be an uncle."

"Really? He told me he didn't think the baby was his." Christina looked towards the road. The conversation was making her uncomfortable already.

"We all know the baby is his, Christina."

"Then why would he say something like that? And why would your grandmother agree?"

"Because my brother's an ass and he was trying to sound right in the eyes of our grandmother."

"Doesn't he realize this isn't a game? How am I supposed to explain his actions to our child?"

"I think we'll all be able to talk to one another about this in time. I'm just hoping you won't hold this against all of us and we'll get to see the baby."

"Of course you will, Roger." She stood and folded her arms looking out towards the road. Out of Lewis' family Roger was the only one that had taken the time to come and speak with her. The others hadn't made the slightest effort.

"I wouldn't keep my baby from his aunts or uncles even if the father doesn't want to be with me."

"I'm sorry about that, Christina," he said, putting his head down. "I can't say I'm happy about how Lewis is treating this situation."

Christina was glad he showed that he cared about what went on between her and his brother.

"It's okay. I understand. Right now I have other things to worry about."

"What do you mean?"

"Butch Curtis bumped into me twice, once at the Tasty Cream, and the other time at my job. It's like he was seeking me out which is strange because I haven't seen him since he came with the police that day to tell me my Dad was killed."

"Do you think he's just trying to heal his conscience because of what happened?"

"I don't think so because he said the reason my Dad died was because he couldn't keep his mouth shut."

"So you think he knows more than what he's saying?"

"Yes. But why would he tell me, and why now ten years later?"

"Sometimes it takes a while for the truth to show up even in people who you least expect."

Christina wondered if there was hidden meaning behind those words. "Are we still talking about Curtis, or are you trying to say something else."

"We needed to have this conversation a long time ago but I guess now is a good time. You need to know the real reason why the family wasn't speaking to one another years ago."

Christina nodded and sat down on the top step. She was determined to know the truth even if it hurt her more than what it already had.

"It was rumored that my mother was a dancehall working girl when I was about eight years old."

"How can that be? Aunt Evelyn was in Maryland for a long time and I really didn't get the chance to know her until recently."

"That's because she was back and forth from here to Maryland every weekend, not just once a month like she told my father."

"How did you find this out?"

"My father told me after she revealed she had fallen in love with one of her sister's husbands."

Christina gasped. "I'm so sorry, Roger. That must've been the reason Mama wasn't talking to her for all these years. She found out Aunt Evelyn deceived one of her sister's. Did she tell Uncle Edmund who she was in love with?"

Roger cleared his throat. He didn't know how he was going to tell her what happened during that time. Maybe the person who needed to explain the full story was her mother. Only the small details needed to be revealed.

"No. And he never asked. It tore the family apart and no one was speaking to one another. She chose to leave her lover after a while, preferring to focus on her family."

"So how does this tie in with me and Lewis?"

"She was teaching in Dorchester County, Maryland in order to help put food on the table. Dad wasn't working during that time and Lewis had to be raised with Mama, being as how she was a teacher and he a slow learner. I stayed here to help Dad."

"How did you two keep in touch over the years?" she asked.

"Mom would come down when she made enough money and Lewis would sometimes be with her or he'd stay with family. Then she'd go back to continue teaching."

"We must've missed each other several times. I don't really remember Mama going over there at all. She told me one day they didn't have much of a relationship and I never questioned why. They didn't seem real close during those times."

"No, they weren't." Roger put his head down. "That was because of the relationship she kept with her lover. What she did separated the family something big for everyone to not speak the way they did."

"It's alright, Roger. They just couldn't get along. And now that I understand why, it seems they were truly at odds with one another. I can't imagine. They seem alright now."

"Yeah, I guess you're right. Lewis only visited when she allowed him to. The family didn't see him much."

"I must've been in school or working in Richmond when he would come down to visit."

"When Mama finally moved back home three months ago for good, nobody recognized Lewis because he'd grown up so much. And no one knew that you two had already met at the fair in Fredericksburg a couple of months before then."

"We would meet in Fredericksburg sometimes on the weekends. He said some of his people were from Virginia but I never questioned it. I never put two and two together."

"He never told you his last name?"

"I only knew him as Lewis. That's what his friends were calling him when we met. His last name wasn't mentioned."

"We were excited when Mom said she was done teaching up in Maryland."

"I was excited when he told me he would be moving to Henry County," Christina said, staring blankly at the ground.

"And it wasn't until he finally came to your mama's house that he figured out who you were. Your mama told him his cousin Christina would be happy to finally meet him."

Christina's eyes closed. She recalled the day when things started to change between her and Lewis. "He must've been humiliated. No wonder he didn't touch me that day."

Roger sat down beside Christina. "He said he didn't want to hurt you when he met with you later that week."

"But he could've told me something. No one said anything."

"He was waiting for a good time to let you know."

"Anytime would've been a good time, Roger. My God, I am humiliated!"

"I should've been there. Maybe things would've been a lot different."

"What could you have done that wasn't done already? Mama thought at first we were just going out until she saw the looks we gave one another."

"She didn't say anything either?"

"No. She thought everything would work itself out all on its own when it just made things worse."

"This isn't anyone's fault, Christina, and there's one more thing you need to know."

"I really don't think I can take anymore news. Everyone is blaming me, Roger." She stood up, clearly agitated at her own choice of words. She gestured to her figure. "I'm pregnant and a disgrace to my family."

"Don't think that way, Chris." He grabbed her in a bear hug with his chin sitting atop her head. "Everything will be okay. It'll work itself out. You'll see."

Now that she finally knew the whole story she still didn't feel any better, only guiltier and far more ignorant for not piecing the puzzle together from the beginning.

The scent of the garden coupled with the farm animals running around the house made her nostalgic. This place had been home her entire life. Even though she was spending a little over a year at Aunt Bessie's, it felt like she would be gone for a long time without the presence of her mother, brothers and sisters, or friends to keep her company.

೧

She heard someone coming down the road that afternoon sobbing and immediately knew who it was. Uncle Jerry. Uncle Jerry was Mama's older brother and a WWII veteran who lived down the road in a log home. He came by the house daily to visit and bring whatever animal he'd killed for the day so Mama could cook it. It was usually a groundhog caught after attacking the vegetables in his garden. Uncle Bill often said the war made Jerry crazy, making his mind seem child-like. Wars took a toll on small towns and Henry County was no exception. During the war, Mama said the women had to substitute at their husbands' jobs while they were overseas, or training.

Christina remembered that time as if it were yesterday. She was young but could recall churches were packed with women and children every Sunday, some praying and some crying. She witnessed women going to work in military uniforms in downtown Richmond, and others even driving small military vehicles with weapons. She was glad her uncle made it home, as so many others didn't during that time. Uncle Jerry never spoke of what he saw or what he did, not even when his sister tried to hold a conversation with him about warfare. It was understood amongst everyone that he didn't want to speak about it and so no one brought it up, not even when he wasn't at the house.

Christina could see her younger brothers and sisters were playing with Jerry, tossing his hat back and forth so he couldn't get to it. The laughter was infectious. Christina couldn't help but chuckle as they reached the middle of the yard.

"Mary, tell dem chiren give me my hat back," he yelled. "I got to hide my bald spot."

This statement was clearly not true, as Uncle Jerry had a head full of gray hair. Why he thought he was balding was beyond comprehension. This made Christina laugh nonetheless as she called his name. Her uncle may have a slow mind, but he always treated her with love and kindness, unlike some others. She also loved the fact that whenever she asked for a song he always seemed to have one. Christina had to call to him twice as she knew he needed time to figure out who she was.

"Sandy Su, is that you?" he asked. He turned to greet her with a smile and hug.

"No, Uncle Jerry, it's me, Christina. Remember little Chrissy?"

His eyes finally registered on his favorite niece. He stepped back a little and smiled. "Camilla Jean. What you up to?"

Christina laughed. "Hi, Uncle Jerry let me get your hat for you."

It usually took him a couple tries to get her name right. For some reason he needed more time to figure out her name today. She had to pry the hat from her little sister telling her to run along while shaking off the dust before giving it back to him.

"Thank you so much, June Bug, you're the only good one here." Christina sat next to him on the porch steps.

Just then one of Christina's younger brothers came back and slapped him on the back of the head before running away.

"Mary, dem chiren gone make me hurt em," he cried.

"Bo, get out of here before I spank your hide," she yelled at her younger brother, enough to startle him. The little boy took the hint and ran to catch up with his sister.

"Thank you baby you the only good one here. Chiren ain't got no discipline. May gonna have to take a switch to their behinds." He adjusted his hat while saying this, scowling at her brothers and sisters as their laughter trailed behind them.

"Uncle Jerry, you got a song for me? I could really use one." Christina sat next to her uncle while she waited for him to answer.

"I surely do. Don't you worry, li'l Chrissy. Love will find you again. And when it do you gone know it, like honey to a bee."

Christina wondered who told Uncle Jerry the news, Mama or Uncle Bill. It really didn't matter now since she'd be leaving pretty soon. They could talk her name up one street and down another for all she cared. None of it mattered now. She'd be going to an entirely different state in the next few days.

"I don't know about that, Uncle Jerry. I kind of just want to be left alone for a while."

"I understand, Chrissy. I was once in love too. Died way before you was born. Patsy was her name and she was a pretty thing." Christina smiled. Uncle Jerry always talked about Patsy. There wasn't a moment she could remember where he wasn't bringing up her name.

"You see, Camilla Jean, love happens sometimes whether we want it or not. When you get it, take care of it, and it will take care of you." Christina pondered that statement for a moment. Was it true? Did love all of a sudden come between two people who least expected it? She wasn't sure if that was possible. Both she and Lewis seemed to have a mutual attraction between one another when they first met and it blossomed from there. Love was stronger on her part, she realized now, than his. Maybe it was more lust on his end than love. She shook her head. Her love was real. It was just upsetting that his wasn't.

Uncle Jerry grabbed his guitar beside him, folded his long legs one over the other and began to sing. Christina immediately recognized the song, "It isn't fair," by Dinah Washington. The words reflected the enormous amount of emotion that was coursing through her body at that moment. She sat beside Uncle Jerry as each verse weighed heavily on her mind and in her heart. Ms. Washington's song could be heard in the house every evening on the radio.

The melody was like a torrential storm on a mission, its aim directly penetrating Christina's soul. Everything she felt from pain to heartache was in that song. Its words sending her head to lay on Uncle Jerry's shoulder while the guitar ended its final note on the last verse and the music faded into the afternoon air. She didn't know why Uncle Jerry picked that particular song, as he usually sang one that he made up five minutes before he got there. She had the impression he was trying to tell her he knew about the Lewis situation, and he was just telling her in his own little way. Uncle Jerry put his arm around her shoulders and squeezed. He supported her and at that moment she felt like crying all over again. She placed her head on his shoulder and closed her eyes. "Thank you, Uncle Jerry."

"You're welcome, Chrissy. Now go on and live your life. You'll learn to love again. It may be here or elsewhere. But remember one of the worse things you can do in life is be afraid to love." He squeezed again and patted her shoulders.

"Okay, Uncle Jerry."

"I want that baby to come into this world healthy and happy."

"You might be the only one. No one else besides Abigail and Roger have said that to me."

"Oh no. It's all of us, Chrissy. All of us want what's best for you."

"What about Lewis' side?" She lifted her head to watch his face for any negative reaction.

But there wasn't a scowl or sign of anger displayed on his weathered face. He didn't give off the hint that Lewis' family was being difficult with the news.

"I'm sure they'll come round. Some are in real shock, some can't believe it, and others are just crazy as hell."

She laughed. Uncle Jerry may talk gibberish sometimes, but other times he made perfect sense. He shifted his position so that he was facing her.

"One thing is certain. Once a babe comes into the world, everything changes. Life goes on as time goes on and things they always gonna change for the better, Chrissy, you'll see."

"Thanks, Uncle Jerry."

"You're welcome. baby. Now go on in there and tell Mary I need my groundhog stew ready when I come back from visitin' Patsy's grave."

Christina made a disgusted face and laughed. "I will."

She watched her uncle grab his guitar and head down the road towards the church, whistling the tune he'd just played for her. If only all of her family were as sweet and comforting as Uncle Jerry, but she knew that was asking for too much. The sun was making its last appearance for the day, dipping in and out of the clouds and leaving its red silhouette against the sky. Christina wanted it to stay like this for as long as possible. She breathed in the country air; its mix of vegetation from the garden and surrounding shrubbery smelled wonderful. Rubbing her upper arms she made her way into the house to prepare for the evening's events.

She chose a blue skirt, which accented her hips and hung down to her ankles for the church honoree program. A white long sleeve blouse hid her slightly swollen breasts and she braided her hair in one long plait with only a few tendrils to surround her face. The outfit was modest at best, plus she didn't want to draw too much attention on herself, as these people focused more on what you wore than the good book itself. Thankfully she wasn't showing too much yet, so the dress fit in the right places with a slight bulge in the middle. She exhaled as she walked through the doors of the dining hall.

Christina felt under pressure, having been badgered by her mama after she unsuccessfully tried to get out of attending the evening's festivities. She finally surrendered and decided to attend one last home event. Christina wasn't at all ecstatic about where the dinner was taking place or the people that were there supposedly celebrating her leave. The expression on her face couldn't quite reach a friendly smile when she saw Lewis' sisters and aunts. And they likewise seemed annoyed at being at an event in her honor.

Her mother probably should've provided a male date just to give a bit more falsehood to the story she already told. She no doubt told them a lie to keep their mouths from yapping about her life, but that didn't keep the gossip at bay, nor did it keep any of Mama's friends from asking questions.

Mrs. Pearl did just that. As soon as Christina walked through the door she wanted to know if she was doing "fine." Others just simply shunned her and wouldn't speak, such as the aunts and cousins of Lewis. Christina overheard some call her a bed wench as she walked by and she had to fight back the tears that threatened to creep into her eyes. As the evening dragged on she realized what the dinner was all about. This was her mother's way of showing her friends that Christina was moving on with her life and not giving a care for Lewis Harris. She made sure she held her head high as she searched for her mother. This was going to be a very long evening. There was simply too much on Christina's mind as she made her way to the honoree's table and sat beside her mother.

She decided to be cordial and grateful for the dinner as the first plate was placed in front of her. At first glance it seemed everyone was enthralled with the conversations at their table, but as the evening went along Christina could see that most of the conversations were about her. There were scowls instead of smiles directed her way, and the occasional nose in the air with a slight head toss was directed at her plenty of times.

Christina watched the clock, wondering how long she would have to endure this. A kitchen helper came just then to refill her glass. The girl looked no more than ten years old with an apron around her waist. The picture she created was one Christina was all too familiar with. She had begun her job in much the same way, serving church folks until one day her mother said she had to "earn her keep" and got her the maid's job she had just left.

Little girls were taught to serve, while also being taught the importance of education until a certain age. Then they were made to work on the farm, in the house, or as a housekeeper. Christina wondered if the girl had been asked about her life goals or even if she was interested in achieving something other than what was expected. Christina thanked the little girl for the water. She found herself alone at the table when dinner was over. Mama was helping clean the kitchen and everyone seemed content with avoiding her end of the table. She wanted to eat but was leery of the eyes darting back and forth towards her, accompanied by whispers. She was just about to slide the cream cheese pound cake towards her when an elder woman made her way to Christina's end of the table. Mrs. Carter was the first lady, Sunday school teacher, and head singer of the women's choir. Unfortunately, hospitality wasn't what she was known for.

"You don't appear too concerned with your condition, dear."

The abruptness of that statement caught Christina off guard. This was the moment that Christina dreaded. Mrs. Carter had a group of mean looking women behind her. Did her mother think that these women would actually not speak openly about this issue? They were church people, yes, but when it came to situations outside the church they could be downright vicious. In another life they must've been vipers, for surely they were spitting venom her way now.

"Excuse me? I have no condition that I need to be concerned with, Mrs. Carter." Christina was infuriated with the woman. How dare they come to her this way in front of everyone?

"You don't think we're ignorant do you, Christina? You came in here with that tight dress probably thinking men were going to be here."

"I did no such thing," Christina replied.

"We each have had more than one child and know the signs, the expanded hips, weight gain." Her eyes travelled the length of Christina with a sneer across her lips. She leaned in closer so that Christina could clearly hear her next comments.

"You don't belong here with these fine women. Girls like you need to go before the church and apologize. Everyone knows what you've done. You've ruined that boy's life," she sneered.

The women behind her nodded their heads in agreement. They were obviously her supporters, more like puppets being told when to speak and when not to. Christina stood up quickly, making her chair slide backwards, screeching against the stone floor.

"I did no such thing. How dare you accuse me?" Her voice escalated loud enough to turn a few heads. She was just about to leave to save herself from further humiliation when her mother suddenly appeared by her side.

"That's enough, Teresa." Her mother stood in front of Christina, blocking her attacker's venomous accusations.

But the woman kept going like she had diarrhea of the mouth. "It's just the same. Her father was as much the whore as she is right now."

Mary Davis gasped and pointed a finger in the woman's face. "You keep my husband's name out of your mouth."

Christina turned to her mother. "Mama, what does she mean by that?"

"My goodness, Mary, didn't you ever let her know about her father? He was much like you, dear quick to spread his legs while destroying families in the process."

"I said that's enough, Teresa."

"She didn't even beg the pardon of the church. And do you know how this will look to other communities? Why, it's just scandalous."

"Christina will beg the church's pardon in due time. I sincerely hope you're asking Lewis to do the same."

"Your daughter is the harlot here. Why would we need to get the young man involved?"

Christina watched as her mother stepped closer to the antagonizing old bat. It was one thing to criticize the act of fornication, but to insult her daughter was something different.

"I suggest you stay away from my daughter and keep my late husband's name out of your mouth if you know what's good for you."

Her mother's voice had changed just that quickly. Just a few minutes ago she was the kitchen helper; now she was a lioness, aggressive and protective of her cub.

"We don't need that kind of trouble around here, Mary. I suggest you find a cell to lock her in before she causes anymore shame to your family's name and this community."

She walked away with her group of supporters following behind her. Their argument had drawn a crowd that was now looking at Christina and her mother. Some were whispering and others were shaking their heads. Christina didn't see a sympathetic face in sight, which made her feel more alone than ever. Mrs. Carter's behavior hurt most of all. She had known her since she was a child. How could she turn from such a sweet woman one minute to a malicious person the next? Clearly she only got half of the story from Lewis' side of the family. And obviously those who knew about what happened had already taken sides. Her mother turned to her with an irritable look in her eyes.

"Christina, go home. Let me set things straight here and I'll meet you there," her mother said sternly.

She wanted to stay and ask what that wretched woman meant by talking about her father that way, but she couldn't bring herself to do it. The tension was so thick you could cut it with a knife.

"Yes, ma'am."

She left the dinner with her head down, feeling like the lowest person on earth. It wasn't enough for these women to know of her indiscretions, but to blatantly display their dislike for her in public and blame her for ruining someone's life was too much. Looking back, the shining lights from the church dimmed as she moved closer to the house and welcomed the thought that by this time tomorrow she'd be far away from this place and these horrible people.

Chapter 7

S he should have left a long time ago. The back seat of the Chevy
Coup was better than the bed she'd slept on her entire life with its
mercury brown striped wool seats and cream colored interior. The car
pulled into the yard during the mid-morning hours, coming to a halt
in front of the porch steps. Christina was dressed and ready by the time
Russell opened the gate, and Mama had already prepared breakfast
along with a light lunch for the road. Only her mother, brother, and
Uncle Jerry were present to see her off. Looking across the field, she
noticed her grandmother standing on the porch with her arms crossed.
Christina placed her fingers to her lips and waved a sentimental gesture they often shared together when one was going away for a while.
Her grandmother repeated the gesture and slowly walked back into her
house. She stood in that spot for a few minutes breathing in the country air, thankful that she had a supportive and loving grandparent.

The goodbyes after that came leisurely and full of emotion. Christina
couldn't pinpoint how she felt. It definitely was a mixture of sadness
and relief, sadness that she had to leave her home and siblings behind,
relief that she didn't have to see that no good Lewis Harris for the next
year or more. Her mother had come from greeting Joseph to give her
a final goodbye hug. Christina couldn't help asking about what Mrs.
Carter had said the night before about her father.

"That was nothing, Chrissy. I took care of Mrs. Carter."

"But she was talking bad about Daddy like she knew something."

"Don't you worry about that now go on and promise me you'll write every week to let us know how you're doing."

"I promise, Mama."

She knew her questions were being avoided but decided not to press the issue. One day her mother would tell her what she wanted to know; she just hoped she'd be able to take the news as it came. Joseph shook her brother's and Uncle Jerry's hand before climbing into the driver's seat. She waved her last goodbye as the car pulled out of the driveway, gazing out the window with her hands centered in her lap. Joseph didn't say much and she didn't know whether to start a conversation or go to sleep. The road to Aunt Bessie's was going to be a long one so she decided small talk would be the best thing to make the time go by.

"How long have you lived in South Carolina?" she asked him.

"I'm spent my whole life in Charleston, born and raised."

"How long have you known Auntie?"

Silence not a word. Okay, too personal, she thought. She could take the hint.

"Before you see your Aunt, young lady, you need to know the history behind the place you'll be staying."

Christina nodded. Actually she would agree to any interesting topic of conversation to make the time go by. It felt like they'd been on the same road for hours already.

Joseph began talking about the history of James Island and the importance of it to its African American descendants. James Island was one amongst four islands, including the islands of Johns, Edisto, and Wadmalaw, which had been homes to indigenous dark skin people before the slave trade as well as ports of entry for many people of Africans coming to America during the slave trade. In the 1600s, some Africans came from West African countries such as Sierra Leone and Ghana, sought after because of their skill in cultivating ice. The relationship between slave and plantation owner developed the town and wasn't without hardship.

There were many cultural differences, difficulties, and mistreatments as Africans fought to work and be treated equally as citizens. Christina thought it was the same today; the issue of equality hadn't changed. They were still making strides for better conditions in the nineteen fifties, much like other cities in the south. Joseph told her that Aunt Bessie's house had been given to her by an elderly woman named Eloise Jefferson, a descendent of a Sierra Leone slave, whose children all moved north to Chicago seeking better opportunities. Africans in the Low Country believed in passing land to their children to keep their history for future generations. However, in this situation Auntie was more like a close friend to the family who was the next best choice for keeping the house and land.

"Didn't the children have a problem with that?"

"As long as the house and land were in good hands, they knew everything was going to be alright. Plus your auntie was a trusted friend. It was a beautiful piece of property anyone would want to have."

"Wow, she was lucky."

"Your Aunt promised Mrs. Jefferson she would take care of the land and keep it until the time came to sell it or for someone in Bessie's family to inherit it."

She had to tell Joseph to stop and use the bathroom at least five times after the history lesson. Her thoughts kept drifting as she watched the scenery change from farms to trees back to farms and cattle. The car continued down the road, loneliness surrounding her like a thick inflexible cloud. Joseph hadn't offered any refreshment other than the water he carried in a jug seated on the floor. She sighed heavily, extremely parched, but thought better of asking for anything. She had no idea how long that jug had been sitting there. The breakfast and lunch Mama packed was consumed quickly two hours into the ride, and she didn't want to ask Joseph for anything, seeing as he really wasn't in a talkative mood. No, he simply didn't say anything after that, stopping only for gas and to relieve himself while she drifted in and out of sleep. She didn't know what waited her in South Carolina but it had to be a hell of a lot better than the mess she had created for herself in Virginia.

As the car sped down the road, drifting closer to their destination, she said a silent prayer that her little miracle would be born healthy, and that her heart would heal from the beating it took before she left. Her eyes were getting heavy again. She tried to get comfortable by resting her head against the window, and her mind drifted to Lewis again. It was always like this when she was going to sleep, as if her mind just wanted to immediately switch to an imaginative world where he was present and everything was better. She didn't want to think about him. She didn't want to think about his lips, or his hands, or how either of them made her feel. She couldn't. She wanted her mind to be free and clear of that monster and his family. Damn him! He was still trying to get to her, and she was over three hundred miles away by now. To forget it ever happened was the only option she had. But how could she forget her first love, even though he was her kin? How would she explain the relationship to her baby when he or she became old enough to understand? She would have to dig deep for strength and transfer what was left of her love to her unborn child.

As sleep finally claimed her, Christina hoped her dreams stayed clear of the recurring nightmare she had when she fell asleep. It was always the same. She was running with a baby in her arms, her hair in wild disarray, calling Lewis and trying to get to him before he was to marry. All of a sudden she slipped and fell, but instead of hitting the ground she kept falling and falling with no end in sight.

Suddenly she was jolted from her dreams by a strong hand. Joseph.

"Wake up Christina. Welcome to your new home."

She slowly opened her eyes. There was water as far as the eye could see; a mix of blue and green were on both sides of the road like a welcoming carpet complete with small boats. They rode past huge homes and yards she would later learn were plantations, very well preserved by the decedents who took care of them. Some of the homes had white pillars standing as tall as trees against brick foundations with white shutters and thick shrubbery. Others were small country homes with wide porches surrounded by beautiful gardens and moss trees.

Christina thought this was the most beautiful place she'd ever seen. They turned on a dirt road and several minutes later pulled up to a quaint cottage nestled on its own land with beautiful shrubberies and trees with moss hanging from its branches. It was a small white cottage with blue shutters and flowers of yellow and red decorating the walkway up to the porch. It didn't look like anyone was home as she got out of the car and noticed the porch wrapped around to the sides of the house, making it seem wider then she initially thought. The quiet seclusion of the area almost reminded Christina of home with the wooded space near the rear. The cool breeze coming from the ocean danced against her nostrils, exposing her to the salty sea air. It was relaxing and almost made her want to go to sleep again.

Why hadn't Auntie invited them to come see her home before now? Or maybe she had. Knowing Mama, the invitation probably stayed with her and her alone. She considered the fact that there were a lot more children in her mother's house and Auntie was a single woman who didn't have experience with children. Still, she wondered after all this time why no one had really seen where or how she lived.

Christina noticed there were two rocking chairs seated side by side and pondered just how close Joseph and Auntie were. Just then the front door swung open. Bessie Washington's face looked stern and unmoving. Christina didn't need to wonder anymore if her mother had told her the full story. Auntie's face said it all. At least she didn't have to worry about explaining it herself. As Christina got closer, Bessie had crossed her arms and was observing her attire, looking her over from top to bottom. Christina hoped she wouldn't be too critical, as she was so emotional nowadays. The least little criticism could have her running back to Virginia.

"Hi, Aunt Bessie."

"In this house you'll cook and clean. You'll raise your child and go to church. Is that understood?" Bessie said sternly.

"Yes, ma'am."

"If by chance you meet a young man, and you might, seeing as you have the Davis' good looks, you must have my permission along with a chaperone to see that you're properly respected."

"Yes, ma'am."

"Now come along. I got supper on the table. Joseph, bring the bags in the house and set them in her room."

As Christina went inside, she didn't witness Bessie looked towards the sky, close her eyes and breathe a sigh of relief. The elder woman said a prayer of thanks and asked for patience in guiding this niece whom she barely knew.

A rush of cool air from the ocean swept through the house and welcomed Christina as she reached the center of the living room. The aroma of cinnamon bread from the kitchen filled her nostrils and made her mouth water. Auntie's house was just as beautiful on the inside as it was on the outside, with two full couches set against a cream colored wall. There were family pictures on every table, with her mother and Bessie being in most of them. The wood floors stretched from the living room toward the hallway.

"I hope this home can be just like your home in Virginia, Christina. I want you to be as comfortable as possible."

"It's beautiful, Auntie. Thank you for allowing me to stay with you."

"You didn't think I was gonna stop you from staying here, did you?"

"No, I guess not."

Christina got a good look at her then. A robust woman, Aunt Bessie was the middle sister and the prettiest out of all her aunts. Her hair, now salt and pepper, was still thick and braided down her back with loose strands hanging around her neck. Her figure was enhanced by the green and white striped dress that tapered around her waist and flowed to her ankles. Aunt Bessie's honey skin hadn't aged at forty years old, surprising considering the hard work she did maintaining her employer's household.

Open arms and a solid chest crushed Christina in a bear hug long overdue.

"My niece is finally here," she said.

"Yes, I finally made it," Christina replied. Her voice was shaky. She was feeling a little nervous since she hadn't seen her aunt in over ten years, and the welcome she had just received put her a bit on edge.

"I've missed you, baby. You've grown like a weed since the last time I saw you."

"Mama says I outgrew my clothes faster than the other kids, so much that she had to ask the rich folks in town for a raise to buy clothes."

Aunt Bessie smiled. "That sounds like my big sis. After dinner, you'll have to tell me about the family on the farm, dear."

"Yes, ma'am."

"Go on to your room now and unpack your clothes. If you need any help just give a holler. We'll talk more at supper." Her voice was gentle and understanding. Christina wondered about the change in her approach as she was ushered down the hall to the small bedroom. The room was quaint, with a bed, dresser, nightstand, and closet.

She was finally going to be able to sleep in a room by herself without the small feet of her younger sisters pushing into her side. The window in the room was facing the rear of the house and she noticed the blue water could be seen through the brush of the trees. Christina quickly said a prayer of thanks. This scenery wasn't bad at all. She opened her suitcase, which Joseph had graciously placed on the bed, and began putting her clothes away and must've been in the room for a long time before Auntie's voice came through the door.

"Christina, are you alright in there?"

"Yes, I'm fine. I'm just trying to get better acquainted with the room." Go wash yourself up now. Dinner's almost ready," she said.

"Yes, ma'am," Christina replied as she walked past her.

Conversation at the table wasn't at all what Christina expected. Aunt Bessie talked about her time in South Carolina and how wonderful the people were. She talked about the farmers markets, her friends, the ocean, and the sea creatures diving in and out of the waves on some mornings as she went to work. Christina was in such a trance with the picture that Bessie was creating with her words that she almost forgot her nervousness. It wasn't until dessert that the subject she dreaded talking about finally came up.

She was halfway done with a delicious coconut pie when Bessie decided to talk about her indiscretion.

"Your Mother told me everything, Christina. So let's talk about it." She knew it would come up eventually. Christina tried to put something in her mouth to delay the conversation, but the coconut pie was just about gone.

"There's not much to tell. I met someone who I thought loved me," she said, hunching her shoulders.

"Oh sweetheart, I'm so sorry."

Christina swatted the air in a nonchalant manner like her mother did when she was trying to explain her feelings. "It was stupid."

Bessie reached out her hand and covered Christina's. "Look at me, Christina."

She could feel her emotions climbing from her stomach to her throat as she tried looking at her aunt. She prayed for a distraction at the moment but didn't receive one.

"Being in love is not stupid. And one day you'll learn the meaning of true love."

"I thought I did. I mean I thought I had it. But it wasn't meant to be," she said sadly.

"That wasn't your fault. Someone should have told you who your kinfolk were before you got into this mess."

Christina could feel the anger and emotion about to pour out of her. She wanted to excuse herself before that happened. "I'm embarrassed, Auntie. Can I go to my room?"

She slowly stood from her seat, trying to fight the tears that threatened to come down and began walking to her room. Bessie sat back in her chair and looked at her with a concerned expression.

"Yes, of course, dear," she replied. "Christina?"

She turned to look at her aunt, who had a distraught look on her face?

"We all make mistakes, honey. What you have inside of you now is a blessing from that mistake. Don't forget that."

"Yes, ma'am," Christina said.

"Wednesday this week we'll go see Doctor Winston. I've already made the appointment so he'll be expecting us." Christina nodded her approval. "Go rest now. I'll check in on you later."

Christina made her way to the bedroom and removed her clothes slowly. The events of the day were finally catching up to her and she felt exhausted. After putting on her nightgown she crawled into bed, placing the soft feathered pillow comfortably behind her head. Tomorrow she would start a new beginning in this place. No more Lewis, no more gossip, no more hypocritical church people talking behind her back. She breathed in the salt air coming through her bedroom window and said a small prayer for grace and patience. In the next couple of months she would need both.

Chapter 8

Michael Rose was finally home. His trip to Savannah, Georgia proved productive, as he had made successful business deals and met new potential business partners. He was physically exhausted when he finally entered the house and set his bag down on the floor just inside the door.

"Welcome home, sir."

"Thank you, George. How did everything go while I was away?"

"Mrs. Rose came by to check on the house, and Ms. Patrice sent a Thank you letter for the roses she received."

"Is there any news about my father's trip?"

"Yes, he sent word that business is going well in New Orleans and he should be home in the next week or so."

Michael smiled. His father never missed an opportunity to acquire new prospects for the family business even if it meant travelling days on end to do it.

As the oldest of four children, Michael Rose was broadly built with wide shoulders, powerful arms, and long legs. His Creole ancestry stopped at the warm cinnamon colored eyes, smooth rich caramel skin tone and southern drawl in his speech. Everything else belonged to Senegal West African, also known as Gullah heritage. His mother would prefer he not claim this side of his ancestry, as it would mean delving into slavery's past, which in South Carolina society meant that you came from a poorer community instead of the wealthy society his parents had claimed for him.

The Gullah were known as basket weavers, a tradition carried from rice cultivation in West Africa to the eastern shores of the Americas, namely South Carolina during the 1680s. They taught the locals their techniques and knowledge of rice growing, while also contributing economically to the rice market of the South.

Michael claimed every inch of his Gullah heritage, attributing his own entrepreneurial characteristics to the culture that sustained so many hardships during that time. They still were a huge part of South Carolina history with one of the largest communities located on James Island. His brothers and sisters all felt the same way, preferring to preserve all of their history instead of only the wealthy part, as their mother would have wanted.

A knock came at the door.

Michael heard George greet the visitor just before a pair of plump breasts came to rest in the center of his back.

"I'm glad you're home," she said, sliding her hands up and down the middle of his pants. Her intentions were clear. Patrice St. Clair was an attractive woman with reddish brown hair, golden highlights around her temples and deep chocolate eyes. Her thick frame turned plenty of heads, and she knew just how to work her feminine wiles on the men who found her attractive. She might've been a good woman on the outside, but she was an experienced woman everywhere else, choosing to be discrete with her lovers and meeting them only at their residences. She could've made someone a decent wife, but she chose lust over marriage, a decision he himself had made not too long ago. Michael knew this and yet he only tolerated her when he needed to release built up tension from long business trips. He wasn't ignorant of the lovers she kept, only requesting that she see him and only him when he was in town. Patrice always agreed, which was a plus for his libido. But today's timing was off. His mother was coming over to have lunch with him before he settled in for the afternoon and he wanted no further distractions. He pushed her hand away.

"Oh come now, darling," she said. "We always have fun when you come home."

"It's two o'clock in the afternoon, Patrice. My mother will be here soon."

He walked away from her, agitated by her lackadaisical attitude. Women like Patrice needed to know they couldn't just disrupt an event no matter what they looked like or what they were presenting.

"Why can't you just tell her you and I are a couple?"

"Because she wouldn't buy that lie, nor do I." Patrice pouted, clearly put off by his answer.

"Well then, maybe I should tell her," she said with a sly grin.

Not taking the bait, Michael looked at her with an emotionless face. "Go home, Patrice. I'll call on you when I need you."

"Don't bother. You're not the only eligible bachelor in town, Michael Rose," she said before turning to leave. Patrice almost knocked over his mother who was standing just inside the doorway.

"Excuse me, ma'am," she said, noticing the elder woman's expensive satin coral dress and matching purse.

"Pardon me, dear."

Not forgetting her manners, Patrice apologized and left a stunned Mrs. Rose in the doorway staring after her.

"Hello, Mother."

"Hello, son. What was that all about?"

"Nothing Patrice stopped by to thank me for the roses."

He didn't have to glance at his mother to see the disgusted look on her face. Patrice wasn't the first woman she disapproved of and he knew she wouldn't be the last.

"Why on earth would you give a harlot a rose?"

"Mother, she's not a harlot."

"Come now, dear, give your mother some credit. It is my duty to know about the young debutantes that show interest in my son."

"And what do you know about Patrice? You just met her a couple seconds ago."

"She spreads her legs like a dog in heat, dear. The next thing you know she'll say she's pregnant by you when undoubtedly she's been around with every eligible bachelor in town. And then the family name will be ruined. I won't have it."

"Don't you think you're being a bit melodramatic?"

"Not when it comes to my children and having their best interests at heart."

He kissed her on the cheek. "Yes, Mother, we know you like to be involved… in all our lives."

"When you have children someday maybe you'll understand."

"When I have children I won't feel the need to involve myself in every aspect of their business."

"At least you can say you have a concerned mother who wants someone better for you than Patrice St. Clair, a woman I'm sure everyone has bedded this side of the Mississippi."

"I really don't know what you mean."

"You know very well what I mean, Michael. She's not right for you."

"Enough with the dramatics, Mother. How was your day?" Michael sorted through his mail while listening to his mother's account of her daily activities.

"It was fairly interesting. We're currently planning festivities for this year. I hope there aren't any surprises like there were last year."

He gave her an exasperated look. "You can't mean the young woman you ran out of town, can you?"

"I did no such thing," she cried defensively. "I merely brought to the attention of a few that she was of ill repute, and that maybe this wasn't the place for her."

"You sent the poor woman crying for the hills."

"I gave her new insight in how to conduct herself as a lady at a social function. She should've thanked me before she left in such a fit."

"All the way from Alabama?"

She raised her eyebrows in innocent surprise. "We do have mail, you know."

"Mother," Michael started. He wanted to say that her behavior was even too much for him sometimes, but thought it best to talk to her about it some other time. Right now he wanted to stop his stomach from growling. The aroma of fresh rolls was coming from the kitchen, making his stomach growl in anticipation. Looking towards the dining area, he saw that Gladys, the housekeeper, had already put place settings on the table. Following his gaze, his mother said, "Ah, I see Gladys has prepared lunch. Good thing. Last time she was terribly late and we had to wait."

She sat down in the chair opposite her son and placed the table napkin across her lap. The flask of alcohol normally seen coming out of her purse at this time wasn't visible today as Michael took his seat, clearly irritated with his mother's comment.

"She was taking the pound cake out of the oven and burned herself, Mother. Have a little sympathy!"

Sensing the irritation in his voice, she changed the subject. The fresh rolls were positioned in the middle of the table, while the baked whitefish was placed in front of her, accompanied by fresh greens and mushroom broth.

Celia waited until the housekeeper left the dinner area before asking her next question. "So how was your business trip, dear? Do you have any new clients?"

Michael buttered his roll, happy to change the subject to something more practical to discuss. "There are some companies that may be interested in buying our products."

"Wonderful. How much money?"

"We have to negotiate first, Mother, and then earnings will be discussed."

"Good, as long as that's at the top of your list."

Michael breathed heavily. He knew he should have patience but sometimes being overbearing was one of the things he disliked most about his mother. She didn't treat his other siblings this way, maybe because she was only allowed in their homes during the holidays. Her criticism and attitude annoyed more than one family dinner to the point where most of them chose not to be around her. "Did your father say when he was coming back?"

"George informed me within the next week or so."

"It would be good if he told me where he was going, or better yet, maybe he could take me with him on occasion."

Michael knew his father needed every ounce of peace and quiet to conduct his business. This was not achievable when his mother was around, as she was prone to asking questions and sticking her nose in where it didn't belong. "Dad is taking care of some things. I'm sure he'll be back sooner than you think."

"Well, if you see him before I do, which you probably will, please let him know I'll be home waiting. It'd be nice to see him before I begin the social events of the season."

Mother was lonely when his father was away. This was why she busied herself in other people's lives, not exactly a good thing. She had her lady's society and a church board she attended every week, but Michael knew she was still looking for something else. He silently wished his father would come home soon, before his mother found further trouble to get herself into.

After lunch Michael escorted her to the door and watched as she drove away.

Walking to his bedroom, he took off his clothes and placed his shoes neatly beside the closet door. Maybe he shouldn't have sent Patrice home; his body felt like it was in need of special attention. As he climbed into the huge four poster bed, he thought about his parents' marriage and how long they had stayed together. He thought marriage would be a nice change of pace one day. But for right now he was content living the life of a bachelor until he met that special someone.

Chapter 9

Christina rocked back and forth in the old chair overlooking the front yard. She sipped the fresh lemonade Bessie made not too long ago and placed her hand over her swollen abdomen. A worried expression spread slowly across her face as she rested the pen and half-written paper on her lap. She wasn't sure what to write this time. Mama hadn't written the last two times she'd sent letters back home, and she wondered if she were avoiding her because of the pregnancy. Hopefully this time she'd write something to let her know she cared.

Aunt Bessie had gone to purchase fish for the evening dinner, and Joseph was busy in the backyard planting rose bushes. Christina knew her days confined to the house were numbered, but she and Auntie had made the decision not to be seen by anyone until after the baby was born. It was better this way so no one would have questions she didn't want to answer. She couldn't take the chance someone might see her. And sure as hell she didn't want the gossip to start like it had in Virginia.

Dear Mama,

This is my third letter to you. When will you write me back? I hope everything is going well back home. Nothing has really changed here except the seasons. Aunt Bessie's house is surrounded by a beautiful array of flowers, and the ocean is not too far from here. The weather has brought a mix of colorful blossoms that produce a fragrance like nothing I've ever smelled before. Charleston is a beautiful place full of history, which I hope to learn more of once I get out of seclusion. The days here are very hot; it's almost unbearable to go outside sometimes. I often sit out on the front porch in the evening when the sun has gone down. My doctor says I'm in good health and will deliver in the next couple of weeks. I hope I hear from you soon. I still feel I'm able to raise my own child, and I want to prove that to you and everyone else. I no longer think of Lewis or his family, and if he decides he wants to be a father I won't hold any ill will against him.

Love, Christina

Christina knew her letter sounded different than when she first arrived in Charleston, as she sealed the envelope looking at the potted flowers that sat alongside the walkway and hung from the rafters. The scenery made for a relaxing atmosphere on the porch. Lewis was no longer her target of hate like he had been before. His family was a distant memory as she now concentrated more on how she was going to earn a living while raising her child. She was stronger also, not the fragile girl who left Virginia unsure of what she wanted. Christina knew what she wanted, and ultimately it was to raise her child. If she had to fight her mother for the right to do it then so be it.

An hour later the door to the kitchen slammed, making her jump. Bessie's voice rang out from the kitchen, "Christina, lunch will be ready shortly."

"Auntie, do you need any help?" Christina scooted to the end of the rocking chair and tried to push herself up but couldn't, so she rolled back and stayed there. She laughed at her own immobility. "I really don't know why I bother trying to help when I can barely move."

"Wait, Christina, while I put these beans in the pot." The clattering of pans were heard being set down on the counter tops, as Bessie didn't waste any time seasoning and tossing the ham hock in before heading to the porch.

"If I could see where I'm placing my feet, I'd have no problem getting up off this chair," she huffed. "Auntie, I need you."

Bessie came through the door and shook her head. "Look at you, Chrissy. You're doing fine until you sit down." She helped Christina to her feet and up the few steps into the house. The aromas from the kitchen made her mouth water as she settled onto the couch.

"Your body automatically relaxes when you're on the rocking chair." Bessie chuckled and set a pillow behind Christina's back for support. "Too bad he isn't here to see how cute you are carrying my niece or nephew around."

"And just who are you referring to?"

"Lewis, of course."

"Auntie, you know he couldn't be here, not that he would ever want to. Why did you mention him?"

"I just think he's missing out on one of the best moments of a pregnancy."

"Well, if he were here right now, I think I would stomp his feet till they bled!" Christina laughed menacingly.

"Now, now. That's not nice, Christina. Remember you two did love each other before the obvious was recognized. And you were planning on getting married, remember?"

"Don't remind me. It was a complete waste of time planning for a future that was never meant to be."

"Christina, you know getting upset is not good for you or the baby. And we've talked about this time and again. What's done is done and the only thing you need to concentrate on is that baby inside you. Nothing else."

"There still is the fact that my mother doesn't want me to raise the baby."

"You may not believe this now, but your mother only wants what's best for you."

"And how do you know that?" Christina asked.

"Aside from knowing her as my sister, I read it in a letter I received from her."

Christina should've been happy about this, but her mother hadn't tried to contact her since she moved to Charleston. Why couldn't she write to her eldest daughter about her feelings? Christina's letters had gone unanswered since she arrived in Charleston, and no one had sent word about the well-being of the family, or what was going on in Mills-town. If anyone should be upset at how things went it should be her, not her mother. Every day she was reminded that she was sent away from her family and friends because to stay would've meant shame and embarrassment for everyone else.

Sensing Christina's aggravation, Bessie replied, "I know you haven't heard from her in a while, but I think you may want to read what she has to say."

Bessie handed her the letter and waited for a reaction. If Christina didn't want to read it then she wouldn't force her. Their mother and daughter relationship had been worn thin over a long period of time, without proper communication. If they needed additional space then she would allow it. Christina looked at the letter for a moment, not sure she wanted to open it.

"The woman didn't even bother to write me a letter when I first came here to see how her child is doing, let alone her grandchild inside me like she promised."

"That woman is your mother, Christina. She did the only thing she could do at the time. And no matter how you feel about her decisions, she truly did what she thought was best."

"By throwing me away like some piece of garbage..."

"By keeping you and your reputation intact while she figured out how to resolve the mess that you and Lewis managed to get yourselves into."

Christina shook her head. She knew her mother meant well, but it didn't mask the hurt that was still there. She remembered girls getting pregnant from her town that went to live with relatives in the same town. They didn't even go before the church to apologize as was expected by unwed pregnant women. Why did she have to be the one to move away? She shifted the pillow for more relief against her lower back and concluded the rocking chair was more comfortable than the living room couch.

"When did you get it?"

"The letter came a couple days ago."

Christina mulled it over. She did miss her mother, despite what had happened between them. Reading that letter couldn't hurt any more than what she'd already been through.

"I guess I'll read it."

"Chrissy, I don't want you to get upset. You're a stronger person because of what happened, and you can't deny that."

"Am I? What am I going to tell my child when he or she comes here wondering where their father is," she asked.

Bessie walked back towards the kitchen leaving Christina alone to read. Was it possible mother and daughter could reconcile via letter? She prayed this would be true. The family had been through enough heartache over the past several years. The last thing they needed was more turmoil, especially between a mother and daughter who clearly loved one another.

Christina sat looking at the letter for a few seconds before opening it. Why did it take her mother so long to write one simple letter? She was the one who had been exiled from her home.

Dear Christina,

Where do I begin? I know it's been a while since we've spoken. The day you left was one of the hardest since your father died, even more so when you asked about him. You were always the curious one out of your brothers and sisters. I guess when you asked me it opened up old wounds I thought had long been buried.

107

I wanted to tell you this before you left. Let me start by saying I loved your father with every part of me. From the day we met he has been the only man I've ever loved. I wish I could say the same for him loving me. But I can't. As much as it pains me to say this I knew that one day the truth would come out. Your father was married to me but had other women on the side. One of those women was Lewis' mother, your Aunt Evelyn.

Christina gave a little whimper and had to read the sentence twice more before it settled in her mind. Daddy cheated on Mama with her aunt? No wonder the relationship between Lewis and her was so scandalous. Everything came full circle from Mrs. Carter's comments to Mrs. Harris's outbursts.

I didn't want to tell you, not even when you grew up, seeing as you loved your daddy so much. I wanted you to remember him as the strong, hardworking man he was, providing for you, your brothers and your sisters. And he was, Christina. He just needed a little more than what I could give him. I doubt that even if your Aunt Evelyn had been with him he would've been faithful. He was selfish when it came to his needs. But surprisingly that never showed when it came to his children. He loved you all with every breath he took. Please remember that. Your father's love was yours and your brothers and sisters, even if he didn't show any to me. At least you received the better part of him.

I'm sorry I haven't written, Chrissy. I've made a lot of mistakes when it came to doing what I thought was best for you, but I thought I was doing something right. I know I could've had three grandbabies instead of one, a fact I hope God and you can forgive me. Please forgive me Christina.

Love Always, Mama

Christina's heart ached. She looked at her aunt, who was standing in the doorway watching attentively.

"Did you know?"

"Yes, we all knew since it happened. Your mother came home crying something fierce that day and told all of us. It tore the family apart."

"Is that one of the reasons she wanted me to come here? She didn't want me to be hurt by someone I loved like she was."

"Your mother saw how much you loved Lewis and it hurt her that he couldn't show you the fullness of that love because of you and him being kin. It was heartbreaking for her, and she didn't want the same thing that happened to her to happen to you."

"Why didn't she tell me about any of this?"

"You loved your daddy so much, Christina. She didn't want you to stop loving him or to look at him in a different way."

Her mother had endured the worst betrayals, not only from her husband but from her sister. And through it all she continued to love her father despite being humiliated by the people she thought truly loved her. Christina took deep breaths, then suddenly inhaled sharply and doubled over in agony.

"Auntie, please help."

"What is it?" She rushed over, her brown eyes expanding as she looked at Christina's wide-eyed expression.

"Oh Lord, it's starting. Joseph," she called out, "go get the nurse!"

"Auntie, please don't leave me. I don't know what to do. I'm afraid I'll mess this up somehow."

"No you won't, Chrissy, you'll be just fine. And don't worry, I won't leave you. The devil himself couldn't pry me away, and you know he is not allowed in my house. Hallelujah!"

"Auntie, please!" Christina moaned.

"I'm sorry, baby. What do you need?"

"I need to lie down. The pain just hit me all at once. Hopefully it won't be any worse than that."

"Oh, you just wait, you haven't felt pain yet," she mumbled to herself.

"What?"

"Nothing, dear. Come on. We'll change your clothes and get you to your room. Joseph should be back with the nurse any minute. Maybe I should go see what's taking him so long."

"No!" Christina cried. "Please don't leave!"

"All right, Chrissy, I'll stay right here. Once the nurse comes I'll get Joseph to boil some water and get plenty of fresh towels and sheets. Don't worry, everything will be fine."

Seven hours later, Christina was exhausted and fighting to stay awake. Her son was being washed and she was trying to get the first glimpse of him before her eyes closed. The pain that had consumed her body not long ago was now a distant memory.

Christina saw Bessie tip-toeing past the room, checking to see if she was okay. She knew her aunt wanted her to rest and didn't want to disturb her, but she was eager to see the baby and finally hold him in her arms. The midwife came in and was speaking to her in Creole language, which she couldn't understand until she switched to English. During the labor she bragged endlessly that the women in her family had at least seven children apiece and could birth a child standing while washing clothes on the hottest day of the year.

Christina told her she was the most insensitive bitch on the face of the earth, to which the midwife had again said something in her native dialect and marched out of the room. This happened on several occasions as Christina's language turned from yelling to cursing, all while each contraction became stronger. Lewis' name had only been mentioned a couple of times while she was in labor and she really let him have it then, something else that should've been done before she left Virginia. The only person who she truly wished was there was her grandmother.

Dr. Winston came in and checked her eyes and heart. He was a kind-hearted man. The only thing she remembered about him was his stubby fingers testing her vagina to see if the baby's head could get through. After all, the baby was slightly bigger than she or anyone else there imagined. Uncle Joseph didn't want to come in during that time, preferring to pace outside the room where it was safe from the yelling.

Why couldn't everyone just exit the room so she could get some alone time with her baby? She had gone through so much in the last several hours, the pushing, prodding, and the endless perspiration of water from every part of her body.

"Ms. Davis, it's time."

She breathed a deep breath and waited. "What does he look like? Will he recognize me?"

"He's a healthy baby boy and you'll do just fine."

"I hope so."

Dr. Winston smiled. He was in his early fifties, of average height with gray hair and a large scar on his cheek that ran from his ear to the top of his lip. It almost seemed menacing until he smiled, as he was doing now. He looked down at Christina as a father would do a child who'd accomplished something great in life.

"I've already cut the cord and cleaned the little one up. You'll need to put him close to your chest for the first feeding."

"Feeding? You mean breast feeding?"

"Yes. This moment is important to the baby and to you. It'll tell whether he'll do well in breast feeding. Now hold his head close to your nipple."

"Okay. Here we go," Christina said as he placed the baby in her arms while she adjusted his head so that his mouth rested right beside her nipple. She couldn't stop looking at him even while he was making such a big fuss. "Why is he crying so much? Is something wrong with him?"

"No, not at all. He just needs your breast." He turned to leave.

"No, wait! What if something goes wrong?"

"I'll be right outside the room, Ms. Davis."

"How do I know when he's done?"

"He'll detach himself when he's finished." Dr. Winston left the room, but left a small crack in the door so he could keep an ear out for when she needed him. He had to let Mom and baby have some quality time together first, and he didn't want to disturb them any further.

Christina was scared but thankful for the alone time it gave her with the baby. She looked at her son with his coal black hair and chocolate eyes. A love she'd never known captured her soul, and she knew she'd never be able to give him up to anyone. Christina cried for him, herself, and the siblings he would never get to see. Maybe now she could think of a name that would best suit him. Isaac came to mind, as it was an old family name from her father's side.

"Isaac," she said. "That's what I'll call you."

Chapter 10

W ord of Bessie Washington's new tenant made the gossip rounds fairly easily due to an upset midwife talking about a young girl's foul mouth over at Bessie Washington's house while at the open market. As soon as she went out to get fresh sheets she immediately fussed about the rude new person barking orders at her like she was the hired help. This set tongues wagging as they wanted to know who was in Bessie's house and why they hadn't been formally introduced.

Weeks after she'd given birth, Christina was finishing her daily walk when she noticed a black town car sitting in Auntie's driveway. She was desperately trying to get back to her old figure and only had a slight pouch on her waist and a few stretch marks on her stomach that gave evidence of her pregnancy. The ointment Auntie had found for her was working its magic as she applied it every day to the areas that needed it the most. The driver in the front seat didn't notice her approach as she eased her way to the back yard to gain entrance through the kitchen.

She was curious about who Auntie might be talking to at this hour of the morning. The kitchen door creaked open slowly as voices from the inside reached her ears. She was careful so as not to interrupt the conversation going on inside.

"Bessie, oh Bessie, it's so good to see you," the stranger said, coming forward with outstretched arms to greet her aunt. Her eyes darted back and forth across the room, trying to catch a glimpse of something.

"Celia Rose, what brings you by this morning?"

Christina could hear the anxiety in Aunt Bessie's voice. She clearly was not falling for the phoniness of her unwanted guest.

"I haven't seen you around and I wanted to invite you and your guest to a little luncheon I'm having at the house. It's just a few friends and neighbors. I thought it would be a perfect time to enjoy the weather and to introduce your guest to everyone. I hear Joseph brought her here all the way from Virginia. Why, the poor thing must be exhausted. Is she sleeping?" Celia asked sweetly.

"No, she's awake. But I'm afraid we'll be in town tomorrow for our own luncheon."

"What a shame. I was so looking forward to meeting her. Are you sure you won't be able to attend? I make a mean sweet potato pie."

"We'll try to make an appearance. I don't want Christina being too overwhelmed by the social activities while she's here."

"Of course. Christina is such a pretty little name." Celia was clearly disappointed she wouldn't be able to reveal any news about Bessie's new tenant. It was one thing to hear gossip from different sources. It was an entirely different thing to see something for yourself, and she needed that evidence to take back with her and confirm.

Not one to bite her tongue, Aunt Bessie gave her unwanted guest a cool stare and stepped towards her. She knew why Celia had come. "There's nothing here you can take back and talk about, Celia."

"Indeed," she said disdainfully, looking around the little house, which was much different than the large home she lived in. "I guess I'll see you two in town or somewhere."

"Celia? If you don't remember anything else, remember this. If you hurt my niece you hurt me, understood?"

"So she's not a guest then. She's your niece. Is that what they're calling them these days?"

Celia turned towards the door, the sarcastic remark not lost on Bessie's ears. "I won't have you speaking bad about her, do you hear?"

"Yes, Bessie, I do. But do you really think you can tell that to everyone in this town?" Celia asked coolly.

"Oh, but I am telling everyone, Celia," Aunt Bessie replied as she walked ahead of Celia and pulled the door open. "Have a nice day."

Celia huffed as she left the house.

Christina finally walked inside the room. If there were more people like Celia Rose around the town, she thought, maybe it hadn't been such a good idea to be staying with her aunt after all. This place, it seemed, was no different than her hometown.

"Aunt Bessie, who was that?"

"Goodness, you startled me. Were you listening? It's not good to listen in on people's conversations, Chrissy."

Christina waited for Auntie to explain. She learned from her mother that patience is a virtue especially when trying to find out things from different people.

Seeing her expectant look, her aunt took a deep breath.

"Don't worry about Isaac. He's been asleep ever since you breast fed him an hour ago. I should fill you in on Mrs. Rose, seeing as you might run across her while in town." Bessie sat down on the couch and began to shed light about the notorious town gossip.

Celia Rose was the wife to Mr. David Rose, a wealthy businessman from Savannah, Georgia. Together they had four children and lived in a two-story mansion on the port of Charleston surrounded by beautiful landscaping and decorative black iron gates. She had been pampered her entire life so it was no surprise she married into a wealthy family.

It wasn't long after the birth of her last child that it was rumored she had taken lovers when her husband was away. It was said that when Mr. Rose went on business trips, Celia would all of a sudden have the need for "yard work" or some type of maintenance that required a young handsome worker to attend to. Nearby neighbors would see her in scantily clad attire while the local landscaper trimmed her bushes.

Yet she still found the time to be a nosy busybody and speak ill of others.

"I know just how to handle women like Celia Rose. Ignore them," Aunt Bessie said.

Christina shifted uneasily. "That woman sounds like a real piece of work."

Auntie nodded. "I want you to understand something, Christina. There's always going to be someone talking about you whether you do good or bad in this world. It's just how life is."

"Yes, ma'am. I just thought by me coming here that things would be different. I guess I was wrong."

"Everywhere you go in this life people will always have something to say about you. It's how you handle those people that will help shape you and define your character."

"Thanks, Auntie."

"You're welcome. Just remember that people who feel they have juicy gossip will spread it no matter if it's true or false, and if I know that woman its already in downtown by now. But don't you worry, baby girl. Everything will be alright." She got up from the couch. "I'm glad you're up so early. We have church in about an hour."

"We do?"

"Yes, we do. Joseph will take care of Isaac while we're gone, so get dressed."

℞

Sunday church in South Carolina was altogether different than the stomping tap your foot music Christina was used to back home. No, this was something almost regal in a sense. The music could be heard as they turned off the main road. It reverberated through the trees, a rich musical progression that beckoned its members as they walked through the door. The church, if that's what you wanted to call it, was one of the biggest Christina had ever seen.

"Is this your church?" Christina asked.

"Yes. This church has a lot of history behind it. It was one of the first churches built after the Civil War for blacks in the South."

Christina noticed the paintings and colors surrounding the pulpit. "It holds a lot of traditional value for black folks here."

Traditional. The word stuck on Christina's tongue like paste she couldn't get out of her mouth. Her church back home was the same. She suddenly felt like turning around and hightailing it out of there.

"What's wrong, Chrissy?"

"Nothing. I'm just nervous in a new place, that's all."

Bessie looked at her, trying to read her face. As they took their seats, Christina noticed the woman who had visited Auntie that morning. Celia Rose was seated two rows up on the opposite side of the aisle. Those seats were designated for the deacon and deaconess of the church, as they were all wearing black and white, the colors of the diaconate.

How could a busybody like Celia be a deaconess of a church like this? Christina wondered. Didn't they know who she was? As the service started, Christina was mesmerized by the singing. These were no ordinary singers. They sang with reverence and deep emotion, their voices like noon bells ringing in the afternoon. You could probably hear them miles down the road. The classical sound was so beautiful Christina was moved to tears several times over the course of a few minutes. When it was time for the pastor to preach, the congregation stood to read the text for the day. She immediately recognized the passage. It was the same scripture her father used to read in church. He always loved this text for what it spoke about. She drifted to that memory for a moment before Auntie pulled her back. Christina felt Auntie tap her leg to get her attention and motion to the scripture being read. It was Psalm 27: The Lord is my light and my salvation; whom shall I fear? The Lord is the strength of my life; of whom shall I be afraid?

As she read the scripture, Christina gripped the bible tightly. Her father's spirit was here and she could feel him. He would want her to be like the scripture described; to have no fear even when people spoke against her; and to have faith that everything would turn out alright even when it seemed like the bad would never end. She knew he was speaking to her, telling her to hold her head up and be strong.

Christina felt like the message for that day was for her and her alone. When the service ended she felt refreshed and was glad they had come to listen to the spoken word. Now all she had to do was apply it to her daily life. How she was going to do this was another mystery.

"Thank you, Auntie. I really needed that today."

"You're welcome, dear. I figured you needed some form of spiritual inspiration." Auntie smiled, took Christina's arm and hooked it through her own.

"Let's take a little stroll to the market place. It's only a short distance from here."

Christina could hear groups of people in front of her talking about someone. They were so wrapped up in their conversation they didn't realize they were drawing a big audience of listeners who could also clearly hear them. Christina listened as they spoke of a new person in town that was already causing scandal to her family.

Bessie looked at her and shook her head as if to say, "See, I told you." She realized Auntie was right. Telling Celia Rose was like sharing your life story with everyone in Charleston. The woman really had a flare for the dramatic. Stories could circulate throughout the town quickly without a hint of truth. This was like home all over again. She took a deep breath. It seemed like no matter where she went people would still talk about her or the person they thought she was. She squared her shoulders and continued walking. If she was going to make it in Charleston, Christina knew she had to take Auntie's advice and ignore people as best she could. She really would try even though it hurt her feelings. It was literally one fabricated story after another. One lie had her being held captive by Aunt Bessie and made to work as a housekeeper to pay for her stay. Another story painted Christina as a chaperone for Aunt Bessie's many lovers that frequented the house. That story was particularly disturbing considering Christina never wanted to think of Auntie as having a lover. As she walked down the street Christina shook her head in disgust. What a bunch of crazy people with too much time on their hands!

They walked through the crowd towards the fruit and vegetable stands that lined the streets weaving their way past men, women and children.

"I'm going to grab some lima beans for dinner this evening," Bessie said, looking at the assortment of beans on the carts. "Don't go too far now. We'll be leaving soon."

"Okay, I'll be over by the fruit stands," she said, leaving Auntie to negotiate prices with the vendor.

Christina had picked up a taste for different fruits since being in Charleston. Uncle Joseph would have her try different kinds every day while she was pregnant and she became especially fond of the papaya and pineapple. Christina wondered how he and Isaac we're doing and was eager to get back to them. He would need her breast in another hour. She walked around each stand, admiring the many different fruits assembled, and thought maybe she could persuade Auntie to make a fruit bowl for dinner with papaya, grapes, strawberries, and chunks of sweet pineapple. Mangoes were also visible and she wondered how they tasted. The vendor broke open the succulent fruit, revealing its yellow juices, which sent a pulsating scent straight to her nostrils.

Stepping away from the mangoes, she went to look at the tomato stand and wasn't paying attention to the solid wall that suddenly appeared in front of her. At least that's what it felt like when she walked into him. He was a rock solid wall with arms that caught her as her backside was about to meet the grape stand.

"Pardon me, I wasn't paying attention."

He was tall, well built, and staring at her with warm whiskey colored eyes. Christina stared back and thought he was one of the most handsome men she had ever seen. His hair was black with tight curls closely cropped to his head. His face was hard and virile. She let her eyes travel down from his face to his muscular shoulders. His chin had a cleft in the center and his skin had a caramel glow to it. Alarm bells immediately went off in her head.

No, she said to herself, off limits. Besides, he was probably married with a couple of kids. She wouldn't get involved while she was here. And she sure as hell wasn't going to make the same mistake she made with Lewis.

"It's alright. You can run into me anytime." He unhooked his arms around her enough for her to wiggle out of them but stayed close enough so that no one could move in between them.

"Excuse me?" She couldn't believe his brazen attitude. His voice was as husky and deep as a wolf.

"My name is Michael, and you are?"

"Not interested." She turned around and started walking toward the place where she last saw Auntie. That place turned into three more places. She turned so many corners that she didn't realize she was walking in circles. And she bumped right back into the hard chest she was trying to avoid.

"Excuse me, please. I'm looking for my aunt." Christina tried to sound as annoyed as possible when really this man made her very nervous. He towered over her and she felt sure he knew he was making her uneasy. It was evident by the smirk on his face and the goose bumps on her forearms and neck.

He stared at her for a couple seconds. She was intriguing, probably the only girl that hadn't swooned at the sight of him. As she walked away from him, he quickened his pace to catch up with her.

Realizing that he was behind her, she said, "Don't you know it's rude to follow people?"

"Not really. And it's not rude considering you're a stranger in my city. For all I know you could be a criminal and I can't let a criminal go without checking them out."

"Right, I'm a criminal. I'm inspecting the fruit stands with little old people so I can steal their money. How very criminal of me."

She turned her back, pretending to look for something that looked familiar to her. Christina didn't see his smile or the fact that he was admiring her body. "And how would you know I'm a stranger here?"

"Because we've been walking in the opposite direction for the past ten minutes, while the woman you walked to church with this morning was collecting beans back at the farmers market stand two blocks from here."

She stopped suddenly, turned and looked around. Christina had managed to wander down the street without clear thought of where she was going.

"You knew I was walking in the wrong direction and you continued to follow me?"

He hunched his shoulders in a boyish gesture that made him look even more handsome. She tried to sound irritated.

"Where are we?"

There were very few people on this end of the street. The buildings weren't at all familiar and she suddenly felt nervous about being alone with a stranger in an unfamiliar city.

"We're near the Old City Market."

He walked up to stand beside her. She was too aware of his physique and size. His scent was all male, like nothing she'd ever smelled before. His arm brushed her side sending shivers up and down her body. "And how far is that from the church?"

"Which church? There are three churches in this area." He was looking intensely at her as if he were trying to figure her out.

Christina quickly looked away, avoiding eye contact. She didn't want to be entranced by this stranger any more than she already was.

"Do you even go to church?"

"Of course I do."

She gathered the courage to look straight at him. Christina thought for sure he could tell he made her nervous. She tried to mask her unease. "Your manners would say otherwise."

He inched closer to her and for a moment she thought he might have the audacity to kiss her.

"Christina, Christina."

She heard her name being called and felt relieved. Breaking her stare with the stranger she answered, "I'm here, Auntie."

He still didn't leave. He just leaned against the wall of the building next to them and waited to see who would come around the corner.

How arrogant. Suddenly very annoyed, she said, "You can leave now."

"Christina. What a very pretty name." The clef in his chin smoothed out a little as he smiled broadly.

Christina heard the alarm bells go off in her head. She rolled her eyes to look annoyed but her palms were getting warm and she couldn't seem to keep her feet still. She didn't know whether to run for the hills or stay in the company of this stranger who at this point had heightened her senses to a fevered pitch. So she tried another technique to get him to leave. "Thank you. It was nice meeting you, Michael."

Christina could feel the curious stares of people nearby. She turned around too fast, almost knocking Auntie over as she approached them. Someone grabbed her arm to steady her. It was Michael. She let out a little gasp when his forearm touched her flesh, and then adjusted her dress. "I must be going."

He looked disappointed as she turned away from him. Bessie had a questioning look on her face as Christina turned her away from Michael. They were walking away when she heard her name.

Bessie nodded in Michael's direction, instructing her to turn around and answer him. Christina rapidly shook her head as if to say, absolutely not.

Michael picked up a yellow flower from a nearby stand and twirled it between his forefinger and thumb. He handed it to Christina and waited for her reaction.

"Thank you," she said, finally turning around to accept the strange bud. "What kind of flower is this?"

"It's called Jessamine and is one of South Carolina's finest flowers."

Christina liked how he said the word 'finest' as if it were directed at her. She quickly cancelled that thought and tried to focus on something else other than the handsome man standing inches from her.

He didn't know the effect he had on her and she wanted to keep it that way. He was a stranger, after all. What could he possibly give her? Passion, ecstasy, freedom from her current solitary state. What was wrong with her?

"I use it to decorate the outside of my house. When the wind picks up you can smell its sweet scent clear across the yard." His piercing eyes never left hers.

Her knees began to tremble. She told herself her emotional state must be a combination of the early morning hours and lack of caffeine. It couldn't be this handsome, muscular, virile man in front of her causing her senses to go haywire. It was a good thing Auntie was holding her steady by the elbow or her knees would've buckled from the emotions soaring through her body. Lord, he smelled good, or was it the flower?

Bessie added to the conversation just then when silence between the two youngsters lasted a bit too long. "I use it sometimes to sweeten my tea. It's a local tradition." She gave her niece a slight shake bringing her back to the present before presenting her hand for a proper greeting.

"My name is Bessie Washington and I believe you've already met my niece Christina."

Christina was glad for Auntie's interruption because she really didn't know what to say to this handsome stranger.

"May I call on Christina later?" Michael asked.

"Why don't you allow my niece time to get used to Charleston. She only just arrived and will need to schedule classes and familiarize herself with things here."

Christina heard the lie and was grateful Auntie spoke up for her. She didn't think she could think of anything quick to say at this point.

"Yes, ma'am." He looked let down.

She finally decided to speak up. "Yes, I arrived not too long ago and would like to rest a bit."

Lord, she sounded like a broken record. Didn't Auntie just say that? He smiled. "Okay. If you need a guide to the city I'd like to show you around, Christina, with your permission, of course, Ms. Washington."

"Bessie. You can call me Bessie, dear. And I don't think that would be a bad thing, do you, Christina?" she said with a slight nod of acceptance.

"No, not at all." Christina could tell Auntie was trying hard not to smile.

"I hope to see you soon, Christina."

"Yes. See you soon. Good day to you, Michael." She quickly turned around and waited for Auntie to start walking with her. When they were out of hearing distance she heard Auntie's surprised voice.

"And what was that about?"

"That was nothing. I accidently bumped into him. I wasn't looking where I was going."

"He seemed quite taken with you."

"He did? Oh." She was trying to sound disturbed but couldn't quite get the surprise out of her voice. They walked arm in arm the rest of the way, the older woman enjoying the sunshine and atmosphere, the younger wondering what just happened to cause her heart to beat so fast. She'd never experienced that type of feeling in her life, not even with Lewis. Goose bumps appeared up and down her arm, which was odd since it wasn't cold. It was the middle of summer, and the extra heat Michael caused should've sent her swooning.

She'd never met a man who looked like that and could still feel his strong hands on her shoulders, hands that were so large she felt like a small girl when they were holding her. His eyes were mesmerizing, looking at her from that refined face, almost too refined, as if he should've been at the market with a chauffeur carrying an umbrella to shield him from the sun. The color of his eyes was a warm honey brown, and when he looked at her she felt as if he were stripping her outward appearance all the way down to her core. She wasn't sure why she felt this way. His hands felt so strong and forceful they could make a woman lose herself and feel protected at the same time.

Christina rubbed away the goose bumps on her arms. Maybe she was getting too carried away with the thought of him. His whole demeanor was just like any other guy when first meeting her, and she was sure he treated all women the same with no exception. But there was just something about him she couldn't quite grasp. Maybe it was his arrogance, or self-assuredness. Maybe she was just tired, as today was her first true outing and she did feel a little out of it. But did exhaustion make your head spin or heart beat to the point where it skipped its rhythmic pattern? Did it make your palms sweaty or your stomach jump up and down like it was on a furious ride? She wasn't sure. But one thing she did know. Michael, whatever his last name, was dangerous and she needed to avoid him no matter what.

They made their way back to the house with the aroma of chicken and dumplings greeting them as they walked through the door. Joseph had started dinner, which, along with the chicken and dumplings, consisted of Okra, buttermilk biscuits, and homemade apple pie for dessert. Isaac was on the floor playing with his feet, rolling his body from side to side. Christina sat on the floor alongside him until dinner was served observing his mission to capture each toe within his mouth, and laughing when it was accomplished. She needed to eat something before feeding Isaac and turning in for the evening.

Charleston was already proving most interesting with the vivacious marketplace and fascinating people. One of those people she may need to dodge for personal reasons, but others she was sure to meet could prove to be good acquaintances or even friends. She felt better about Charleston after today. The city was beautiful, and the ocean was so soothing. She could hear the waves crashing against the sand and took a deep breath, smelling the salt air. This place had a calmness about it she liked very much, which was something she had never really experienced, always running after her brothers and sisters back home to make sure they didn't get into any mischief. Christina realized this was what people were talking about when they mentioned peace and quiet because surely this was a peaceful place.

It didn't take long for Isaac to go to bed after his feeding and she soon followed. With her head nestled against the feather pillows she went to sleep with thoughts of the people she met today, including the handsome stranger at the market.

Chapter 11

Christina sat and played with Isaac while watching the trees dance back and forth against the breeze. She looked down at the flower given to her by the handsome man. Charleston was a big enough area where she could find activities that wouldn't allow her to run into him that often. She was contemplating whether or not she really wanted to run into him again when one of the chattiest females on the face of the earth came strolling up to the front porch.

"Hi, I'm Sandra. You must be Christina. My mom and your aunt are good friends. You probably know they go to church together. I mean, how you couldn't since you're practically living here in her house. My, but you're pretty. Are you mulatto?"

Christina just stared at the chatty girl in front of her. Isaac, noticing his mother had stopped playing with him, swatted her arm to get her attention.

"No, I'm not mulatto."

"What's his name?" Sandra gestured.

Christina shook herself out of Sandra's chatterbox trance to answer her question. "Isaac. His name is Isaac."

"What a cute name."

Sandra Wright was a petite girl with coffee brown eyes and coal black hair braided to her shoulders. She was wearing a black and white checkered dress that flared out to just above the knees and stared at Christina, waiting for more conversation.

"Yes, it's one of my favorite names," Christina said uncomfortably. She shifted in her seat, trying to think of something to say to fill the awkward silence.

"Auntie told me you might be stopping by today. I wasn't expecting any company." Christina hoped Sandra would take the hint that she wanted to be left alone.

"Your aunt mentioned you may need someone to talk with. That's why I'm here."

She plopped down on the swinging bench right beside Christina; it creaked under her weight. Christina hoped the bench would support both of them, as she didn't think she could take falling down right now. She looked at Isaac as he stared curiously at the stranger next to them. The hint of wanting to be alone was definitely missed.

"Hair as soft as yours and a keen nose like that can only mean one thing."

"What's that?" Christina asked, curious as to what this strange girl was trying to say.

"If you're not mulatto, you must be mixed with something."

Christina laughed a little. No one had actually pointed out race or heritage where she was from, so to have someone state the obvious was a bit amusing. "My father's people are Igbo descent and my mother's people are black natives to America. So I guess I am mixed with different cultures. I just never thought about it."

"See, I knew it. My people are from here too, and West Africa as a matter of fact. You ever heard of a place called Sierra Leone?"

"Yes, I have," Christina replied. Thanks to Uncle Joseph's brief history lesson she was becoming more and more familiar with Sierra Leone and its descendants.

"My parents were sponsored by my great aunt in Sierra Leone to become missionaries. They decided to go to Libya to spread the gospel for a couple of years before they moved back here to start a Christian school. You'll meet them soon enough. They always choose young women to sponsor for the debutante ball we have every year."

"That sounds exciting."

"You'd be a positive shoo-in."

"A shoo-in for what?"

"You'd represent your family as a new debutante at the debutante ball. That would mean you and I would have to find dates and all that. You wanna go get something to eat? I can fill you in on the social events and latest fashions if you want."

Christina took her time before answering. It would be nice to get out and walk around to see the area with someone who was more familiar with it. She definitely would prefer Sandra over that stranger she met in the market. What was his name again? Michael?

Oh, don't act like you could forget that handsome face.

"Let me take the baby inside to Auntie and get my umbrella," she said.

Christina doubted she'd be able to get one word in, but she decided that was okay since she didn't really want to talk much about herself anyway. As they walked along the dirt road she felt more relaxed. Maybe it was because of the atmosphere and surrounding beauty of the island, or the fact the talkative girl walking beside her hadn't asked her about the baby she saw not too long ago in her arms. But at that moment she felt more at home than she had felt when she first arrived.

"Have you met Arlene Turner or Carla Richards? Their families are some of the oldest on James Island. They're very good people. I'll introduce you to them."

"That sounds nice."

They walked along in silence for what seemed like forever but it was only a couple minutes. Christina decided to pick Sandra's brain for more information. She was curious about some of the people of Charleston.

"What do you know about Mrs. Celia Rose?"

Sandra came to a sudden halt. Her eyebrows raised and her eyelids closed for a second before she said, "Celia Rose? She's just about the meanest busybody this town has ever seen."

Christina could tell she hit a nerve by the way Sandra's face turned from smiling to rather annoy.

"Is she really that bad?"

"She's the worst, absolute worst person on God's green earth."

Christina was almost sorry she brought the woman's name up, but since she was on this path she might as well figure out who she was dealing with. The woman had made her feel very uncomfortable, especially when she showed up at Auntie's house unannounced and looking for her. How did she know she was even there?

"She stopped by Auntie's house to see what I looked like the other day. It was all very strange."

"Don't give her any information, Christina. She'll use it against you."

Christina shook her head. "I didn't get the chance to actually speak with her. I was going for a walk when she came by. I'm still wondering how she knew I was even there."

Sandra let out a sigh. "She does have the eyes and ears of Charleston. I mean literally she has people watching for newcomers and listening for new gossip. It's sickening, but that's how she operates."

"Why is she doing this? Aren't there people against it?"

"Of course, but you can't stop people from talking."

Auntie's words came back to her as clear as day. Why were there people in this world whose only goal was to manipulate and humiliate people?

"Let me share something with you to help you understand who you're dealing with."

Christina listened intently. She didn't feel comfortable with Celia asking questions about her and needed to know how to stay away from her.

"Celia once befriended a young lady from Alabama. One day at a social function she saw her walking with Edward Fisher, one of the not so gentlemanly men in town, and started a nasty rumor. It was so bad the poor girl went crying all the way back to Alabama."

"That's awful!"

"That's Celia Rose. She doesn't care about hurting anyone. You watch yourself around her, Christina. She's a snake in the grass, and if you don't watch her she'll jump up and bite you."

Christina felt queasy. She was even more desperate now to keep her life in Virginia a secret. New people in an unfamiliar place tended to cause more attention than people already established in the same area. She just hoped her secret would stay that way long enough for others not to notice. Christina wanted to tell Sandra about Michael, the man she had met in town, but she thought better of it. She didn't want to take a chance that anymore gossip might get started, even though she had no reason to distrust Sandra. They walked and talked until they reached the small corner store a mile from Auntie's house.

"Hey, would you like a sandwich or something?" Sandra asked. "Mr. John makes a mean barbecue with extra fixin's."

"That sounds good. I may need two of them, I'm so hungry right now," Christina said.

Sandra smiled and slid a chair out for her. "Good. Sit right down here while I order."

Christina sat in the rusted-colored chair. Her appetite was on over-load and she felt like she could eat the whole pig. Whatever Sandra decided to order she would gladly eat it. The girl was proving to be nicer than the other people she encountered, and she was thankful for her company. By now her stomach was growling something fierce and she needed something before going back to Auntie's house.

The sound of hoofs hitting gravel drew her attention and she noticed a white carriage making its way down the street past the store the driver tipping his hat when he noticed she was looking. All five brown and white horses were hooked together by shining leather straps. The carriage looked like something out of a picture show seen on the big screens. Christina shook her head. She really was in a different place, a wonderful place, where seeing horse drawn carriages was a part of everyday life.

Sandra came out with a tray of sandwiches packed to the max with barbecued pork and what looked like coleslaw and black beans with bacon on the side. The aroma was making her mouth water something fierce.

"So, was that your baby you were holding?"

"Excuse me?" Christina had to swallow some water before she choked on her bread.

"Don't be mad. Your aunt told my parents everything. Plus he looks a lot like you, with his similar skin coloring and everything."

Christina was shocked and a little frightened. Who else did Auntie tell?

Sandra continued, oblivious to the surprised look on Christina's face. "I guess since you have people here like Celia Rose spreading gossip like wild fire, your aunt thought the truth would be much better than hiding it, which is a good thing since she only told people she could trust."

The news of her baby had to be revealed because of one nosy person. This was deja vu all over again. She suddenly wanted to leave and go back to Auntie's house, bury herself underneath the covers, and not come out, for fear someone else might discover her secret.

Sensing her friend's distress, Sandra tried to alleviate the tension she had just caused. "You don't need to worry about stuff like that while you're here."

"Isaac is my baby," Christina admitted. "I got pregnant back home in Virginia and my mama decided it would be best for me to move away so I wouldn't embarrass anyone in the family."

She may as well admit it to someone rather than not say anything at all. The chicken had already flown the coop, as her uncle would say. Afraid to look up, Christina sat back with her hands in her lap and tried to concentrate on the plate. She had devoured her sandwich in mere seconds and she really wanted another one. As if on cue, Sandra pushed her plate towards her. A slow smile spread across Christina's face as she picked up Sandra's half eaten sandwich. "Are you scared?"

Christina nodded before answering. "Yes, I am. I don't know how I'm going to be able to take care of a child, let alone myself. My family can only do so much. The rest is up to me." To hear herself admit the truth, Christina was relieved she could finally get it off her chest.

"What about the father? Is he still involved?"

She gave a slight head shake. "No. Some of his family, like his brother Roger, would like to be involved. I don't know about anyone else."

"It's a shame he has to act like that."

"Yeah. It was great when we were ignorant of what was going on. Things changed quickly after we found out."

"Do you want to talk about it? I promise not to judge you in any way." Christina looked at her. If she were going to tell someone Sandra would be a good start. She reminded her of the friends she left behind in Virginia. Besides, she had to try, as everyone was bound to know at some point that Isaac was her baby. She just hoped their judgment wasn't as harsh as it had been back home. Christina exhaled slowly. "It started last summer. The fair was in Fredericksburg, Virginia, and my friends were going to be a part of the swing dance contest."

"Oh, I love to swing dance, but it's mostly shag contests down this way."

"Yeah, me too. Everyone was going to the fair to have a good time. When we got there we stopped by the lemonade stand to buy drinks and there he was sitting with his friends."

She tried to tell the story with as vivid a picture as possible to get Sandra to see what and how she felt. When Christina finished she wasn't the only one with tears coming down her cheeks and was surprised her crying wasn't like before when she first found out. It was a final release that she needed to get out. Was she finally over what happened? This was a welcome feeling to be sure.

"He was horrible to you," Sandra said.

"Yes, he was. But what could we do? We're kinfolk. We should've been introduced when his mother first came to visit her sister, my mother."

Christina paused for a reaction. Back home when people found out, they had disgusted looks on their faces, followed by shock and disappointment. But she didn't see that on Sandra's face. It was something else. Pity.

"I'm so sorry, Christina."

Christina shook her head. She really wasn't looking for anyone to pity her and she had enough blame and negativity delivered her way to last a lifetime. No, what she really wanted was someone to hear her side and not judge her. She wanted empathy and a perceptive mind that quickly figured out that this was not all her fault. Sandra proved to be just that person as she reached out her hand to Christina to offer support.

"Relationships between kin are just not done where I'm from," Christina said. "And everyone wants to be quiet until you do something wrong, whether you meant to or not."

"That's how it is here sometimes," Sandra replied, hunching her shoulders.

"Sometimes you have to ask because there's so many close related kin here, if you know what I mean."

"I should've asked and then headed for the hills, which is pretty much what he did once he found out." She let out a slight laugh.

"But he could've supported you instead of running off like that."

Christina shook her head again. "He did what his family wanted him to do. I really can't blame him for not wanting to be with me. It would be scandalous to the family name."

"Do you think he'll want to be a part of his child's life?"

"He's probably too ashamed and embarrassed."

"He should be a part of the baby's life. I always say a child should have both parents even if they don't live in the same place."

"He should be married now. His family wanted him to come off as the responsible person in all of this."

"Well, that's laughable. Anyone can see you've been more responsible than he has."

"Have I? I traveled miles to come to a place I know nothing about to have my baby when I should've stayed in Virginia where my family was. Does that sound responsible?"

"But Christina, being responsible sometimes means putting the needs of others before your own. Yes, you took a chance coming down here, but I'm guessing this place is far less stressful than the place you left. Am I right?"

"Yes, you're right."

"Are you taking better care of Isaac?"

"Yes."

"Have you thought about Lewis since you've been here?"

"No, not really."

"See? And I'm sure you want to raise the baby instead of letting a relative raise him."

"I do still want to raise my baby even though he might grow up without a father."

Tears made their way into the corners of her eyes again. The thought of her baby growing up without a father scared her even more than the thought of raising him by herself.

"Do you still love him?"

Christina hunched her shoulders. "I thought I did. I thought I was in love. Now I think it was more the excitement of a boy being interested in me for the first time in my life."

Sandra nodded. "I was in love once when I was thirteen, but he moved with his family to Florida."

"Thirteen? Is it love when you're thirteen?"

"Yes, I thought so at the time." Sandra chuckled. "Or it just might've been gas."

They both laughed out loud.

"Lord knows, that boy's breath stank like hot hen ass."

Christina doubled over with laughter. It felt good to laugh out loud and to release stress while they were at it.

"Besides, for women it's different. Mama always said a woman loves so hard sometimes she forgets herself. That's why sometimes women wind up hurt first, unable to get past the pain."

Christina thought about that statement. Was she so blind in her love she forgot how she should feel in the relationship? His actions did throw her for a loop. One minute he was in love with her and she could do no wrong. The next minute he barely looked her way, not even acknowledging his unborn child. What kind of a person does that? She was glad Sandra was here for her to talk to so she could get that heavy emotion off her chest. This was the first time she had ever told the whole story to someone other than her family, even admitting relief that what was shared produced understanding towards the situation. She decided to change the subject.

"So, Sandra, what can I expect at a social luncheon around here?"

"You can expect a whole lot of food and a whole lot of rich men."

They both laughed at that statement, one admitting to needing only food and the other stating a man wouldn't be too bad at this point in time. They remained at the diner until the late afternoon, both enjoying each other's company and promising to meet at least once a week at that spot.

At the house she went straight to the kitchen hoping to find Aunt Bessie so she could talk about the day's events, but no one was home. A note was placed on the counter. "Gone to the ocean with baby; be back soon." Christina poured herself a glass of water and sat down at the table. She felt relieved that Sandra hadn't judged her or her circumstances like so many other people did. Christina said a quick prayer of thanks. Her new life here was showing progress, and with that came new friends and social events. She would have to tone down on the social events for a little bit, as the need to take care of her baby was a must before she went back home to Virginia, but for the first time she was sincerely glad Charleston was the place she could call home. She made her way to the bedroom. Her eyelids felt heavy and before she closed them her thoughts again drifted to Michael, the handsome stranger, wondering when she would see him again.

Chapter 12

A letter from the Ladies Society of Charleston came in the mail for Bessie and Christina. It was an invitation to a charity function held annually every September to raise funds for orphaned children. Bessie was surprised and skeptical that it took the women's group this long to invite her to an event, especially since she told her friend she wasn't concerned with joining after being asked several times. She had been in Charleston more than fifteen years now and wasn't interested in joining any clubs or groups, preferring not to be obligated to attend an event every time they had one. She suspected this had something to do with her niece and instantly knew who the person was that sent the invitation. Celia Rose. Bessie shook her head. If Celia wanted to pick on Christina she'd have to go through her first. She decided to accept the invitation. Dresses, shoes and accessories would need to be purchased from the shops downtown. Christina would need autumn colors that would highlight her features and newly reformed figure.

Bessie smiled to herself. Celia had no idea that her son had eyes for Christina or that they'd met. How interesting, she thought. Love does find a way when its least expected. Her mama's words rang true. She just had to figure out how to hide Christina's secret until she felt comfortable revealing it to those around her. Bessie smiled to herself. Of all the men in Charleston, South Carolina that could've taken an interest in Christina, it had to be the son of one of the most well-known businessmen in the region with a gossipy busybody for a wife.

Had this been a setup? It was rather interesting that Christina met Michael the day his mother paid a visit. Was it a coincidence or fate? One thing was for sure; if Celia Rose wanted to play games then she would be the one writing the performance.

ↄ

The social gathering was more like a high class gala with the latest fashions, wine tasting, laughing, and music available to all that attended. It was at an historical brick mansion with willow trees that formed a welcoming entrance as the guests pulled into the circular driveway. String quartet music met everyone through French doors as they made their way to the courtyard. Rolling hills seemed to go on forever with a gazebo and lake leveling out the sprawling estate landscape.

The reason Sandra wanted to attend this soiree was evident to Christina when she saw the beauty of the social setting. Christina felt more out of place here then she had anywhere else. The latest fashion style was the hourglass shaped bodice with small waistline, full skirt and high heels. Her dresses weren't even close to these styles, and she didn't have a thing to wear to such a fancy affair. Mama had packed her weekly clothes, which consisted of plain dresses, stockings, and shoes. The only colors available out of those dresses were brown, blue, and black cotton with long sleeves and a round neckline, not the pink chiffon or white satin material she saw worn on the streets. She definitely would need new clothes. Christina was glad when Sandra offered one of her dresses for the afternoon. How could she say no? Sandra, God bless her, saw her lack of wardrobe right away and offered a satin navy blue dress that accented her skin tone beautifully.

"Wow! You look wonderful. Everyone will be talking about you this evening. The last time I put that dress on I resembled a cow in its final stages of pregnancy."

Christina laughed. The blue dress had a high-necked collar that opened at her chest, which accented her cleavage and tapered around her waist. It filled her out in all the right places and she noticed the fashion complimented her features tremendously. Her hair was piled high in a loose bun with curly tendrils coming down against her neck, the style very popular amongst the women in the area. Her thoughts turned to Michael. Would she see him this evening? And more importantly could she handle being around him without turning into a puddle of mush.

A rather large crowd had gathered to celebrate the evening's event, and the mood was festive yet refined. The ballroom was lit ceiling to floor with candlelight. Several young men with instruments was playing by the fire place as servants threaded their way through the crowd balancing silver trays of hors d'oeuvre and drinks. She used the time to scan the room noticing people from every class and occupation including soldiers dressed in uniform.

Michael was in the process of answering yet another business question from one of his father's co-workers when he happened to glance up and see Christina easing through the crowd towards the backyard. He stopped his conversation in mid- sentence and watched as every person she passed stared openly at her lovely face. While he had noticed her shape before, the tender curves of her body were more obvious due to the cut of her gown, thinking it showed a bit too much cleavage, he seriously considered dragging her by the hand out of the area and away from the men now gawking at her openly.

Damn, he wanted her.

Christina took one look at the faces surrounding her and noticed no one seemed to have a voice let alone a polite 'hello'. Only Celia Rose, who came from behind them decided to speak and she felt a sudden urge to put on a cloak of holy armor as the lady made her skin crawl.

"Hello, Sandra. Christina, I'm so glad we finally get to meet."

"Hi, Mrs. Rose. How are you?" they said in unison.

"I've just arrived from a social luncheon down in Savannah. I had such a wonderful time, but of course I had to come back and see how my event was being received by Charleston patrons."

"This event is very lovely Mrs. Rose." Christina didn't know what else to say to the woman. The attention she was already receiving was mortifying not to mention the woman in front of her was assessing everything from her hair to the shoes on her feet.

Christina was at a loss for words. She was about to excuse herself from the conversation when Sandra interrupted. "We must be going. Mother would like to see Christina before the evening is over," Sandra chimed in.

"Yes, of course dear." She spoke directly to Christina. "We must sit beside each other at dinner time. I'd love to hear of your life in Virginia."

"Yes, Ma'am, that would be nice."

"It was nice seeing you again, Mrs. Rose," Sandra cut in quickly, steering Christina in the direction of her parents.

"You too, dear."

As she walked away Christina could feel Celia's eyes boring into her back and decided she would try and skip dinner time to avoid any more questions from people like Celia. She was determined to learn all there was to know about South Carolina culture: the way people lived, the food, music, dress, and traditions. There was no way she could go anywhere else without educating herself first, so the next time when someone asked her about educational topics, or even politics, she would be ready. One thing was for certain; she had no problem admitting she wasn't used to this type of life.

The charity event was hosted by the Ladies Society of Charleston. Each member contributed her time and energy in creating an environment where everyone could mingle and donate their funds to a worthy cause. Today's fundraiser would help children whose parents were deceased or who had been abandoned at an early age. It was also a great opportunity for the wealthy of Charleston to come together for a good cause. Christina wondered if this was just another social gathering to see who had the most money. Back home some people in the neighborhood would talk about how much they put in the collection plate at church. This wasn't the same thing, but it was bragging about how much someone could give nonetheless.

Later afternoon the luncheon turned into an evening of music and dancing fairly quickly. Christina saw the dramatic change take effect when the string quartet was replaced by a twelve-piece ensemble. Musicians performed from the terrace while butlers made sure champagne glasses were filled, as guests trickled in through the front door. Tables were set up along the verandah with stacks of hors d'oeuvres, including stuffed shrimp, tuna tartar, and an enormous fruit stand. She recognized some of the dishes from her days working at Mrs. Evans' house. She wanted to sample each one and revel in the flavors produced from them. The roasted hog looked like it had just come from the oven, the steam rolling from its skin like a thick cloud. The tables were covered with Cornish hens, roast beef, huge hams, greens, turnips, squash, and what looked like shrimp and grits with small buttered croissants on the side. The food layout was impressive and she couldn't help but wonder if all social events here were this organized.

Christina looked up from the sumptuous spread and saw a familiar figure come around the corner. It was Michael. He walked with an arrogant air surrounding him. She noticed some women stop in mid conversation with their male companions to stare as he walked by. He was so handsome her hands were shaking from nervousness and he hadn't even seen or spoken to her yet.

"Would you care for a waltz, Ms. Davis?"

"Yes, I would."

He was a balding man with eyeglasses and a toothy smile. It was the perfect opportunity to take her mind off the man that seemed to have gained every woman's attention in the room, including hers.

Her dance partner's name was Edward Wright, a prominent land owner on James Island who was growing rice as a cash crop and father of her new best friend, Sandra.

"I must apologize. I'm not very good at dancing," she said.

"Nonsense, just follow my lead. You'll do fine."

She was led in a dance which she'd never heard of and never danced before. Back home it was mostly hopping around outside Mama's house to whatever Uncle Jerry was playing at the time. She hoped her current partner wouldn't notice. When the music started, Christina tried to follow as best as she could. Her feet felt like they were made of cement and when she went to move them they found the top of Mr. Wright's shoes. She was sure the winces on his face were from her shoe prints.

"You dance very well, Ms. Davis."

"I'm sure you say that to all the young girls who step on your shoes, Mr. Wright."

"Only the one's with sweet charm such as yours."

Christina smiled. She knew he was sparing her feelings but she accepted the compliment anyway.

"Are you enjoying your stay in Charleston?"

"I am. Charleston is a beautiful place."

"Yes, it is. I believe you've already met my daughter Sandra. She's spoken very highly of you."

"We've had lunch together. I enjoy talking with her."

"I'm surprised you got a word in, dear. She can be rather chatty. She gets that habit from me, I suppose. My wife and I have lived here over twenty years. It's a splendid town. Have you had your coming out celebration?"

"Coming out celebration?" Christina didn't know what that was. She was having difficulty dancing the waltz, let alone thinking about any celebration.

"Yes, a debutante ball, dear. It's a simple coming of age event an introduction to society, if you will."

"I'm not sure I'll be here for that long, sir."

"Nonsense. It's this February. Sandra had mentioned you'll be staying here quite a while. Is that true?"

"Yes, but I'm busy with things at my auntie's house."

Christina heard the lie come through her teeth and immediately regretted it. She knew Mr. Wright could sense the lie because a smile came across his face.

"Humor an old man, dear. We sponsor five lucky young women each year. And we don't mind footing the bill. Our own daughter will be one of the five. Allow me and my wife to sponsor you."

"Yes, but…"

"Good, it's settled. I'm sure your aunt wouldn't mind. She's a very nice woman as well. My wife would be delighted to assist in the matter. She's the president of the Lady's Society of Charleston and enjoys influencing lovely young ladies such as you. They offer classes teaching cotillion, which is dance classes."

"Mr. Wright, I must be honest with you." She wanted to tell him about her child and the reason she couldn't attend classes while taking care of Isaac. It would be too much for her to handle. She was still breast feeding, although she wasn't producing as much as when Isaac was first born.

"I already know what's going on, dear," he quickly said. "I like your honesty, but don't you worry about that. We'll take care of the situation on our end."

Christina's cheeks turned crimson. "I don't know what to say."

"Thank you, to start. I've seen girls go through similar situations in Africa, dear." He leaned in closer towards her ear. "We are no strangers to the unpredictable ourselves." He pulled back to look at her with a mischievous gleam in his eyes.

Christina laughed. She liked Mr. Wright already. He had introduced himself to her only a second ago and chose not to judge her. The same couldn't be said about the people who had known her all her life. As the last bars of the dance music drew to a close, Christina promised to accept the invitation for brunch at the Wright's home.

"May I cut in, Mr. Wright?"

She knew that voice. It was the same voice that made her nervous in the market place; the same voice that was making her heart skip a beat now. She got so flustered she missed a step at the end of the waltz, which got her dancing partner's foot tangled with her own.

"Oh, I'm sorry." Christina looked up and saw him standing there with a smug look on his face. He knew he was making her uncomfortable. She tried not to show it as she commanded her feet to stand still. Christina watched as he maneuvered his body to stand just inside her and Mr. Wright's circle. She let out a little gasp when his forearm touched her flesh.

Her hands began to tremble as she heard Mr. Wright answer. "Yes, you may, Mr. Rose." He took her hands, bent down and kissed them.

"Thank you, Mr. Wright, for the dance," she said.

"I'll see you tomorrow afternoon, young lady." He gave a slight nod of his head to her next dance partner before exiting.

Michael took her right hand and placed his left on the lower half of her back. She wondered if this was appropriate as she noticed some women look on in surprise at their stance.

"You look beautiful, Christina."

"Thank you." She didn't know what else to say to him so she tried to start with light conversation, being sure to choose her words carefully.

"Are you helping with the charity today?"

"No I help my mother with the set-up and take down chairs and tables once the event is over."

"That's very nice of you."

"Yes, it is." He looked down at her then with such warmth in his eyes Christina had to look away.

"What brings you here to this little gathering, besides me?"

She laughed a little. "I was invited as a guest by Mrs. Margaret White, and I don't even know you."

"Oh but you will, soon." His emphasis on the word soon was enough to get her heart racing a bit more than it already was. The intensity in his eyes made her look away.

Christina hesitated a little, careful not to reveal too much to this stranger. "I'm staying with my aunt for a while on James Island." She tried sounding matter-of-fact, keeping her voice level and attitude cool. "Charleston is such a beautiful place. You're lucky to live here."

"Yes, I am. I keep one of my father's smaller farms near John's Island. The house is my parents until I decide to move. I'm thinking of building a house of my own out there."

"That sounds lovely," Christina said. She was picturing him shirtless, cutting wood and wiping the sweat from his brow. His muscular physique would be glistening in the sunlight as she touched his... Christina quickly jumped back to reality, reminding herself not to get too entranced with this man.

"Yes, it is," he said.

His eyes made her feel heated again and she knew he wasn't talking about the farm the way he was looking at her. Her stomach felt like it was doing somersaults. As the dance continued, Christina noticed his left hand had inched its way to just above her tailbone while his thumb slowly made circle designs. Across the room she noticed a few people had stopped to look at them dancing. One of those people was Celia Rose. Oh lord she probably had something else to gossip about after seeing them together.

"May I come by sometime, Christina?"

"I don't know if that's a good idea."

"I promise to be on my best behavior."

She let out a little laughter. "I highly doubt that. Besides, I'm supposed to be going to Mr. Wright's house tomorrow." She was scrambling at this point, trying to tell him just about anything to discourage him from coming to see her. "I'll be attending the debutante ball this year and classes are starting this week."

Normally he would've cringed at the thought of any young girl mentioning the word ball around him. He avoided the social event, preferring to gain mistresses after the event than before. Young debutantes tended to be clingy and looking for husbands, a title which he definitely wasn't ready for. However, Christina wasn't just any silly little debutante, and the thought of another man escorting her didn't sit well with him at all.

"Do you have an escort to the event?"

"No, but I'm sure Mr. Wright will choose someone for me. I'm new to this whole thing and not sure how it's supposed to be done."

"Allow me to escort you. I promise you won't be disappointed." He wouldn't take no for an answer and followed the last sentence with a mischievous grin.

She wasn't falling for it. That grin said it all. It spoke of every naughty thing he was probably thinking of at the moment. Who did he think he was: Charming yes, handsome yes, a devil, and hell yes. She put on her best I know what you're trying to do look.

"I'm spoken for, Mr. Rose." Indeed this was half true, as her attention was set on one male, Isaac, but he didn't need to know that. "And I'm sure you already have plenty of other options to choose from."

"Not at all, and please call me Michael." He stared straight into her eyes and brought her right hand to his lips. All she felt was immense desire as he lowered his warm moist lips while at the same time bringing her hand to his mouth. Everything went hazy. Those lips when planted against her skin were full and wet. Her knees felt weak, and she wondered how long they'd be able to support her. His chest may have been separated somewhat from hers but she swore she heard his heartbeat echo her own. The tops of her thighs suddenly felt hot and humid; her breathing was slow and rhythmic. Had his fingers touched her lips at that moment they would've felt the trembling sensations her body couldn't bear to hide. His left hand suddenly came up and stroked her cheek lightly. With his index finger he drew a path from her cheek to the outline of her lips, first along the underside of the bottom, then from the top, tracing to the corner of her mouth and down to lightly hold her chin. Her eyes followed his while her breathing became labored. Christina swallowed the sigh in her throat. Clearly he knew what he was doing. No one did that with such finesse without some experience, especially in a room full of people. There must've been a couple of girls he'd done this to before and she refused to be categorized as one of his girls.

This thought brought her back to reality. The music faded softly before speeding up with another dance. They stood in the middle of the floor, oblivious to other couples.

"Thank you for the dance." She tried to turn and walk away but he still held her to him.

"You didn't answer my question."

"No?"

"No."

"I thought I did."

"You didn't."

"Alright then, no."

"No?"

"No, thank you."

"At least allow me to take you to dinner."

"I'll be too busy, Michael, with the debutante classes. Have a good evening."

She quickly moved out of his arms and away from the dance floor.

Michael stood there for a moment with a perplexed look on his face. After a while he chuckled to himself. Did she just dismiss his advances in front of a room full of people? Ms. Christina was proving to be a lovely challenge. No woman had ever left him standing in the middle of the dance floor gazing after them. And like with all challenges he faced, Michael was determined to win.

He didn't notice there were two women who didn't appreciate that little scene at all. The first was his mistress Patrice, who saw the display of affection and quickly noted that Michael had never looked at her the way he looked at this girl. Jealousy quickly spread through her like hot shrimp and grits on a cold day. Who was this girl? And why did she have the attention of one of the most eligible rich men in town? Not to mention the one she was sleeping with. But it was more than that. She didn't want to share with another woman what she'd worked towards getting for herself for the past two years. Men like Michael Rose didn't just appear out of thin air every day, good looking and rich. Patrice had to get to the bottom of this before her chances with Michael were ruined for good.

Across the room another set of eyes was shooting daggers at the couple on the dance floor. Celia Rose watched her son with newfound alarm. This new girl was good at playing the innocent, but she was no stranger to women playing at being unsullied when it came to her son. She deemed herself a very good judge of character and this girl was a manipulative little weasel. She was the only one who knew what was best for her son and this girl was clearly not it. If Celia was going to find out anything about this girl it better be soon. The look her son gave the young woman just now made her sick, which meant he was interested, which also meant she would lose him, and that was just not going to happen. She needed an informant, someone to find out more about this newcomer so she could warn her son against the gold digger. But who could it be? Who could be that conniving and manipulative to get her the evidence she needed against the potential love interest of her son besides herself? She needed someone to be her eyes and ears, to be her snoop. Celia scanned the room and her eyes connected with Patrice, the whore of Babylon.

Patrice still couldn't look her in the eyes, and so Celia gave her a salute with her champagne glass and a slight head nod to let her know it was safe to come and talk to her. Patrice's eyes went wide and she immediately hiked her dress up and walked quickly over to Celia. A few ladies frowned on that error, as ladies should never reveal any type of skin at a social function such as this. Celia herself watched the girl's error with disgust and noted her ignorance, but at this moment she didn't care as Patrice came to a halt in front of her. If she was going to get information she would need someone on the inside to do her dirty work, and what better someone than a jezebel like Patrice St. Clair?

Chapter 13

Michael paced back and forth, his thoughts racing. Last night's sleep proved to be challenging, as he couldn't get Christina off his mind. She was intriguing. And it was hard for him to concentrate on anything else, especially projects he should've been working on today instead of standing in front of Bessie Washington's front door feeling like a lovesick puppy. He stiffened. What if this was the wrong house? He told Mr. Wright he had the best intentions when he asked where Ms. Washington lived. The older man seemed a bit overprotective of Christina, which was strange given they had only met yesterday. He questioned Michael for over an hour before telling him where the house was located. It could be just his imagination, but the man acted more like a father figure than a nice host. He could only hope Christina wouldn't be put off by his brazen move to see her. The temptation was just too good for him to pass up. Michael knocked on the door. He knew he was taking a risk calling on her without her knowledge, but he was willing to take that risk just to see her again.

The image of how she looked at the social gathering was all he could think about lately. Her eyes were like velvet, so soft and lustrous it made him forget where he was. When he saw her dancing with Mr. Wright he almost felt like snatching the old man from her embrace. Dancing with her only heightened his senses when her body perfectly

conformed to his. He took note of her supple breasts and how they gently brushed his chest when they twirled about the room. But her body was nothing compared to her face. Those chocolate eyes could hold a man steady in his place, and that mouth was made for kissing. If they hadn't been on the dance floor surrounded by people, Michael would've taken the liberty of kissing the breath out of her, which probably would've invoked a slap afterwards. It would have been worth it, he thought, just to feel her mouth pressed against his. He shook those thoughts away for the time being and concentrated on not exciting himself too much before he saw her.

The last time he had felt like this was ages ago with his first love Hanna, who decided to marry a wealthy man twice her age. She couldn't fathom marrying a merchant marine who had been at sea for an extended period of time. That part of his life had been over for quite some time. It was a delicate subject that even he was reluctant to talk about.

Christina was different than the other women he encountered. She was innocent in some ways, but had a raw magnetism that drew him to her. And soon he hoped she would come around to see he wasn't that bad of a guy as well.

An older man came to the door dressed in overalls and shoes that were caked in dry mud. For a second Michael wondered if Mr. Wright had given him the wrong address.

"Can I help you?"

"Yes, I'm here to see Christina Davis."

Joseph gave the man once-over look before letting him in through the door. "Come on in."

"Thank you."

"Joseph, who is it?"

Michael recognized Ms. Bessie's voice from the market.

"Hello, ma'am. Remember me from the market? I am Michael Rose."

"Yes, I know who you are. You're Celia Rose's son. Does she know you're here?"

"No, ma'am." Michael sensed his mother had made a not so nice impression on Ms. Bessie, given her question.

"I hope I'm not intruding on anything here."

"No, not at all. In fact, we were just going to the market to get some fish for dinner this evening. What can we do for you?"

"I'm here to see if your niece would like to go for a ride, with your permission, of course."

"Of course," she said, curious as to why Michael decided to come by today so suddenly after seeing Christina last night. Usually gentlemen callers waited a day or two. This one hadn't even waited twenty four hours.

"Before I go get her, would you like something to drink?"

"Yes, ma'am."

"We have iced tea."

"Iced tea would be just fine."

As Bessie went to the kitchen, Michael could feel Joseph's eyes on him, studying his every move. He decided he should make light conversation to ease the slight tension in the room. "This is a lovely home you have here, Ms. Washington."

"Thank you," she said, handing him the cold glass. "I must say I've lived here for quite some time, but I haven't seen you around this area."

"I left Charleston when I was twenty-two to join the merchant marine. I wanted to see some parts of the world. After that I decided to help my father build the family farming business."

"A working man. That's good, very good," she said. "Let me go get Christina." She made her way down the small hallway, knocked on the door, and went inside.

"You can have a seat."

Michael had almost forgotten Joseph was in the room because he was so quiet. He took a seat and sipped his tea slowly. He noticed the older man didn't say much and wondered if he was a hired hand that worked around the house or something more. Judging by the way he was seated in the chair Michael guessed it was something a little more. The door to the room came open and Bessie walked out.

"She'll be out in a little bit, Michael."

"Thank you, ma'am."

Thirty minutes later, when Christina emerged, she was sure she would find an empty room. Instead she found Michael seated and undeterred by the long wait. Thankfully Isaac had been put to sleep before Michael came to the door. It took several outfits and three hairstyles for her to finally settle on a peach dress with short sleeves. She chose a pair of flat blue shoes with her mother's pearls as accessories, and hoped it looked halfway decent for her first day at debutante class.

"Hello, Michael."

"Hi, Christina. You look beautiful."

"Thank you. What are you doing here?" She really wanted to ask him how he found out where she lived, since she hadn't given out that information the last time she saw him.

"I thought you and I could go for a ride and get to know one another." Christina's guard immediately went up as she folded her arms and looked at him. Was he really trying to get to know her, or was he looking for something else?

"I have my debutante class in another hour."

"Yes, I know. I saw my mother's society schedule on the ball and wanted to drive you there myself."

Her eyes looked skeptical as she met his gaze. "Just think of me as a temporary chauffeur," he said, giving a slight bow.

Sensing her niece's apprehension, Bessie said, "Christina, why don't you go with Michael? Joseph and I can pick you up later on."

Christina's face revealed a panicked look. She wasn't sure if she should be alone with this man, and her instinct told her he was more rascal than anything she had ever encountered.

Before she could protest, Michael thanked Bessie for her hospitality and escorted Christina out the door. They rode in silence for the first few minutes. Christina made sure she didn't look at him, and her body was as close to the door as physically possible. She kept her focus on the passing scenery so as not to give any indication her nerves were something other than calm. He, on the other hand, didn't mind talking.

"Before we become better acquainted, I need to apologize for my behavior last night. If you were embarrassed please accept my apology."

Christina drew herself up stiffly. "More like I was manhandled by a lion."

"Ouch! Are you always this approachable?" he said sarcastically. "I'm glad you came with me. Besides, I'm not here to harass you, Christina. I'd like to get to know you, a little better." His voice sounded gentle, which helped put her mind at ease. There was nothing conniving or manipulative coming from his mouth.

She bit her lip and glanced over at him. Maybe she was being a bit harsh, but it was better than succumbing to his charms, which made her feel like an immature school girl. And she knew better than to feel that way again, as it drew memories of Lewis from which she spent the better part of a year trying to forget. One mistake had already been learned, and she didn't need to make another one. It seemed easier to pretend to be surly than an over eager woman looking for a lover. At this moment she needed to be as in control of her emotions as possible. "I'm sorry. I guess I'm still getting used to being in a strange place and strange people."

"Charleston isn't so bad once you get to know everyone."

"That's not what I'm talking about."

"Well, I'm not bad once you get used to me." He said the last sentence with definite intent.

She adjusted her seating. "Virginia is so different from here. I was worried about trying to fit in, which is why I took Mr. Wright up on the offer of being a part of the debutante ball."

"So the pressure got to you and you gave in."

"No, not at all," she said a bit forcefully. "I thought it would be a great way to get to know some of the people here and possibly make a few friends." She glanced at him again to see if he understood what she was trying to say.

"People will be drawn to you anyway, Christina. You're a very appealing young woman."

Christina felt her heart quicken. The silence was making her more nervous than the conversation.

"After your class, please allow me to take you to dinner. You haven't had real southern food till you've eaten here in Charleston."

"Auntie and Joseph are going to pick me up after class."

"I'll drive back and let them know I'm taking you." He waited for her to answer as she thought about it for a moment. His behavior was definitely better, he was keeping his hands to himself and she knew she'd be hungry afterwards.

"That would be alright. Could you come around seven?"

"Seven it is," he said as they pulled up to the Wright's three-story townhome.

Sandra was waiting by the gate and waved when she saw them pull up.

"Have a good class, Christina."

Turning around she caught him smiling before he pulled away. As she walked up to a curious Sandra, she hoped he would keep his hands to himself later on this evening. But could she do the same?

❧

James Island turned into a peaceful getaway when the sun went down. Christina was glad Michael decided to be in her company as they pulled into a small dining shack overlooking a salt water marsh. The tables with white and turquoise linens had lighted lanterns that created a warm romantic atmosphere. The host gave them a critical stare before Michael stuffed money into his pocket and asked for a seat overlooking the bay. He pulled her chair to sit down and ordered their meals simultaneously. The names of the dishes sounded incredibly difficult to pronounce yet Michael seemed at ease with speaking directly to the waiter and she noticed the server was equally impressed with his command of the language. He began calling out the order to cooks immediately, who hurried to prepare the food.

"J'espère que c'est bien avec vous," Michael said to her.

"What did you say?"

"I hope that's alright with you."

"And what language was that?"

"French. My mother taught me the language when I was a boy."

"Is your family French?"

"No, Mom made sure we learned to speak another language other than Gullah, which is what my father's people speak."

"What does the Gullah language sound like?" she asked. Christina had heard the Gullah people originated from West Africa, but wanted to know more about the language and who the people were.

"Oonuh 'ooman done fuh smaa't," he said.

"And what does that mean?"

"You, woman, are really smart."

Her lips curved into a slight smile. "It's nice of you to say so." He can speak different languages, she thought. Very impressive I wonder what else he can do.

"Would you want to order anything for yourself, or are you okay with what I ordered?"

"If I knew what you ordered, I should say yes. Is there fresh fruit on the menu?"

"Yes, there is."

Light music was coming from the patio area as she swayed in rhythmic motion with the tune. He noticed the wind had loosened several strands of her hair, and blew them around her face. The picture it created stirred his soul, as the moonlight captured her, and held it beautifully just for him.

"May I have this dance," he said standing and offering his hand. She took it without question and noticed other women were staring as she and Michael maneuvered their way past their tables towards the dance floor. Michael seemed at ease with the way he placed his hand on the lower part of her back as he drew her closer to him. He was extremely good looking and it was obvious that every female in the place thought so too, as she saw the pairs of eyes scan his masculine frame. He had on blue trousers, a navy blazer with white buttons, and a white cotton shirt that opened at his collar bone to reveal his muscular chest. Christina stared at that 'v' opening for a long time. Did he have any idea what effect he had on her? She felt his arm wrap around her waist and the faint tug guiding her close for a slow dance. It felt so good to be held. Christina hadn't realized how much she missed being in a man's arms or how long she'd gone without it.

Her longing for affection seemed to diminish as soon as Michael pulled her close, pressing his hard chest against hers. They swayed back and forth for a while, speaking very little to one another and letting the music communicate for them. She was glad for her dance classes today as she was able to follow his lead with every step and turn. His intent was clear in the way he stroked her back and the underside of her arm. He wanted her. His whole body told of his adoration for her as he slowly moved closer and closer. She felt her own body temperature rise as their bodies continually brushed back and forth against each other. When the music ended he reluctantly escorted her back to their table, where dinner was waiting. "This looks wonderful," she said, observing the delicious plates set before them.

"I hope you like it." Michael dipped his papaya lightly in the parfait and handed it to Christina.

She looked at it warily, not sure if she should allow this man to feed her in such an intimate way. She opened her mouth slightly, feeling his fingertips before the fruit was imbedded between her teeth. The juices made a slight river down her chin, but she didn't seem to mind. Their dinner was all about tasting and giving to one another as he made sure she got her fill of the dishes that were offered. Christina thought the night couldn't get any better.

The food was tasty and the man sitting across from her was as handsome as anyone she'd ever met. Not wanting the evening to end, she didn't know how to relate that to him, and began to talk frivolously. "I had a good time, Michael. The food was wonderful, wasn't it? I don't know the last time I had a meal as good as that. Thank you for escorting me. I felt a little out of pla—"

He stroked the side of her face to stop her incessant chatter. "I wanted to show you a different side to Charleston in hopes that you'll want to enjoy it with me often."

She knew he meant that he wanted to keep seeing her. "This is beautiful, Michael, but I think I have to go now. Auntie will be worried."

"Of course." Laying a few dollars on the table, he led her out the door towards the car. It didn't take him long to climb in after closing the passenger door, but when his eyes found hers again he put his hands on either side her cheeks, dipped his head to the side and placed his lips on hers. Her eyes couldn't seem to stay open as they glided closed and she sampled for the first time what he tasted like. She kissed him first with a bit of uncertainty, not knowing how he liked being kissed, but then passion took over, as did an overwhelming sense of urgency. She placed her fingers on his chest and wanted to relay the feelings he brought out in her, hoping he could read what she was trying to tell him. She kissed his mouth over and over while sliding her tongue against his bottom lip and pushed against him slightly to see if the feelings were mutual. He growled his disapproval of that action and pulled her against him once more for a very long and profound kiss. His mouth slanted over hers again and again. They stayed like that for a while until they heard laughter coming from outside and knew they had to break contact before something else happened that they didn't want the public to see. He reluctantly pulled away from her lips, the moistness of them not wanting to become a distant memory as he struggled with wanting to pull her towards him again. Her mouth was so sweet and it took everything he had not to pull her head forcefully for another impassioned embrace.

Putting the keys in the ignition, Michael started the car and slowly pulled out of the parking area. If he wanted to be with Christina he'd have to do it the right way. She wasn't like the other girls he encountered in his life and he didn't want to treat her like he treated the others. He had to figure out his next move as he tried to calm his head as well as his loins down to a respectable size. The last thing he needed was Christina running away from him because he couldn't control his urges. She in turn was a little disappointed as the car pulled up to Auntie's house. The porch light was on and she noticed the screen door was still open.

"Thank you, Michael, for the dinner and the ride home." She turned towards him for another kiss.

"Are you sure you don't need an escort to the debutante ball? I promise to keep my hands to myself."

"You mean like you did a few minutes ago?" She laughed, knowing that kiss was not only enjoyed by him but by her as well.

"You didn't like the kiss?"

She looked away from him, noticing they had an audience. Joseph had come out of the house and stood on the porch with his arms crossed. She turned back to the handsome man awaiting her answer.

"Yes, I did. But don't make this a habit. I have to concentrate and attend classes for the next couple of weeks and don't need distraction."

"So I would distract you?"

"You know what I mean." She bit her lower lip. Did he actually know what she meant? He was proving to be an alright host, and maybe she ought to give him a chance. "Maybe you can help me with the history and culture of Charleston."

He smiled. She thought her legs were going to melt.

"Great. Go inside. I'm sure your aunt will want to know the details of your evening."

"Good night, Michael."

"Good night, Christina."

She watched the car drive off until it could no longer be seen down the road. The lump in her throat didn't seem to want to go down and she knew when passing Joseph she'd have to explain where she was all this time. The blush on her cheeks expanded as she went into the house; she was letting the events of the evening replay in her mind.

"And just where have you been at this hour?" Joseph asked.

"The dinner with Michael took a little longer than I thought after class. It was nothing, Joseph." She tried to reassure him.

"Make sure it stays that way. He don't know 'bout li'l Isaac yet, do he?"

"No, he doesn't," she replied, looking away from him.

"Your baby needs more attention than that boy, Christina. You be sure to remember that before going out next time," Joseph said before turning to walk back down the hallway.

She knew he was right. Isaac was more important than any man right now. She would have to wait to display her feelings to him some other time. She would eventually have to tell him about Isaac, but she wanted to get to know him first. No other man needed to come into her life and mess things up, especially when she was trying to raise a little man of her own.

Chapter 14

Christina spent the next day with Aunt Bessie and the Wrights, walking the streets of downtown Charleston and reveling in the city's charismatic atmosphere. Horse carriages shuttled people back and forth while cars slowed to allow shoppers to cross in front of them. The city blocks were alive with people from different cultures and backgrounds. Some were selling goods made from family farms, while others were out for an afternoon stroll and engaging in light conversation with one another. Christina learned that while Charleston had its roots in the slave trade and working plantations, it also allowed many African Americans the opportunity to maintain their own businesses, thereby adding to the economic development within and around the city.

In truth, Charleston was much like Richmond with its historic sites and the ethnic diversity of its neighborhoods. Christina might have moved several hours away, but it was to a place that was exactly like Virginia, as everyone worked and contributed to their respective communities. There was little contrast between the two cities and while she noted the similarities there was one distinct difference that Richmond didn't possess: Michael. She might not have liked Charleston when she first came, but she certainly held a different view now that she had spent so much time here amongst the people.

Tomorrow she looked forward to her etiquette class at the Wright's home. And with a little luck hopefully she would run into Michael. The way he touched her last night made her forget all the pain and anger she had felt *this past year. And his lips...*

I'm thinking about him too much. Maybe I need to slow down before things get out of hand.

Last night's image made a lasting impression on her even as she attended church services with the Wrights. There was no mistaking the physical attraction she felt for him or how her heart seemed to find its own rhythm when he was around.

My God, am I falling in love with him?

Christina's throat tensed and she shifted uncomfortably in her seat. She'd accepted the chemistry between them, but love? Love was something entirely different. It was tricky, elusive, and downright awful, especially if it wasn't reciprocated. Christina knew the ramification of love when this happened and there was no way she'd let anything like that happen again.

Sunday wound on into a dinner at the Wright's majestic country estate. The surrounding landscape made for a delightful ending to a fulfilling day. Mrs. Wright played with Isaac, who clearly saw her as a willing participant in capturing bugs and wrestling them away from his grasp. His infectious laughter had everyone smiling and joining in on their fun.

"Dinner was lovely, Mr. and Mrs. Wright. Thank you for inviting us to your home today," Christina said appreciatively. "Isaac is having an especially good time."

"We enjoyed having you join us. Next time bring Joseph along with you. I haven't forgotten our bet of who can catch the most fish," Mr. Wright replied.

"I'm sure Joseph would like that bit of news."

"I've stocked the lake with plenty of fish, so there's no reason why the challenge can't go on. Unless Joseph has pressing matters he needs to attend to," he said playfully.

Bessie chuckled. Christina knew Joseph would be thrilled to participate in the contest, and she was sure he'd be in attendance the next time the Wrights invited them over for dinner. Sandra chimed in suddenly and could barely stop rattling on and on about her father's fishing accomplishments. She promptly received a hush from Mr. Wright when he could no longer tolerate it. Christina smiled at her friend, but all her thoughts were on Michael. She wondered where he was and if he was thinking of her.

They headed towards the house for tea, which Mrs. Wright insisted on after dinner. "Tea after dinner is a long tradition with our family, Christina. The men adjourn in the chamber area and the ladies into the library." Only this time, the men consisted of Mr. Wright and a little boy whose ages were separated by almost five decades.

Sandra pulled Christina's arm and gestured towards the kitchen, whispering in her ear that the 'elder' ladies needed time to gossip. Christina laughed at her sarcasm and politely excused herself from Mrs. Wright and Auntie.

Bessie waited until Sandra and Christina went into the house. Their laughter over something Sandra said followed behind them into the kitchen before she broached the subject.

"Where was Cynthia today, do you suppose?" Bessie asked, trying to sound casual.

Mrs. Wright pursed her lips. "I haven't the faintest idea. Although I'm sure she's up to no good now that Michael is interested in Christina."

Bessie smiled. She knew her friend was just as perceptive as she was when observing Christina and Michael. "You saw the look she gave Christina after they left the dance floor? I thought she was going to spit fire out of those eyes of hers."

"How could anyone miss the daggers that woman was shooting at the girl. It was absolutely terrible. I've never seen such a display and at a social function in front of everyone."

"She probably thought no one saw her," Bessie replied warily.

"Trust me, everyone in the room saw the look she gave Christina. And if memory serves me correctly, that's not the first time I've seen that look on her face."

"Are you referring to the young girl from Alabama? That was just awful. The poor girl's reputation was ruined."

"Celia was warned after that incident that if she ever put another young woman's reputation in jeopardy she'd have to answer to the women of the group."

"Do you really think Celia Rose is going to listen to anyone? I doubt she heard a word you said when you told her that."

"Celia listens through action, and if our words can't get across to her then dismissing her from the ladies society surely will."

Bessie raised her teacup. "I will toast to that," she said.

❦

The next day, Michael tried to exercise restraint, yet he had a great need to proclaim Christina as his in more ways than one. Remembering their kiss, her body yielding to his own, the taste of her lips was still on the tip of his tongue.

She was soft, gentle, generous with her sweet kisses and easy to talk with. Christina was the first woman in a long while with whom he felt comfortable. After his time at sea, he'd been eager to come back to the mainland and begin a new life. Keeping company with women came naturally and he didn't find it hard to keep his bed warm at night. But even that became boring after a while. Was he now looking for someone to tame his restless heart? Christina proved she could do just that. Michael watched as the yard workers tended to the landscape. He always thought the house and land were a bit much for just one person to have. A family should be here, not a bachelor with only the hired help to keep him company. George came into the room and set a pair of shined black shoes beside the bed.

"George, how's everything going today?"

"Good, sir. The house be nice and clean 'bout the time the day be over and done."

"That's good to know. Are there any messages from my father?" Michael asked. He hadn't heard from him in a while and it was unlike him not to stay in contact.

"Mr. Rose came in the other evenin while you was out with Ms. Christina. He say to tell you he'll meet you for lunch."

"Thank you, George. Did he suggest a time?"

"Round this afternoon and you should prepare for some real big news."

Michael was instantly curious, as he knew his father had been diligently pursuing new clients to feature their food products in stores. It was a lucrative business, one that his father had been in well over thirty years. And now that Michael was working with him, they set their sights on areas beyond South Carolina to market merchandise.

"Sounds good, George."

He heard the butler clear his throat and turned around. "Your mother sent word that she wishes to meet you in town tomorrow for brunch."

"I'll be with Ms. Christina tomorrow."

A terrified look crossed the butler's face, and Michael almost felt sorry for him.

"Mrs. Rose don't like it when you tell her no."

"She'll just have to get used to it. I expect to see Christina a lot more now that we've become better acquainted."

"Very good, sir. I'll see she gets the message," George said. "Ms. Christina a fine looking woman, sir. My Hazel saw her and Ms. Washington out and about yesterday with the Wrights."

"So, you've been checking out Christina, have you?" Michael teased. "And to think I thought you were a faithful man, George."

"Yes, sir, I am been with my wife for thirty-four years. Seems like fifty sometimes, and I wouldn't trade her in for no one."

Michael noticed George's expression when he talked about his family and he envied the man. George had been with Michael since he was a young boy, and he was almost like a second father to him, considering the amount of time they spent with one another.

"I hear you, George. Maybe one day I'll have the same thing." George walked towards Michael and put his hand on his shoulder.

The older man's face was worn and tired, but there was something else in the way he looked at him almost as if he was looking at his own son.

"I'm going to tell you like my father told me. When a man find a wife he find a good thing. Take time to know Ms. Christina and everything else will fall into place." George affectionately patted his shoulder and left the room.

Oddly enough, Michael felt as if he'd already found that good thing George just mentioned. The man's affection pulled at his heart strings. He remembered as a young boy how he'd wished his father showed just a tiny bit of interest in him as George did. His parents lavished their wealth on him, and he could have anything he wanted, but more times than not he wanted fatherly affection.

As the black town car pulled in front of the restaurant, Michael got the distinct impression this wasn't going to be an affectionate lunch hour between father and son. "Good to see you, Dad," Michael said, giving his father a hug before sitting at the table.

At fifty-five, James Rose had aged fairly well, with only the slightest hint of grey at his temples. He maintained a toned physique, and at six foot three the man could still turn a head or two when he entered the room. Michael inherited his father's cinnamon-colored eyes and muscular build, but that's where the similarities ended. James Rose had dark smooth skin that resembled melted chocolate, in contrast to the lighter brown complexion of his son. His skin color made him seem somewhat menacing, as some stereotypes portrayed, until the elder Rose opened his mouth to speak. His deep baritone voice put most of his counterparts at ease and seemed even now to set the tone of their conversation.

"Your mother sent a letter telling me you've taken an interest in a young lady unbecoming for a man of your wealth, is she correct in her statement?"

Michael shook his head. "No, she's not. Mother feels the need to point out the woman's flaws before getting to know her."

"Your mother does seem to go a bit overboard in her judgments. She loves you, son, and her intentions are purely out of love."

"Yes, I know."

"But enough about that I came here to discuss the next plan of action in our food distribution business and I need your input."

Michael knew this was the real reason for the meeting. His father was always eager to grow their business outside of Charleston. "The southern clients seem enthusiastic about the terms we're offering. Are we expecting any future clients?"

"Yes, we are. There are numerous western companies that have sprung up in the past few years."

"And you think there's a possibility they would have interest in our products, too."

"I don't see why not. We have the best produce throughout the south thanks to our farming techniques."

The company he and his father shared had been doing quite well since he took over the financial aspect of the business. The elder Rose handled sales and shipment. If there were more profits to be made by going out west then he was willing to take the risk. The only drawback would be his father taking more trips away from home, which wouldn't sit well with his mother at all. That was probably why he didn't broach the subject.

"Have you contacted any clients?"

"We didn't need to. Our reputation for superior service has preceded us. Business orders started coming in yesterday, which is why I needed to talk to you today."

Michael smiled. Western clients made sense if they were trying to expand the business. The accounts receivable and payable would indeed increase, which meant he'd need to hire additional workers.

"I think expanding the business is a good idea. We'll need to hire workers to keep up with the paperwork."

"I trust you can handle that end," his father said, as he handed money to the server.

Michael nodded his agreement. When it came down to business his father was clear, concise, and to the point. He never extended anything past the point where there was nothing left to talk about.

"I'll be at the house if you have any questions." He picked up the jasmine flower centered in the middle of the table and twirled its stem. "Your mother loves jasmine. The scent always puts her in the perfect mood."

Michael knew his father missed time spent with his mother. The business took him away quite often, and he didn't think his mother realized just how hard her husband worked to give them the life she was accustomed to. He would have to see Christina later in the week. Business matters now took precedence and they would have to formulate a plan to compensate for the added paperwork. As he got into the car, Michael couldn't help but wonder whether this scenario would be similar to his parents' relationship. Would he treat his relationship the same as his father did his mother, always putting the business first? He certainly hoped not.

Chapter 15

Celia Rose felt euphoric as the young stud withdrew his penis from inside her. What a wonderful way to start the afternoon. She had been exhausted when she went home and was going to relax with a cold glass of lemonade when a knock came at the door. He was disgracefully filthy, the dirt stains accumulated from the top of his head to the sodden brown shoes on his feet. And yet when she saw him, heat built in her like a kerosene lantern, and she immediately threw herself at his body. He fondled her breast through the silk blouse she was wearing making her nipples harder with each touch. His mouth came down to replace his hands and ecstasy claimed both of them once again, just as it had multiple times before. The large four-poster bed provided a delightful scene of debauchery and perspiration with its rose silk sheets now damp with sweat from their lovemaking.

She remembered a time when she and her husband had spent their days lying naked with one another. Those days were full of affectionate touches and sensuous kisses. Now, she was lucky if he spent an hour in her presence before going to one of his business meetings across town or out of state.

Celia moved to the dresser adjacent to the window, noticing pictures in black frames. There were several of them, one of James and herself, and others of their children running and laughing at family gatherings.

She lightly touched the first picture with her fingertips, wondering where the young woman and man disappeared to. The woman had an innocent look, staring at the handsome man with adoring love in her eyes, eyes that were exactly like her son Michael's. Was this the same man she'd been in love with these past forty years?

"Come back to bed," the young man said, startling her. Celia turned to answer him but heard a familiar voice downstairs. Her husband James was home. Everything happened in a flash. She quickly opened the window and motioned for him to exit through it, her arms flailing wildly. The bedroom sheets would have to be washed later as she threw the covers back in place as neatly as possible, before dashing into the bathroom and climbing into the large tub. Celia didn't check to see if he had gotten the message, but she was reassured when she heard the guard dogs bark their usual warning when a stranger was too close to the gate.

A loud thump in the bedroom jolted her back to her present state and she sat upright in the porcelain tub. When no other sounds came from the bedroom, she realized that James had set his suitcases down in the room. Celia relaxed and waited for the opportune time, not wanting to leave the room even after she knew James had left. But her impatience was already getting the best of her and she was finding it difficult to keep from moving.

Celia opened the bathroom door cautiously, but no one was there. The suitcases were against the window, and she noticed the curtains had been drawn back. Did James see her lover escaping through the brush? She shook her head in disbelief. James couldn't have seen him that soon after entering the room. Or could he? Celia called in the maid to change the sheets before finding her evening attire. She quickly got dressed, hoping to catch him in the study, but paused when the bedroom door opened.

James stood there in the doorway, barefoot, wearing only his slacks and a towel wrapped around his neck. He had shaved off his beard and looked as handsome as ever.

"You're home early, dear."

His eyes never wavered from hers. "You sound surprised."

"Not at all. You normally don't arrive on the weekends, and so naturally I wasn't expecting you."

"Business took an unexpected direction. Aren't you happy to see me?" He slowly closed the door and walked towards her.

"Of course I am," she said, nervous tension already claiming her vocal chords. Celia tried to calm her nerves, but he seemed too cool for the moment. Not only that, but she just had another man inside her ten minutes ago.

"Then may I have a smile along with a proper greeting from my wife?" He kissed the side of her neck.

"I'm sorry, you just startled me, that's all."

"Did I startle you or the young man running through the bushes?" Silence. Celia tried to search for the right words but none came to her. She wondered how he saw her lover from the upstairs window unless someone had already hinted to him being there.

"Would you like to explain, wife, or should I guess at your infidelity," he said in a cool tone, sitting on the edge of the bed.

She felt cornered. How dare he make her out to be the guilty party? It was his entire fault after all. "There's nothing to explain. I've been by myself here in this house without so much as a letter or postcard from you, James. How am I supposed to cope with being by myself for weeks on end or months?"

"I'm supposedly the one responsible, Celia? My wife, who whores around with the hired help, and I'm being held responsible."

"Don't you dare blame me for that, damn you!" she retorted angrily, her mocha eyes flashing. "If you'd stay home long enough, I wouldn't feel the need to go outside our marriage for something I never get at home." She paced in front of him with her arms folded across her chest. He was being too calm with her and she didn't understand why. Shouldn't he be raising his voice or showing some semblance of emotion?

"I work for hours on end to keep you in a life of luxury and for what?" he replied. Looking around the bedroom, James was disgusted by his wife's lack of respect and propriety. "I'll sleep somewhere else then. I'm afraid there's a lot to consider from this."

"You'd rather not talk to your wife than communicate about what's been wrong in our marriage for years," she replied.

"There's no need to talk right now, Celia. I'm tired and I'd rather get some sleep elsewhere."

She started for the door. "There's never been a need to talk about anything, has there, James? It's always been about the business. Don't bother sleeping somewhere else because I've already started," she said condescendingly over her shoulder.

James sprang after her and caught her arm. His grip felt painful as he swung her around to face him. She had never seen this side to her husband and was instantly afraid of him.

"You're not going anywhere," he said harshly. He pushed her back into the room. "This is the place you and your lover shared and this is where you'll sleep."

Celia staggered. When she managed to regain her composure and look up at him again, he was gone. He had tossed his wet towel onto the bed, and the moisture from it had made a damp spot where he sat.

She picked up the towel, smelling the aftershave coming from its fabric, and threw it onto the floor. Damn him! How dare he fault her for wanting the comfort of another human being? A wave of emotion clouded her mind and body to the point she had to sit on the side of the bed to gain composure. She prided herself on maintaining grace and self-control in the midst of chaos, but at this moment all she wanted to do was throw a chair out the window. Celia breathed deeply and placed a hand across her chest to steady her beating heart. The car would be coming around soon to take her to Michael's home. She needed to check in on him and confirm their luncheon for tomorrow. Could she look her son in the face? After all, his eyes resembled the very man who had been disappointing her for all these years.

A muffled voice came from behind the door. "Mrs. Rose. It's me, Maude, ma'am."

"Yes, Maude, come in."

"I just received this note from your son, ma'am. He say to tell you he can't make lunch."

First James, now her Michael.

"What?" she replied, her face red with anger. "What else did it say?" The maid wasn't sure if she should read the rest of the letter. Mrs. Rose's typical arguments with Mr. Rose usually ended with someone getting fired. She herself had been let go at least three times already.

"Maude, the rest of the letter now!" Celia said, her voice rising in frenzy.

"Mr. Rose say he having lunch with a Ms. Christina Davis. I believe that's Bessie Washington's niece," she explained, her knees now trembling.

Celia felt her blood pressure rise. The little bitch was trying to steal what little family she had left.

"Would you like me to send a reply, Mrs. Rose?"

Celia almost forgot the maid was there. She was too busy picturing Christina Davis being sent home in a ball of fire. Walking towards Maude, she snatched the note from her hands.

"I will contact him myself, thank you! Please tell Curtis to ready the car. I'll be leaving shortly."

"Yes, ma'am."

Celia pulled her thoughts together, watching her maid walk away from the room, her eyes narrowed turning black as night. Curtis started the car as she arranged her hat and selected matching jewelry. She straightened her back firmly and walked through the front door. Damn that girl for ruining a mother and son moment! She was stunned when he declined their lunch date, and she felt even more hurt when she found out who he had dismissed her for. As the car exited the driveway she instructed the driver to take her to the home of Patrice St. Clair. If anyone knew of any recent gossip, it would be the town jezebel herself.

Chapter 16

It was only lust, he told himself, and he was determined not to let her know that she had any effect on him. Although his being there contradicted that statement thoroughly, the feeling that he received thinking about Christina was a far deeper emotion. Lust was a fleeting sensation brought on by attraction so intense it had to be put out quickly. After it was resolved it no longer became important to pursue. This was definitely not lust, but something else.

Michael turned into the Wright's driveway and sat there going over his plan of action. As tired as he was, he was still determined to see Christina even if it meant staying through each one of her lessons.

That morning he entered the flower shop on New Market Street as soon as it opened. Inside, it looked like a Garden of Eden with different flower species, along with vases and glass cases in the middle of the room. The door against the back wall led to another area that held an array of flowers and what looked like fertilizer to maintain gardens.

"Does she prefer hydrangeas or red roses?" the florist asked as she walked behind the counter.

"Red roses. She would love red roses."

"Roses are the perfect flower for the one you love. It's also the perfect centerpiece for an evening dinner. Who is the lucky young lady?" she asked.

"Her name is Christina. She's a part of the Wright's debutante class, and I thought I'd surprise her by bringing flowers as a gift."

"That would be a lovely gesture. How long have you two been courting?"

"Not long at all," Michael said. He wanted to change the subject, not feeling comfortable in talking with a complete stranger about his and Christina's relationship. At least not yet.

"Oh, Lord, where are my manners? Of course you'd want to keep that to yourself. I hope I haven't embarrassed you too much."

"No, ma'am, it's alright," Michael said with a smile. Perhaps he was being too cautious in revealing his feelings, but he wanted things to run as smoothly as possible and with the way the gossip mills ran around town he didn't need anyone guessing at his relationship status. "Don't mind me," he heard the florist say. "I'll wrap your flowers up nice and pretty for your lady companion."

That made him feel better. The sooner he left the florist's shop the sooner he'd be in the company of Christina. "I'm no good at picking flowers. They're like foreign objects to me."

"Nonsense. Every man thinks they'll have a hard time deciding on which flower to get, but they eventually get it right. It takes time."

Michael nodded his head in agreement. "You're absolutely correct. How much for the flowers?"

"Fifty cents."

He reached into his pockets and withdrew the change. "Thank you for your assistance. Have a great day."

"To you as well."

Now his hands were shaking as he reached over to grab the flowers he had placed in the passenger seat. He couldn't stand the anticipation any longer and decided it was a good time to go into the house.

"Michael Rose, is that you?" Patrice asked, sashaying down the sidewalk. Her hips seemed to have a mind of their own as they drew attention from everyone on the street coming towards him.

"Hello, Patrice. How are you?" He kissed the side of her cheek.

She was wearing a golden yellow dress that highlighted her skin tone and buxom figure. Her dresses usually had him wanting to take them off as soon as he saw her, but things were different now.

"What brings you down to the Wright's home?"

"I thought I'd drop by and visit."

"With flowers?" She gestured to the red roses in his hand. Now was not the time for him to be besieged with her questions. He didn't notice her hurt expression and decided to change the subject.

"That dress looks lovely on you, Patrice."

Not one to pass up a compliment, she placed a hand on her hip and showcased her attire. "Do you like it? It was a gift I couldn't refuse."

"I'm sure the poor bastard that gave it to you is currently crying over his empty pockets."

Patrice laughed haughtily. Michael always seemed to bring up her suitors when he saw her in a new dress. Could he be envious of the attention she was getting from her other lovers? The thought of him being jealous made her giddy with excitement.

"Michael Rose, do I detect a little jealousy? You know the only reason I wear new wardrobes is to entice you," she said seductively.

"Really? I thought the only reason was to get new male prospects to pound on your door."

"I seem to recall you doing the most pounding, Michael."

"That was a different time, Patrice."

"It wasn't that long ago. You've forgotten how much fun we had together," she said, coming close to him.

He shook off her hands before they came towards his face. This wasn't the direction he wanted the conversation to go, and he was wasting precious time talking to this woman. Michael didn't spend his nights in restless dreams, plagued by sexual memories of this girl. Nowadays he thought of only one woman. Trying to keep up with her schedule and his drew most of his time and thoughts. Not this desperate repugnant woman in front of him.

Looking at Patrice, her eyes searching his wantonly, he suddenly felt sorry for her as she clung like a fly to his shirt. When he first met her, she was like any other woman, curvy with very little to say, the way he used to like all of his women.

But during his pursuit of Christina he found he didn't want the quintessential woman who remained quiet to satisfy him. Or a woman that used every inch of her body to get what she wanted. He wanted someone to come home to, someone who understood his mind as well as his body. And he was willing to bet Christina was going to be that girl. He smiled to himself. Clearly Patrice was never going to be that type of woman.

Michael stepped away from her grasp, nearly having to pry her hands off his shirt. She clearly didn't want to let go.

"I have to go, Patrice," he said. "Will you be alright out here by yourself?"

"Actually, I was going to be picked up by Frank Greene. He owns several businesses in town as you well know."

"Ah, yes, I know Frank. How's his wife Carmen?"

"She's not here, I'm afraid." Patrice's blood began to simmer. He was deliberately trying to piss her off, damn him.

"I'm his partner for the evening," she said matter of fact. "Perhaps if you worked twice as hard as he does, you'd have more money to entertain young ladies instead of spending it on withering roses."

"Insulting me won't make you the bigger person, Patrice," Michael said. "Especially when everyone knows the job title you hold."

"You son of a bitch! I was the best you ever had, Michael Rose," Patrice retorted, pointing her finger towards his face.

Couples walking along the sidewalk had ceased their conversation as Patrice's voice rose, and watched the scene play out before them.

"Perhaps you should lower your voice, Patrice."

"What? Why should I lower my voice?" she demanded, obviously not caring who heard them. "Are you embarrassed by our relationship? Is that it?"

"This is not the time for this conversation." Patrice suddenly forced a smile to calm herself down. She would get nowhere by yelling emotion filled statements at this man. Time to change tactics and smooth over this whole ordeal. She had to remember that Michael was the one she wanted to keep all to herself. Satisfying her ego and his mother at the same time was proving to be an exhausting task. But raising her voice at him would do no good either. She straightened the front of her dress and patted her hair from the side.

"I'm going to pretend this conversation never took place, Michael Rose." Rich men needed to feel they were on top of muddled situations. Michael was no exception.

"Since Mr. Greene isn't here at the moment, maybe you and I can sit for a spell until he gets here."

Michael looked at her in confusion, trying to imagine what caused the sudden change in attitude. She went from one extreme to the next, then settled on a cool temperament just to appease him. Something was amiss with this girl.

"I can't, Patrice," he said, looking towards the Wright's front door. "I have an appointment at the moment that I don't want to miss."

"If the appointment you're referring to is Christina Davis then you may want to inform her that you and I are involved."

"We are no longer involved, Patrice. Our rendezvous ended a long time ago. And besides you've moved on to richer pastures, ones that you just stated I could never measure up to."

Patrice ignored his sarcasm. "I was wrong."

Michael stared at her. He should've ended this conversation a while ago, but she kept up her poignant exchange as if she really gave a damn about who he was going to see. "You have nothing to do with who I see or court at the moment. If you will excuse me, there is someone I'd like to see before the day is over."

He turned to walk through the gate.

"Did you ever have feelings for me, Michael?" she asked a forlorn expression on her face. This seemed like her last chance. If Michael had a hint of feeling, which wasn't hard for a man, she would slowly guide him back to her bedroom. She stood at the gate entrance anticipating his answer.

"No, I'm sorry, Patrice. I never loved you."

He didn't even turn around when he said it, but kept walking up the pathway to the front door. She did her best to hide the pain he had just inflicted, but it felt like a solid blow to the stomach as she walked the few feet to sit on the iron bench. Mrs. Rose wouldn't be happy when she heard this bit of news. Her son was positively under Christina's spell and there was no pulling him back. How was she going to explain this to Mrs. Rose? More importantly, how would the woman handle Patrice after she had failed in her attempt to lure Michael back to her side? As Mr. Greene pulled his town car in front of the iron bench, she had only one thought. She hoped Mrs. Rose wouldn't keep her off the social soiree lists. That would be horrible for her reputation.

Michael sat patiently as the next debutante class began. It had been a full week since he last saw Christina and it was driving him insane. Her stunning looks and passionate kisses fired his blood like no woman ever had. How long had it been since someone occupied his every thought? She worked on his senses the entire week to the point where he couldn't stand it any longer. Having to stifle his own smoldering inclinations was new to Michael, as wanting a woman so much he couldn't engage a singular thought. He thought by going to one of her classes he could catch a glimpse of her, satisfying a portion of his lust, and then leave. Not so. As soon as he walked through the door, he knew staying was the only option.

He wasn't a stranger to these types of classes, having been to at least three of them with his sisters. Arriving early before everyone else, he was able to see who was in attendance and who wasn't. Mr. Wright immediately welcomed him and asked that he be used as a mock escort just in case the younger ladies needed some assistance in dancing or table etiquette. The only person he was there for arrived shortly before class started. His gaze stayed with Christina the entire time. She was being taught which piece of silverware to use when and for which dishes and looked positively beautiful as she memorized the place settings. He tried to get her to notice that he was there, but her focus was completely unbreakable. Her facial expression went from complete concentration to excitement as she got each question right.

He was so entranced with her he almost didn't hear Mr. Wright. "Young man, can you come sit beside Christina to give her an example of how an evening would proceed?"

"I'd be happy to, Mr. Wright." He made his way to the opposite side of the table and stood there waiting for further instructions. She didn't look up until Mr. Wright introduced him to the class. Her eyes read shock at first and then something Michael wasn't used to seeing in a woman when he was around, composed demeanor. Christina kept her body as relaxed as possible. She tried to keep her focus on the task of memorizing the table setting. If she lost track of it they would have to start over again. She could smell his male scent as he was given a chair and pushed it close to hers. His hand brushed the side of her arm, giving her goose bumps.

"Oh my, what was I thinking?" Mr. Wright said. "We have to get you a table setting also. I'll be right back."

Once he was out of earshot, Michael wanted to get her attention quickly before he came back.

"Christina? I have something for you."

"I think these place settings are lovely, don't you?"

"I'm not interested in the setting, Christina," he said as he reached over and handed her the roses.

She was still looking down, trying her hardest to memorize each fork. "What are you interested in then, Michael?"

He stood up, grabbed her hand and brought it to his lips, kissing her palms. She felt the slight wetness of his tongue as her eyes fought hard to leave his. Christina had plenty of time to say no, but desire held her in place, and she didn't feel like thwarting his advances, especially since she wanted to reenact their first kiss that night in his car. Michael must have read her mind as he pulled her up from the chair and kissed her with a passion she'd never known before. Amazingly the goose bumps on her arms were travelling upwards like electricity straight to her heart. It was a jolting surge of energy throughout her entire body that she couldn't keep still. The kiss was intoxicating, and she couldn't get enough. His mouth not only sampled but suggested she do the

same, until it was a free-for-all with lips, tongue, hands and more wanting to feel every inch. It was so intense that she was positive clouds were
forming beneath her feet to give her the sensation that she was floating.
Christina wanted to stay in his powerful arms without letting go.

Someone clearing their throat drew her back to reality and they separated before resuming the lesson.

Christina thought of the kiss the entire next day while she and
Auntie were enjoying their day out. She shook her head again and
again. How in the world had she let him get that close to her again?
One moment she was trying to memorize dishes and the next minute
she was wrapped in powerful arms being deliciously kissed. The car
glided down the road towards their destination but she hardly noticed
her surroundings or where they were going. Her body felt as if it were
overheating from the memory of Michael's kiss and she tried fanning
herself to get it to cool down. This was absurd. It was just a kiss a
long, moist, satisfying kiss that I shouldn't be concentrating on at the
moment. Christina tried to roll down the window to get some air, but
it stopped at a slight opening, clearly not wanting to cooperate. The air
inside the car was stifling, but thank the Lord they only had a couple
of minutes before reaching the downtown area.

"Auntie, when was the first time you were in love?"

"Why do you ask, Christina?"

Christina decided to confide in her Aunt. She needed to talk with
someone about what happened and, except for Sandra, Auntie was the
next best candidate. "Michael and I kissed the night he took me out.
And I never felt that way before, not even with Lewis."

Silence. Neither woman knew what to say next. Christina looked at
her and wondered if she had said too much. Bessie wondered if the kiss
had already led to something else. She cleared her throat.

"What you felt for Lewis was puppy love, Christina, and sometimes that can be mistaken for real love. When you were with Michael how did you feel?"

"It felt really nice. All we did was kiss but the way he made me feel was wonderful."

It took every ounce of strength for Bessie not to holler with glee at this news. Thank God it hadn't gone too far. She would have to talk to Christina about how to conduct herself from here on. She knew Michael was interested in Christina, but this was more than she thought would happen.

"He makes me feel desired and I can't help but want to give him the same thing."

"There is Isaac to think about, you know."

"Yes, I know." She looked down at her palms, not wanting to ask the inevitable question, but she needed another opinion. "How do you think he'd feel if he knew I had a child?"

"I'm not sure. You two obviously are attracted to one another. Give it time and see where the relationship takes you."

"Auntie, you didn't answer my first question." Christina looked at her with expectation. Her relationship with her aunt had grown close over the past year and she valued their conversations. If only she could've communicated with her mother in much the same way, their relationship would've been better.

"I've been in love with the same man for the past ten years and, Lord willing, we'll be in love for ten more."

Christina laid her head back against the seat and allowed the small amount of air to rush at her face. She thought about that statement for a while. How wonderful it would be for someone to love her and share her love in return.

The day had started fairly well, with Uncle Joseph placing new flowers at her window. He had taken Isaac to their favorite spot by the water to play until they returned from town, while Auntie coaxed her out of bed to go to the dress shop for her ball gown measurements. It seemed others had the same idea, as the shop was packed with young women and their mothers all looking for the perfect fabric for a ball gown. Christina recognized Sandra's mom immediately; she was negotiating a price for her daughter's dress.

"Hi, Bessie, are you and Christina out today for a little shopping?"

"Yes. Christina needs some measurements for her dress and today was as good a time as any."

"Oh good. Bessie, come with me, would you? I need your opinion on these shoes over here."

Christina watched Auntie walk off with Mrs. Wright and started looking at the different fabrics herself. She noticed there was a distinct difference between the more expensive silk gowns and the wooly mammoth gowns her mother would've made her wear.

"Are you looking for something in particular?"

Christina turned and came face to face with a very beautiful girl with red hair.

"No, I'm just admiring the pretty fabrics you have here."

"Oh, I don't work here," she said with a laugh. "I'm just here to pick up my dress." The girl was looking at her as if she were under a magnifying glass. Christina suddenly felt like she was being observed a little too much.

"Where are my manners? My name is Patrice St. Clair." She held out a neatly manicured hand.

Christina shook it lightly, being careful not to squeeze too hard. "It's nice to meet you."

"Likewise."

"Are you going to the ball, as well?"

"Why yes, I am. My long time beau, Michael, just asked me and I just had to say yes. He and I have been dating for a while. Do you know Michael Rose?"

Christina was struck speechless. She didn't notice the slight smirk Patrice had on her face. All she heard was that Michael was dating another girl at the same he was trying to sweet talk her. The man had some nerve. She tried to keep her emotions in check and her voice as calm as possible.

"Would he be tall, handsome, and own a farm on John Island?"

"That's the one."

"I only met him once." And that was enough for her. She felt like such a fool. The enchantress in front of her was smiling from ear to ear and all she could think of was the kiss they shared just the other day. How could he have kissed her that way, knowing he had someone else on the side? She guessed he had kissed other women often enough that there was no remorse on his part. Well, there wasn't going to be another time for him to do it with her. She was done.

"We will have to make it a point to introduce our dates to one another. That way everyone can get to know each other better. By the way, who are you going with?"

Feeling a little uncomfortable, Christina tried to excuse herself, but the girl kept talking.

"My apologies. I do get carried away when I talk about Michael. He and I have been dating for a while. I'm almost certain he's going to pop the question any day now, because he's so in love with me."

Christina managed a half-hearted smile and said, "That's very nice for both of you."

She really didn't mean it. How could he be such an asshole? One minute he was trying to see her, the next minute he was about to marry someone else! She listened to Patrice for the next five minutes before excusing herself, feigning the need for some air. Christina quickly walked outside and took in several slow deep breaths. How could she be so stupid? Did he really think she wouldn't find out? Apparently he did. With her being new to town he was probably betting she wouldn't run into any of his girlfriends while she was there.

Auntie's voice called to her from inside the shop. She turned around to respond, but Christina wanted to stay outside. Going back in and bumping into Patrice again was out of the question. She didn't think she could disguise her jealousy. She was sure a disgusted look was plastered across her face and it didn't feel like it was going away any time soon. She would give Michael a piece of her mind when she saw him again. But for now she pulled herself together and went back inside the store, careful to avoid Patrice's side of the room. Auntie was speaking to the seamstress about how long the dresses should be and motioned for her to come over.

"Where were you, Christina?"

"I was just outside to get some air."

"Look at this white fabric with blue undertones. I think it would look beautiful on you in a long-sleeved princess style gown with a v-neck."

"That fabric looks nice." Christina wasn't really interested in what color her ball gown was going to be. Her mind was somewhere else.

"Are you Okay, dear?"

"Yes, I'm fine. I like the gown, Auntie."

"Good, because I'm purchasing it in that lovely color." She continued to look at other colors, picking out some deep yellows, hunter greens, and burgundy fabrics. Christina didn't know why Auntie suddenly wanted her to have so many dresses, but she gave her opinion anyway. She wasn't going to let the news of Michael and Patrice ruin her day, not now and not ever.

☙

"I'm glad I finally caught up with you."

Christina was in town on a grocery run for Auntie and thought that by avoiding the main market she wouldn't bump into anyone she knew, namely Michael. She was wrong.

"I don't want to talk right now."

"Okay, I'll just follow you around until you do."

"Don't you have somewhere to be?"

"No, not really. I finished my work early and thought I'd take a stroll. As luck would have it I bumped into the prettiest girl in Charleston."

Christina almost laughed at that loaded statement. "I'm sure you have plenty of pretty girls you can talk to."

"No one with substance, and certainly no one with a spitfire attitude like yours."

She turned towards him with a look that said I don't believe you. "No?"

"No."

"No one?"

"No one."

"Not even Patrice St. Clair?"

He paused for a minute and tried to recover, but it was too late. Christina, seeing his hesitancy, decided to walk away. Michael hurriedly went after her. He should've told her sooner about his relationship with Patrice but didn't feel the need because he had ended it as soon as he met Christina. Catching up to her he turned her around by her shoulders to face him.

"Patrice is someone I've dated off and on for some time now."

"So how come you didn't tell me that when we first met?" Their voices were raised, drawing a crowd of curious onlookers.

"Because it was nothing serious."

"Just like I'm nothing serious." She turned and started walking in another direction. He was doing a very poor job of lying to her face and she didn't want to put up with it any longer.

"It's not what you think, Christina."

"It's not? You could've fooled me."

By this time everyone in the market had stopped to look at them. He pulled her to a stop for a second time to look at him.

"Look, I'm not interested in Patrice St. Clair."

"Again, you could've fooled me. She had plenty to say about your relationship."

"Dammit, woman, what do I have to do to convince you?"

"Nothing, since your impending nuptials basically tell me that we'll no longer be seeing each other."

And with those last words she walked away from him and their audience. A few people were whispering about the arguing couple; others just looked to see what was going to happen next. Michael looked at Christina's back until it disappeared around the corner. He scratched his chin at what had just transpired. He would have to find out who told her about his relationship with Patrice, and then figure out how to get her to accept that he was falling for her. This wouldn't be an easy task, but again he was up for the challenge. Michael just hoped Christina would stop her stubbornness and realize he had real feelings for her.

❦

"Have you lost your mind?"

Celia came storming through the door, handing her gloves and hat to George before coming to a halt in the living area. Michael hadn't anticipated any company for the day and was sitting by the fireplace, sipping brandy while going over what Christina had revealed to him. Patrice was the number one culprit, as she could've easily seen Christina somewhere and given her the news of their relationship. This made more sense than some random person giving the same news. It must've been important for Patrice to embellish on their relationship so as to get Christina upset. The damn woman was a nuisance.

He hadn't spoken to her since the day she'd bumped into him at the Wright's house and tried to get a reaction out of him. To her utter dismay it didn't work and she'd received the hint that he was no longer interested. So why then did she go to such lengths to tell Christina of their affair? The question was: what did she really have to gain from all of this? His mind was so focused he almost didn't hear the knock at the door.

"Hello, Mother. What brings you by?"

"You and that floozy were arguing in the middle of the downtown market, that's what. Are you trying to bring shame to this family?"

"First of all, she's not a floozy and second of all, Mother, no I'm not trying to bring shame to this family." He got up to pour more brandy into his glass. It seemed he drank more when his mother was around, a similar action he noticed his father did as well.

"Michael Rose, don't take that tone with me. I did not raise you like that and I won't have this family's name tarnished just because one of your little escapades went awry."

Michael was good at ignoring his mother, but this time he wasn't going to let her speak badly about a person she didn't know, especially someone who he was very interested in.

"I understand your concern, Mother, but Christina is a wonderful girl. I'll not have you talking about her that way."

"Christina? You mean Bessie Washington's niece?" Feigning ignorance wasn't her strongest suit, but she had to or else their plan wouldn't work. Celia needed Michael to think she was ignorant of his and Christina's relationship, so that when the time came for him to be comforted over her leaving the area, Celia would be right there picking up the pieces. "Is that who you were fawning over? Absolutely not! That's out of the question and I won't have it."

"I'm a grown man, Mother. And just what is wrong with her? You barely know her."

"I know enough to conclude that she's not the right girl for you. What about that lovely girl from North Carolina you met last year?"

"The possum in the woods is smarter than that girl."

"But she comes from a wonderful family. She doesn't really need to produce intelligence, just a couple grandchildren for the family lineage."

"So that's what it's all about, Mother. Heirs?"

"Yes the right heirs from the right kind of family to carry on the family name. It's about the right kind of blood, dear. You can't mix a thoroughbred with a pig. They don't go together."

He walked away from her then. His mother really knew how to get under his skin with all of the wealth and prestige talk. He wasn't at all interested in that and she knew it. To try and force it on him was a mistake because he'd never fall for it.

"I like Christina, Mother. I like the way she makes me laugh, and I can talk to her. We have a lot in common and I'm not going to base what we have on titles and rank."

She took a deep breath, clearly frustrated at her son's poor choice in women. And Patrice was doing a horrible job on her end of convincing the girl that Michael was already spoken for. Maybe she needed to intervene at this point to get their plan back on track.

"Okay, dear, we'll talk about this later. Just think about what I said. I have to go meet the ladies for lunch." She kissed him on the cheek and put her gloves and hat back on. "I'm only trying to look out for your best interests, dear."

"Yes, I know, Mother, but my best interests right now would be for you to stay out of my love life."

She completely ignored that last statement, but decided to placate him for now. "Of course, dear. I'll talk to you soon."

Michael watched his mother walk to her car and gracefully get in. He waved from the doorstep and watched the car pull out of the driveway. Somehow he knew his mother wouldn't let this go. She always found some excuse to meddle in his life. But right now he couldn't worry about her. He needed to see Christina to tell her that his relationship with Patrice was over and that he wanted to be with her. She was being stubborn and he needed time to talk with her so she'd listen. He decided to call on the one person he knew he could talk to his father.

Chapter 17

A week and a half later, Christina was still reeling from her encounters with Michael at dinner and later at the market. Even at her debutante dance lessons she was thinking about him so hard she squeezed Mr. Wright's hand to the point where he asked, "Are you alright, Christina?"

She apologized and excused herself to the ladies room. How dare he try to diminish his relationship with that girl? She wasn't going to be part of his little game no matter how much he tried to deny his involvement. Christina was determined not to fall for his charm, but there was just one thing nagging at her. Patrice didn't know her well enough to divulge any information, so why had she told Christina her personal business after just meeting her for those few seconds? She decided to ask Sandra about her. Since she had been gracious enough to tell her about Celia Rose, maybe she knew something about Patrice St. Clair. The class had a fifteen minute break before the social etiquette and manners class was to begin.

Christina sat beside Sandra as she pulled her dance shoes off. "Would you happen to know a young woman by the name of Patrice?"

"Patrice St. Clair? Yeah, everyone knows her. She's not exactly a woman of virtue, if you know what I mean."

"No, I don't know what you mean."

"Christina, she's loose, a jezebel, floozy, or what some might call a frisky bed wench. She sleeps with men, and then they in turn buy her things."

"I didn't know that. She seemed nice when I met her at the fabric store a week or so ago. But it was a little strange."

"Why is that?" Sandra was desperately trying to get her left shoe unbuckled but couldn't. Her toes had conformed to the top part of the shoe due to countless hours of dancing and remained stuck. Christina motioned for her to give her the uncompromising shoe. She began to tug at it and the shoe finally slid from Sandra's foot. Sandra immediately did the same for Christina.

"Out of the blue, she was telling me she'd been dating this guy and I'm not sure if she was telling the truth or if she just wanted to hear herself talk."

"Whoever the guy is he has some competition on his hands when it comes to that girl." Sandra laughed.

"What do you mean?"

"She has more suitors than Celia does in one week while her husband is away."

"What?"

"I'll tell you later."

"So I'm not sure if she was being sincere or trying to make me jealous which is absurd because I don't know her at all."

"That's strange. So who's the guy she's trying to make you green with envy about?" Sandra helped Christina up from the seat.

"His name is Michael. He's the guy I told you about, remember?"

"The one that you've been seeing?"

"Yes."

"You never told me where he's from."

As the time wound down, Christina and Sandra gathered their things and walked to class.

"He's from John Island. But that's not all. He was the one who took me to dinner the other night."

She didn't need to turn around and see Sandra's face. The silence said it all.

"Oh my Lord, that's the man you were dancing with at the luncheon. Oh Christina, he is so handsome."

"Sandra, I can't see him again. Patrice, whatever her name is..."

"St Clair."

"Yes, that. She's dating him. He didn't tell me that."

"How did you find out if he didn't tell you?"

"She mentioned it."

Sandra frowned for a couple seconds before laughing hysterically. "Christina, Patrice was at the luncheon when you and Michael were dancing, wasn't she?"

"I'm not sure. I didn't see her."

"Well, she was. In fact she was shooting daggers at both of you. Even Mama saw it because she commented to her ladies society on the jealous looks you two received."

"Then why did she act as if we just met?"

"Because she's jealous, silly. She told you that to get you angry and out of the way."

"Why that little liar!"

"She has the hot's for him and that's why she told you that. It's the oldest trick in the book."

"Has that happened to you before?"

"No. It's just something I've heard over and over again. I thought it would fit the occasion."

They both laughed. After class was over Christina said goodbye to Sandra and her parents and waited for her ride. She realized that she would definitely have to be more careful the next time someone tried to sabotage her relationship. If the women here were brazen enough to confront you by fabricating their own lies, she wondered what other things they had up their sleeves.

Christina noticed a burgundy town car sitting directly across from the Wright's home. The driver got out and opened the rear door on the driver's side. She saw a woman in a crimson hat with matching suit and shoes walk toward the Wright's home.

"Good afternoon, Ms. Davis."

Christina recognized the woman immediately. "Good afternoon, Mrs. Rose."

"And what brings you here this afternoon? Is Bessie finally taking lessons on how to be a lady?"

Christina didn't miss the sarcastic dig. Mrs. Rose was certainly a piece of work, determined to humiliate people at every turn. Well, other people might cower to her but she certainly would not.

"No, Auntie doesn't need lessons in that department, but I'm sure other women do."

Celia chuckled. The little miss had spunk, clearly not lost on her end. "I came by hoping that I would see you here."

Christina looked put out. "What can I do for you, Mrs. Rose?"

"You seem to have taken an interest in my son. I'd like to know if this is true."

"Who is your son?"

"Oh come now, Ms. Davis. Do you take me for a fool?"

Christina looked at her dumbfounded. The woman actually thought people cared about her family life.

Celia let out an exasperated sigh. "Michael Rose. What is your interest in him?"

The smirk quickly disappeared from her face. Christina couldn't believe her ears. Michael was this woman's son? Well now, that made sense, and as the pieces began to fall into place Christina had a couple of questions of her own. Why was this woman seeking her out because of Michael's interest in her? This was between her and Michael and the bigger question was what Celia Rose had to do with her son's love life. She wasn't about to give her any information.

"I'm afraid I can't answer your question, Mrs. Rose."

"And why is that?"

"Because it's none of your business what your son does with me or any other girl he chooses to see."

"My son doesn't know what he wants, so his being around you is only causing him confusion, if you know what I mean."

"No, I don't. Your son is a big boy. He chooses who he wants to be with."

"I'm not asking you, Ms. Davis, I'm telling you."

By this time Christina had stood up from her sitting on the bench. This was not only a bully but another word she didn't want to say at the moment as there were others standing nearby. She wasn't going to be bullied by anyone, especially by someone who didn't know her at all. "And I'm telling you, Mrs. Rose, that your conduct here is unappreciated, as I've done nothing to warrant such hostility from someone I barely know."

"Maybe I haven't made myself clear. Stay away from my son."

"And maybe I haven't made myself clear. It's none of your business if your son and I are involved or not."

Christina's voice had changed the moment she stepped closer to Celia. It wasn't the notion she had come unannounced; it was the impression the woman gave that she stop her from seeing Michael. No one was going to intimidate her into doing anything ever again.

"Michael is a well-respected man in this community. He doesn't need to be tied to some backwoods nobody."

"Well, if that's all I am, I wonder why you came all the way down here and sought me out."

"You have my son walking around like a lovesick chicken without his head, that's why."

Auntie's car pulled up at that moment.

"It was nice talking with you, Mrs. Rose."

Celia grabbed her elbow. "You backwoods people are all the same. You always want something for free. Well, you will never have my son. I'll see to that," she replied.

"Christina, are you alright?"

Celia chose at that moment to leave before things went in another direction as Christina watched her walk back to her town car.

"Yes, I'm fine I just had a little run-in with you know who."

"What did she say?"

"Oh nothing," Christina assured her as she got into the car. "Just that she wanted to know if I was the object of her son's affection."

"And are you?"

She couldn't answer that question but her heart said she sure wanted to be. Christina didn't know what to make of that encounter. Why was she so concerned with who Michael dated? Was it like this with all the women he was interested in, or was it just Christina?

As they drove away, Christina filled her aunt in on what had happened. When they reached the house, Michael was waiting on the porch steps while talking with Uncle Joseph. One leg was perched on the bottom step, and Uncle Joseph was leaning backwards in hysterics. Michael was telling him something that he obviously found funny. Christina saw Isaac being held up by Joseph as he played with his clothes. What was Michael doing here? She hoped it didn't have anything to do with the conversation between her and his mother. Enough drama had occurred for one afternoon. Joseph excused himself with Isaac as Christina and Auntie approached the house.

"Hello, Michael."

"Hi, Ms. Washington. How are you today?"

"I'm doing just fine, thank you. I'm going in to get dinner ready. If you find the time to stay, I make a mean apple pie."

"Thank you, ma'am. I sure will think about it."

Christina handed her belongings to Auntie and waited for him to start speaking. If he was going to chastise her for speaking to his mother rudely then she could take it. What she couldn't take was the awkward silence that followed Auntie and Joseph's exit into the house. He just stood there looking at her with what could be described as a slight smile on his lips. His eyes travelled from her feet to her head slowly, making her breath quicken while he scanned every inch of her. He stared at her with those warm whiskey eyes so intensely that Christina couldn't move.

Michael left the porch, his eyes never leaving her face. "I'm sorry about Patrice. I should've told you earlier about her."

"It's okay. If that's what you want in your life who am I to judge?"

"But she's not who I want. Let me explain."

Christina listened as he told her of his strange relationship with the girl. Their love affair was simply that, an affair. She almost felt sorry for Patrice as she had no more ties to Michael than a stranger on the street. "I haven't spent time or dated her at all since I was introduced to you."

She stood there looking into his face for some sign of falsehood but couldn't find any. He was telling the truth.

"I'm going to kiss you, Christina."

She couldn't say anything. The next thing she felt was his lips on hers, warm and supple. He pulled her into his arms and her hands immediately went to his hard firm shoulders. This man was making her feel things she'd never felt before, which scared the hell out of her. He was so forthright in his need to tell her how he felt that it made her feel guilty. If he could tell her about Patrice, she needed to tell him about Isaac. Pulling away from the kiss, she knew now was the time to tell him.

"Michael, there's something that I have to tell you."

"Anything, Christina, you can tell me anything."

He said this while kissing her cheeks. She couldn't get her thoughts together. Every time his lips touched her face her train of thought left and all she could think about was kissing him even more. She inched her face away from his so there was room for thought.

"It's just that…"

"By the way, no one has ever stood up to my mother before."

"How did you know I spoke with her?"

"Her driver gave me the details, before I came here."

"Oh," she said, feeling a bit embarrassed for how she reacted. "I'm sorry for seeming disrespectful, but it seems her interest in your love life is a bit inappropriate."

"Mother has her ways about her that I seldom like, but she's trying to build this family dynasty and I'm just not interested in that." He looked towards the door of the house and then back at her.

"Hey, I have a question of my own."

"There's something you need to know first before this can go further."

"Okay." His face was thoughtful, concerned. Christina briefly considered lying, but she had done that enough. It was time to come clean.

"I have a baby, Michael."

His eyes revealed this shocking news before his mouth spoke the words. "What?"

"I have a son."

"Yeah, I heard you the first time. Why, how–?"

"I know it's a shock, but I'll tell you everything."

He rubbed his head and turned around, trying to find a place to sit down. "I'm listening."

She sucked in a deep breath and let it out slowly. "Before I left Virginia I was seeing someone I'd met at a county fair. We had a brief relationship and a couple of months into it I found out I was pregnant. My mother was devastated and that's how I came here. She sent me here so I wouldn't destroy the family name."

There was a nauseating silence. He was staring at her as if she were a different person. "Is that all?"

"No, that's not all." Had he even heard what she just said?

But before she explained further, he shot up from his seat as if someone had lit a fire underneath him. "You lied to me!"

"I didn't lie to you. I just didn't feel the need to tell you why I came here."

"But you never said you had a baby my God, Christina!"

"I didn't know I would meet someone. That wasn't the plan at all. I couldn't tell you because I wasn't sure how you'd react." She gestured to his rigid stance. His hands were rubbing his curls from his head so much Christina thought they would be straightened out if he continued.

"So what you were trying to do was trap me into falling in love with you so you could have a father for your baby?"

"No! Not at all! Isaac is my responsibility. I'm not asking you for anything."

"Save it, Christina. I need to go."

"No, Michael. Don't go, please."

"How do you expect me to deal with this?" He asked while pacing back and forth, his hands running through his hair again, a distraught look on his face. He finally stopped to look directly at her.

"I need time to think."

Michael left her standing there, a scene she was all too familiar with but one she thought she'd never be in again.

❦

In the weeks that followed Christina distributed time between educating herself on how to be a debutante, sampling different dishes created by Aunt Bessie, and being with Isaac. He was a healthy baby, growing every day, and extremely active, which made her trips to town decrease. His daily regimen of food consisted of fresh squeezed goats milk, fruits and mashed vegetables. She especially loved dishes that she could try with him. Auntie would make butter beans, shrimp and grits with sweet peppers for her, and squash and lima beans for Isaac. Other Charleston dishes she quickly took a liking to were peach cobbler and buttermilk pie with graham cracker crust. Not one of these dishes compared to the one thing she often craved but couldn't have— Michael. The absence of his kisses made her sigh many times during the day, so much so that it made

Aunt Bessie look at her peculiarly. She felt lonely without him and wondered if he felt the same.

❦

Across town, Michael couldn't sleep. Her face kept creeping into his mind when he tried to close his eyes at night and she was the first image that came to his mind in the morning. It wasn't enough that she was just on the other side of town; he had to have her in his house, in his bed. She was like an addiction he couldn't shake even if he wanted to. This was absurd. He fought the urge to see her every day, delving into his work to take his mind off her mouth, those eyes, and that body that conformed to his own when they were close to one another. He hadn't seen her in weeks, choosing to stay away from her so as not to confuse the situation any longer. At least that's what he told himself. He really didn't know how to handle a baby and thought by not seeing her it would make it easier to forget her.

It was October in Charleston. Fresh rain had fallen the night before, its lingering proof a thick blanket of fog covering the city and adjacent plantations. It was days like these Michael loved going to the ocean to wade chest high in the water. But it was something else also. Every time he closed his eyes he saw her. He heard her. He even smelled her, a rich spicy perfume like nothing he had ever smelled before. By eight he was eating a light breakfast. By ten he was going over the accounting books. By noon he was getting rip roaring drunk. What a way to start the day, he thought, and it was all Christina Davis's fault.

Christina was feeling similarly overwrought. She went into the kitchen to talk with Bessie and Joseph about a plan she had concocted. She'd written a letter earlier to explain her feelings as well as apologize, and she needed to put it directly into his hands. It might not be one of her smartest ideas, but she needed to know what they thought before she went through with it.

"Christina, I'm going to town for a while. Why don't you come with me? Mr. Andrew down the street has a carriage and I know you like his horses."

"Auntie, I have to talk to Michael."

"I think you may need to stay away from him for a while, sweetie. At least until after he's cooled down."

"But if I don't go now I'll never know if he's still angry with me."

Deja vu again? I sincerely hope not. Would this time be different?

"I saw his butler earlier today. George say he drove him down to Brisco's this afternoon. The bar is over there on King Street," Joseph said. "Not a place for a young lady such as yourself to go into."

"Thanks, Joseph, but I can take care of myself." Christina reached for her shawl.

"I suppose I can escort you down there. It would be nice to get out of the house for a while," he said, looking at Bessie before reaching for the car keys.

Christina had the feeling he was going to go with her anyway, whether she liked it or not. The unspoken message between him and Auntie was clear enough.

She heard Bessie exhale slowly. "I suppose Isaac could come with me to town to visit some people. It will be nice to show my handsome nephew off."

As Christina and Joseph got into the car, she felt glad for his company. Being in an unfamiliar place could be potentially dangerous, and at the moment she didn't need any more dramatic confrontations.

☙

A cloud of smoke greeted her and Joseph as they entered the dingy looking hole-in-the-wall club. They took a seat at the lengthy bar and looked for Michael. She noticed the women had on scantily clad dresses worn off the shoulder with their breasts pushed upwards past the point of straining. Christina wondered how they were able to breathe. The men didn't seem to mind as they openly groped them, laughing and whispering lord knows what in their ear. This was not the place someone came with a spouse; no, this was the place you came to forget your spouse for a time with either a stiff drink or an experienced pair of legs. Christina had never been to a place like this in her life. She sometimes wondered what it was like when Grandma Esther had her parties back home. Stories about the Do-Drop Inn had made her sick to her stomach when she heard some of the girls at the parties would have more than one man screwing them, with no one being brave enough to stop it from occurring. The Do-Drop Inn was the closest thing to a club in the neighborhood. Grandma Esther's nickel a shot glass and one dollar ice buckets were all you needed to have a good time at her house, as everything else was provided for on a first come first serve basis, and that included women. She couldn't believe the similarities between her home and Charleston. In a beautiful place like this, why would there be such a horrible club? Searching for Michael, she noticed the room consisted of round tables and a couple of booths that filled the dimly lit space. Games were being played at the rear of the club, while a rhythm and blues band kept the guests entertained at the front. Stairs led to a second floor where Christina guessed a different form of entertainment took place, the kind she only heard about back home when no one thought she was listening.

"I don't see him," she said, looking at Joseph as he ordered a shot of whiskey and downed it quickly.

"I don't like this, Chrissy." He had a worried look on his face as he looked around at the other club patrons. "We need to find him quickly and get out of here."

"Okay. Just give me a few more minutes. I have to talk to him."

Christina knew he regretted coming here as soon as they pulled up to the place. He must've thought that once Christina saw the club she would be hesitant about going in, but unbeknownst to him, she had already known of such a place and what went on in the midnight hour.

Joseph finally spotted Michael and made a groaning sound followed by an "Aw shit". Christina followed his gaze and noticed a working girl rubbing her breasts against his back, trying to get more than attention for the evening. She felt a pain go through her chest immediately and pondered whether she needed to go over and speak to him. Uncle Joseph ordered another shot of whiskey and prayed that the next moments would run as smoothly as the car that got them there.

Michael drank until he couldn't feel his teeth. He'd been drinking shots of corn liquor one right after the other. George had taken him to the club when he realized he couldn't make it on his own in his current state of mind. His body felt numb, completely devoid of any emotion, and he wanted it to remain that way. No emotion meant some semblance of peace from thinking of Christina every damn minute. The waitress kept rubbing her tits against his upper shoulders, which should've sprung his manhood to attention like it normally did, but this time it only annoyed him until he finally turned around to ask her to leave. She was pissed, mainly because he was an easy target and money would come naturally given his current condition.

Before coming to the club, Michael had walked around the house until his legs felt like heavy stones and his feet were crying for rest. He still hadn't figured out a way to get his emotions under control; his thoughts kept going back and forth from Christina to the news of her baby. He didn't even know if she was still in Charleston, preferring to stay away from Ms. Bessie's side of town to avoid any confrontation. She might've already gone home or found some other sucker to lie to. He had even tried to find her doctor for some answers, but he couldn't locate him.

Sitting in the seat, he stared at a spot on the table where someone had obviously put out a burning cigarette, the charred black spot contrasting heavily with the brown cedar wood. Had she gone back home to the father of her child? She was too stubborn to go back to that asshole. Maybe she was really innocent in all of this. He laughed to himself. The woman almost had him believing that she was pure until she told him about her baby. She must've thought he was a fool. He shook his head again and rolled the remainder of his drink around in the glass before downing it in one gulp.

Thinking clearly wasn't the name of the game for the moment. As a matter of fact, ever since he met the illustrious Ms. Davis he'd been thinking about starting a family of his own. That was until she told him she already had a child. Now he didn't think he was ready for a child, or was he? And did he really want to raise another man's baby? If he saw the guy today he would definitely give him an ass kicking till he was blue in the face. That fight would be worth the torture he was going through right now.

He looked around the bar, noticing the women that were trying to get money from the club patrons. He let out a little humph. His mother was right; give them an inch and they'll take your money. There was one thing that gnawed at him though. If she were planning to have him as the father to her child, why didn't she make it a point to tell him from the beginning? Why did she choose to keep it a secret? He started thinking about their first encounter. Was that all a set-up as well? She was certainly mean enough to do it. He stared straight ahead, noticing another girl looking at him. Careful not to give her any encouragement, he half turned and motioned the waitress to get him another drink.

At the bar, Christina tried convincing Joseph she would be alright talking to Michael even if his current state said otherwise. "I'm going to talk to him."

"I don't think that's a good idea, Chrissy. Look at him. He's flying without a pair of wings right now."

Christina saw that Michael's head was down and swaying from side to side. It looked like he was talking to himself.

"Uncle Joseph, if I don't go he'll never know how I feel about him, about us."

"Alright, but I'll be watching."

Maybe this wasn't the best idea but she had to try, Christina thought bleakly. She made her way to the table and noticed a few couples kissing, totally oblivious to their surroundings, and other groups of people laughing at anything that sounded great while drinking liquor. She felt awkward and out of place, for she was literally the only one there not exposing a great deal of her breasts. Christina stood beside Michael's chair and noticed one of the working girls flounce up to Michael to ask him for a dance. He tried to shoo her away, but she wasn't taking no for an answer.

"Michael, I need to talk to you."

He turned around to look at her with eyes that looked red and glazed over.

"Came to finish me off, huh? Well maybe I don't want to talk to you." He grabbed the girl's hand as he said this, hinting that he wanted the whore to stay at his table.

Christina sucked in her breath. She knew his meaning. "You're a bad liar, Michael Rose." She reached into her purse, grabbed the letter and threw it down on the table.

"I came here to tell you that I love you, but since you have other plans I guess I can't now." She pointed towards the letter that now lay half crumpled on the table. "Read that if it suits you, but I'm sure you'll be too busy to even do that."

Michael looked at the letter and then at Christina. "Yeah, be too busy," he said in a nasty tone.

"I guess assholes have better things to do with their time then," she said, before turning around and walking back to Joseph at the bar.

Michael watched her as Joseph guided her to the front door and left. He let the woman's hand go with a slight jerk and picked up the letter, staring long and hard at the envelope. He was transfixed by the handwriting.

"Was that your woman?"

Michael heard the girl ask the question and looked at her warily, but he couldn't find the words to answer. He wasn't exactly sure himself if Christina was his woman or if she still wanted to be. He admitted the baby surprised him and not in a good way, but that wasn't the worst of it. The worst part was that she hadn't told him when she first realized they were becoming serious. He at least wanted the opportunity to choose before he fell more deeply in love with her than he already was. And there it was: the admission that needed to be said months ago.

He loved her.

From the moment she bumped into him at the market Christina Davis had made a permanent impression on his heart. He let out a blistering curse that made the working girl jump a little. He then got up slowly, stuffed the letter in his pocket, and downed the last of his drink. Michael sluggishly made his way past the bar and slammed the money down before leaving. He would need to sober up tomorrow before going to Ms. Bessie's house to apologize. Hopefully Christina would accept his apology for acting the way he did. If she didn't he would have to come up with another way to do it. But one thing was certain. He needed Christina in his life, in his bed, and in his world.

Chapter 18

I f Michael could be grateful for anything, it was the basin of cold water and hot cup of coffee waiting for him by the side of his bed the next morning. He sat on the edge of the bed with his head in his hands, willing the pounding to stop so he could focus clearly. His head felt like someone was slamming it against cement blocks. Thank God Mrs. Gladys hadn't made scrambled eggs for breakfast; the smell would surely send him to the bathroom sink for relief.

What had happened last night? He knew he went to Brisco's to try and make sense of his life. Wait, did Christina show up? He groaned as another pain hit his head. What the hell was she doing in a place like that? Michael willed himself to recapture the night's events so he could get an idea what went on. He groaned inwardly again, remembering his drunken rambling, and knew it wasn't good. He realized right off he'd taken his behavior too far in the way he had treated Christina. She had looked so beautiful with her hair flowing in waves down her neck. When he saw and recognized her through his drunken haze he immediately was aroused, and then cursed himself for being turned on. That's when he grabbed the whore's hand to keep from manhandling Christina. It only made things worse as he saw the hurt look in her eyes before she slammed that letter down on the table.

He reached for his coat, which he'd thrown across the bed last night, and retrieved the letter from the side pocket. Maybe this was her way of explaining what had happened. Whatever it was, he told himself that he would still love her no matter what. Then again she could be trying to let him off the hook easy, which he didn't deserve. He took a deep breath before opening the letter.

Dear Michael,

I want you to know that I love you, that I still love you even though I know it's too late to regain your trust. You've been nothing but wonderful to me and I will cherish that always. As soon as the baby is old enough, I'll be going back home to Virginia. Please find it in your heart to forgive me for not telling you sooner. It was never my intention to hurt you.

All my love, Christina

He crushed the letter to his forehead and shut his eyes tightly. How could he be so stupid? She still loved him even after he treated her coldly with little regard. He could've spoken to her earlier and given his support, taking her into his arms and kissing all the hurt and pain away that he knew she'd gone through before coming to South Carolina. Instead he ignored the one woman he'd fallen in love with. A knock came at his door.

"Christina?"

"Mr. Rose, it's me, George, sir."

Michael opened the door for his butler.

"The day is getting away from you, sir. I thought I'd come up and check in, seeing as you couldn't quite make it up the stairs last night."

"Sorry, George, I lost track of time. Did Mrs. Gladys let you in?"

"Yes, sir. She's in the kitchen cooking a mean breakfast."

Michael's stomach felt queasy. Maybe this wasn't the best time to eat. He doused cold water in his face and quickly dressed.

"I heard Brisco's was the top spot last night, sir."

"Oh yeah? Who told you that?"

"Murdoch told Jennie Su who told Pearl who told my cousin Shug who told me."

"That many, huh?"

"Yes, sir." He smiled, looking at his employer's haggard look. "Are you still upset about Ms. Christina?"

Michael wondered how George knew about his relationship and further how he knew things weren't going well. The help knew more about his personal business than he cared to know. He decided he'd talk to George about the eavesdropping later on.

"She gave me a letter telling me how she felt." He pointed towards the letter and his arm felt like it weighed a ton. George picked the letter up and handed it to him.

"And how do you feel?"

He didn't have to say how he felt. His face said it all. Michael put his head in his hands. He wondered how things could have become so complicated so soon. He hoped it wasn't too late to beg for forgiveness for being such an idiot and looked at the clock.

"I have to go. George, please see to it that the others get a hearty breakfast. I'm sure Gladys will understand."

"Thank you, sir. The workers will be much obliged. Gladys's hotcakes always put a smile on my face." He headed out the door, going past a confused housekeeper as she stacked a hearty helping of hotcakes on a serving dish.

❧

Across town, Sandra arrived at Bessie Washington's house and knocked on the door.

"Christina, I know you're in there. Your Auntie wanted me to come by and cheer you up, and I'm not leaving until I do."

Christina heard Sandra outside of her window. She believed the surrounding neighbors heard her as well, and a smile came over her face. She couldn't have asked for a better friend than Sandra.

"I'll be out in a minute," she replied. Gathering her shawl, she headed outside.

"I'm here to escort you to the last class," Sandra said as soon as Christina opened the door.

"I'm really not feeling up to it today, Sandra."

"I know. But just think: this will be the last class before we're escorted by gorgeous men down a lengthy staircase and given away like brides on a beautiful glorious day."

Christina laughed. "That's a lovely fantasy."

"I'm not making it up; it's true."

"In case you haven't been listening, the man I want to escort me isn't on the list at the moment."

"He'll come around. Once he sees he's made a mistake he'll wrap you in his arms and whisper sweet nothings in your ear."

"I can't say that I blame him. I'm not sure I'd want to be involved with someone who already has a family."

"But you're not just someone. You are Christina Davis and you have a beautiful son named Isaac."

"Thanks, Sandra."

"You're welcome now, one quick question. Do you think everyone around here dances in dresses with a tiny waist?" Sandra asked, measuring her waist with her hands.

"In Charleston, yes and from what I've seen the tiny waist is something to have around here."

Sandra shook her head. "My cousin Lula May didn't have a tiny waist and she got into a debutante gown. She looked like two cows passing in the night."

Christina laughed. Sandra always knew how to cheer her up.

"So you see you don't have to miss the ball because you don't have a partner."

Christina looked at her friend and was thankful for her presence. "Where were you a year ago when I found out I was pregnant? I sure could've used a friend like you then."

"Well, you have one in me now. Come on, let's go."

❦

Thirty minutes later, Michael pulled into Bessie's driveway. He wasn't sure what he should say. Apologies were in order, but he felt like he needed to be on his knees spouting off soliloquies or love sonnets. He hoped his letter of apology would do some good. Christina was probably furious with him for treating her the way he did, just another thing he chastised himself for.

He noticed Joseph outside fixing the stone pallets leading to the front door.

"Hi, Joseph."

"She ain't here."

Michael paused a minute. He had almost forgotten Joseph had accompanied Christina to Brisco's. He'd seen that whole incident from last night, and clearly was not happy to see Michael today.

"Do you know where I can find her?"

Joseph looked at the young man for a moment and smiled. This was the man that Christina needed, not some drunken asshole wasting his life away in a bar.

"You gone treat her nice?"

"Yes, I certainly am."

Joseph looked him square in the eyes and nodded. "She's at her last class before the debutante ball."

"Thanks, Joseph."

"If Christina come back and tell me she upset, I'm gone be real upset. We got an understanding?"

Michael nodded. The implied threat wasn't missed. "Understood."

"Good. Now go get her, son."

Michael jumped in his car and sped away. He prayed Christina would still be at the Wright's house when he got there. If not, he'd find her wherever she was.

$$\mathcal{C}\mathcal{D}$$

"Pay attention, Sandra."

Mr. Wright was getting frustrated with his daughter's short attention span. "Remember that the man leads, and the woman must follow. This is the waltz, not the boogie woogie."

Christina watched her friend make error after error when it came to dancing. It was either her feet wanting to go one way or her dance partner wanting to go another.

"Sorry, Dad," Sandra said between giggles. "This dance is so confusing."

Mr. Wright let out an exasperated sigh. "Maybe you're just thinking too much." He looked at Christina and motioned for her to come to the dance floor. "Christina, please come here and show Sandra the correct steps."

"Yes, Mr. Wright." He replaced the Bing Crosby recording with one by the Nat King Cole Trio. The sun was at its peak, painting vibrant colors along the parquet floors of the ballroom and yet it remained surprisingly cool on the dance floor, despite the sequenced movements of the dancers.

Paintings of past family members decorated the wall on one side of the room while the other was adorned with fresh cut flowers. The atmosphere was comfortable and depicted not only a learning ambience, but a feeling of romance, as each couple danced with the other. She stood in front of Sandra so she could see every step Christina made. Sandra smiled as her friend started the box step; stepping forward, to the side, and back, closing the feet together. The rise and fall of the movements made Christina look graceful and delicate as she glided along the floor.

"Slow, quick, quick, slow, quick, quick, Sandra, remember? One two three, one two three," Christina repeated as her feet imitated the counts she directed. She remembered the open dance figure waltz that Mr. Wright had taught her, which included open rolls alternating between her leads to the left and to the right. She didn't have a lead at the time so she compensated by pretending someone was in front of her. Christina imagined the lead's right arm provided the right direction for her to go. She began her box step with her right foot and did a backward half box, followed by a forward half box.

Christina loved this dance. It reminded her of the first time Michael had held her in his arms.

She imagined she was surrounded by lush greenery in the middle of a field with the sun's warmth against her face and the wind beckoning her to dance. Christina was so absorbed with the steps that she didn't pay attention to the hand at her back, but did feel a sudden jolt forward. She heard Sandra's outburst and knew then she had to open her eyes to see what all the commotion was about. She was mouthing the steps for Sandra's benefit when she heard the same steps being repeated against her face. A low melodic baritone voice harmonized with her own. "One two three, one two three."

She opened her eyes to find familiar warm brown eyes staring back at her. Her imaginary leader now had a face and body to match. Michael. What was he doing here? He started the dance over again, leading with his left foot and executing a forward half box. She matched his movement and did the exact opposite, starting with her right foot. They glided across the floor as if they were the only two people in the room. She couldn't take her eyes off him and noticed his thumb was gently stroking the middle of her back. It felt wonderful to be in his arms again. She felt cherished, safe, and in love.

"Have you been waiting long?"

She couldn't take her eyes away from his. Michael wasn't smiling but looking at her intently as if he wanted to absorb her every expression. A little embarrassed at his brazen act, she glanced around to see if anyone was watching them, and they were. Sandra had her hand over her mouth, looking very emotional, and the others were all smiling. Without missing a step he continued his conversation, not waiting for an answer.

"I needed to speak with you."

She averted her eyes and concentrated on the side of his jaw, which seemed safer than the intensity his eyes made her feel.

"You have a lot of nerve coming here after the way you treated me."

"I deserve that. I read your letter, Christina, and figured I owed you an explanation about how I reacted. Please hear me out."

Her mouth refused to open for a rebuttal because she was curious to hear what he had to say. "I see you're not going to answer me." He sighed. "I made a complete ass of myself and hurt you in the process." His eyes tried to hold hers but she refused to look at him. "I hope you can forgive me, Christina, because I can't take another moment without you."

She didn't know if she could either. Christina knew in her heart she loved Michael, but how could she trust that he wouldn't leave if changes or other bad news suddenly came along? She doubted he'd be able to handle the future struggles that would come.

"How can I trust that you can handle situations like this without running away?"

"It was just a shock to hear about your son. I've never been with a woman who has a child. I didn't know how to react and I ended things badly." His eyes were pleading with her to understand, but all she could see was his rejection and drunkenness.

She shook her head. "I don't know if you'll be able to take the bad with the good if we were to be together. Having a child in your life isn't like courting someone where they're here one day and gone the next. It's a completely different responsibility." She wanted to walk away from him but seeing his expression compelled her to stay and hear what he had to say.

"Christina, I may not have handled things as I should have, but just give me another chance. I know that I need you." He changed the dancing style at that moment and swayed slowly back and forth in place, stroking her cheek with the back of his hand. She turned her face away from his grasp.

"You can't keep doing that, you know."

"Doing what?"

"Touching me, distracting me. There are things that need to be addressed before we move forward." By this time the music had stopped and they were standing in the middle of the dance floor.

Christina heard Mr. Wright clear his throat.

"Maybe we ought to take this conversation to the parlor area," Michael whispered.

Christina looked at her host's curious expression. "Mr. Wright, please excuse us. We're going to adjourn to the parlor area, if you don't mind."

"Certainly, Christina. Sandra, please pick up where Christina left off."

Sandra looked as if she wanted to go to the parlor with Christina but thought better of asking. The scene that played out just now was better than any play she'd ever seen and she wanted to see the final act. "Okay, I'll try." Sandra made a face at Christina and took her position in the middle of the floor while the music started over again. Christina and Michael walked side by side until they reached the parlor.

"There's also your mother to consider. How can I be in your life when she's determined not to let that happen?"

"Let me handle my mother. She's no threat to this relationship."

"Isn't she? How do you know she hasn't figured out I have a baby."

"She hasn't said anything to me about it. And I haven't heard anything around town that would say otherwise."

"Still this seems like the calm before the storm. Just because you haven't heard anything doesn't mean something isn't coming."

"Does this mean you're accepting me back?" he said with a grin. She missed that about him. His ways of making her feel good in spite of everything.

"I didn't say that."

"Or it could mean you're a bit paranoid and scared of a relationship with me."

"Yes, I am scared, which I have every right to be."

Michael took a deep breath. This wasn't how he imagined the conversation to go. He wanted Christina to immediately forgive him and run into his arms while he kissed the breath out of her. The kissing would have to wait, he supposed. Right now he'd have to assure her that he wanted to be with her regardless of his mother's actions.

"Why are you so concerned with what my mother says or does?"

"I know firsthand how a mother can influence your life. It's one of the reasons I came here to Charleston."

"Your mother forced you to come here?"

"Yes, she did. She claimed it was in my best interest."

He heard those words more times than he cared to admit from his own mother. "Why didn't you tell her you wanted to stay in Virginia?"

"I tried a couple of times but once Mary Davis makes up her mind there's no changing it."

Michael finally understood why Christina was so worried about his mother. She reminded her of her own. He grabbed her hands and looked into her eyes.

"Christina, nothing and no one will succeed in influencing me to stay away from you."

She wasn't convinced. Celia Rose was a bulldog when it came to her son. She knew of another one in Virginia who when she wanted to get her point across would insist on it whether you agreed or not.

"I love you, Christina. I've felt this way from the day we met. And I don't want to lose you to this or to anything else."

"You love me?"

"I certainly do. And I'll love Isaac as if he were my own."

Christina couldn't stop the tears from coming down her face. She was overwhelmed with emotion. How could this man accept all of her, and even Isaac, a child who held no blood relation to him?

"I love you too, Michael. I was so scared to say it because I didn't know your feelings."

He wiped her tears away and kissed each cheek where the tears had formed wet paths.

"What do we do now?"

"Well, I can kiss you like I planned to when I first came here, or we can go back to your aunt's house and I can kiss you there."

She smiled at his unabashed answer.

"Would you care to kiss me now?" she asked, expressing her own forwardness. The question she knew would lead to some long overdue kissing but she didn't care. She was so happy he finally admitted his feelings that the fiercest lightning storm could blow the entire mansion down and she wouldn't care. She was so in love with the man sitting across from her that nothing could sway her.

"Christina, are you alright?" Mr. Wright called from the opposite end of the parlor.

"Yes, I am," she answered, never breaking eye contact with Michael. The host's doubtful eyes sprang back and forth between the young debutante and her beau. When he was satisfied nothing was amiss, he nodded his head and left the room.

"Where would you like to go?"

"We could go over to your house."

Michael groaned inwardly. "That probably wouldn't be a very good idea."

She laughed. "Okay, let's go back to Auntie's. I'm sure she's in the kitchen by now, cooking up a storm."

"Wait! What about my kiss?"

She turned towards him and planted her lips on his. The kiss quickly built to a fevered pitch and was so full of emotion he had to break contact, knowing he would take her right there in the parlor.

"Come on, we have to go before something else happens."

They hurriedly left in his car, both elated and happy that their feelings were mutually and totally shared.

ভ৩

Michael's letter came a couple days later. She didn't need to read it, as she sat looking at it in the living room. His feelings for her were clear from the way he had kissed and held her the other day.

"Christina, may I speak with you in private? It'll only be a minute." She recognized that voice and stood up. How did she get in? Joseph must've left the screen door open. She had to admit that she knew this was coming. Celia sashayed into the living room and stood in front of her.

"Hello, Mrs. Rose. Come in. Would you like some refreshment?"

"Let's skip the formalities, dear. You know why I'm here."

"No, I'm afraid I don't. Our last conversation wasn't exactly pleasant."

"When a mother hears that her only child is involved with a ready-made family it doesn't excite the senses, if you know what I mean."

"And when a man decides for himself that he wants to be a part of a family, then it is his decision alone and no one else's."

"What do you know of a man's decision? They are so fickle. One minute a man is in love with you, and the next he is in love with someone half your age."

Christina sensed Mrs. Rose was talking about something more than just their conversation. Whatever it was it temporarily held her attention until she turned back to refocus on the current subject.

"I must say I'm not too thrilled with the idea of Michael being involved with a girl who had a baby with another man."

Christina noted her change in approach. The discussion transformed just that quickly from her being the culprit to Celia's concern that Michael would be raising a child that wasn't his. She could feel her temper rising and had to take deep breaths to calm herself. It would do no good to rile herself up as she continued to listen to Celia's comments.

"It's disgraceful, and I must ask you to stop seeing him at once."

"Why don't you ask Michael, or is your control only limited to his potential partners?"

"Don't be naïve, Christina. I have more control than your pretty little head could fathom."

"Then I wonder why you're over here and not talking to Michael."

"I know the powerful influence of a woman. A woman can make a man forget himself as well as his duties. And so I'm here to make you an offer."

"And what would that be?"

"Since I have more influence on the social and business affairs than any other woman in Charleston, I'll let this little matter go and your reputation will remain as solid as before."

"And if I don't?"

"Then any future dealings you or your aunt may have with any employer in Charleston will be null and void. Do I make myself clear?"

"You're telling me that you would destroy me and my aunt's work activities here just because you don't want me with your son?"

"I've done it once and I can do it again, easily. Women of a rather adulteress nature cause problems for decent men here in Charleston."

"And is that through prior knowledge of other women or through experiences of your own?"

"Don't get crass with me, young lady. I'm not the one wanting another man to be my child's father instead of the actual parent. How do you think that looks to others?"

Christina wasn't surprised by her opinion. As a mother she had the right to her view of the situation. As a woman she was the most brazen mean-spirited person she had ever met.

"Mrs. Rose, the relationship I have with your son is personal and I will not discuss him any further with you. The business that I have here in Charleston is totally my own business. Show your threats to those who give a damn. Good day."

She opened the door and stood beside it, waiting for Celia to leave. "How dare you! My son is not going to marry some jezebel who slept around only to be shipped off to another house of ill repute."

That was it. Christina had had enough. It wasn't enough for Celia to insult her; she now was disrespectful to her Aunt Bessie. And if her parents taught her anything it was to always be protective of your family, especially when there were those trying to speak against them.

"You know nothing of my life, Mrs. Rose, or of my family's. Just like I know nothing of yours, although I'm sure you'll agree that a gardener is not normally used every weekend even after the grass has been cut."

"Why you little bitch," she snarled as she pointed within inches of Christina's face. "We'll see how my son reacts when he figures out who and what you truly are. You will not put my son in a situation where his name will be just as tarnished as yours."

Christina stood her ground as Celia stared at her for a second before pushing past her through the screen door, leaving a seething Christina behind her. She shook off the tension Mrs. Rose had caused. The woman was definitely a pain in the ass. Instead of allowing her son to be happy, that woman would try everything in her power to make sure he wasn't. The car door slammed shut before the driver could get out of the driver's seat. Its occupants felt the impact as the car shook from side to side.

"Drive, Mr. Curtis."

"I see that didn't go well," Patrice added, observing the elder woman's emotional state.

"Shut up, Patrice. If you had done your job correctly I wouldn't have to waste my time coming over to this slum of a place."

Patrice hunched her shoulders, giving the impression of a child just scolded by her parent.

"It's rather quaint actually," Patrice said, looking at the house with its wraparound porch and lovely flowers leading to the top steps. This house wasn't at all bad compared to some of the places she had frequented in her earlier life.

Celia looked at her with disgust, before removing her flask from her purse. This event truly called for drinking, and liquor was her only form of comfort these days. Not even her lover could get her this worked up.

"So, did the little miss agree with your demands?"

"No, she didn't. She insulted me and insinuated I was having an affair with the gardener. Can you believe that?"

Patrice suddenly had a bout of coughing take hold of her. She raised her gloved hand to her lips, her eyes wide with that little bit of news, hoping Celia wouldn't notice. Everyone knew of Celia's dallying with her gardener. In fact it was the running joke in town that the landscapers in the area could sure get a "good job" over at Celia Rose's house. She knew Celia tried to be as discrete with her relationship as possible. The only problem with this was Charleston was a small town, so everyone knew each other's business no matter how discrete someone tried to be. Her denial was comical at best, and also a little sad. In fact the newest rumor was that Mr. Rose had moved out of their home into a townhouse across the street from Mr. Willis' funeral home. Patrice knew Celia was trying to keep up appearances. After all, who would want their personal business out there for everyone to gossip about? Not Patrice.

"Just where is the little miss from anyway?" Patrice asked, clearing her throat.

"Virginia. It's unthinkable how a slut could come from such a wonderful place."

"Indeed." Patrice looked at Celia, waiting for her to talk more about the conversation that took place. It obviously had upset her to no end, which meant the girl had stood up to her and didn't back down. Celia could be quite intimidating when it came down to it and even Patrice knew not to get in her way. She was the one who got you into the social events, and also the one who could clearly keep you out. One word and you could be cast out indefinitely, which is why she wanted to do this favor for her. Patrice knew in order to stay on Celia Rose's good side she'd have to do some questionable things. The last person she wanted angry was her future mother-in-law. Why risk getting her upset? Besides, she met and engaged new suitors in the art of lovemaking during each function. Patrice knew not to cross this woman. It was bad for business.

"It looks like I'll have to take a little trip and try to save my son from making a huge mistake."

"How are you going to do that with the number of events coming up this week alone? Won't anyone miss you from the women's club, and won't Michael notice you're gone?"

They pulled into the mansion driveway. "No. Unfortunately no one will notice I'm gone. Michael is exactly like his father when it comes to that."

Celia got out of the car and immediately motioned to her butler to make arrangements for a trip. She would need to stay in a nice hotel in Virginia, preferably close to a place called Henry County.

Chapter 19

Celia Rose sat in the burgundy town car for what seemed like hours. Personal investigations in a foreign town were both dangerous and time consuming as there was no guarantee the residents were going to accommodate her questions. She was praying that someone would be able to give her the answers she so desperately needed to expose Christina Davis. She had to convince Michael that she was the wrong girl for him, and what better way to do that than uncovering a few secrets the tramp could be hiding. The dust from the gravel road created a heavy cloud behind the car's sleek tires as it pulled to a halt in the churchyard. Celia's spies had useful skills when finding where Christina previously lived, from her prior residence to the church she and her mother regularly attended. It was easy to complete the job now that the legwork had already been done. Her employees might even be considered assets she'd acquired from the last situation in Alabama, ridding their town of another harlot and potential scandalous situation. Most importantly, Michael couldn't hold the offense against her, once he discovered the truth, which was refreshing. Sometimes she felt he emulated his father's actions as if it were a brand, even though Michael never so much as alluded to wanting to be like his father. The apple usually never fell far from the tree. Indeed, Michael was the image of his father. That was the problem. Celia couldn't control him, it seemed, just as she couldn't control James. A cushy life growing up in her hometown had hardly prepared her for such a life with James. But all would be lost if she handed everything over to a lying, vile little snippet.

"Mr. Curtis, please keep the car running."

Celia emerged to find a sea of curious onlookers standing there in church attire with black and white suits, dresses, and for the women white knitted head dresses that indicated either they were of the diaconate or she had the wrong church. "Who is that?" she heard several of them ask. They obviously weren't big on whispering to one another, which she found rude and typical of backwoods poor people. They were all eyeing her luxurious vehicle like gawking fish. She supposed she did stand out, wearing her new indigo suit accessorized with matching designer shoes and pearl earrings.

"Good afternoon. May I speak with someone in charge here?"

One of the women was ushered through the crowd like a queen intending to speak with her lowly subjects. She had an overly made up face with coal black hair, dyed at the hairline to maintain some youthfulness about her. Celia almost laughed, thinking that as women embraced their senior years some chose to delay the inevitable with dyes and other white powder makeup. This woman clearly had this idea with her unfashionably braided hair and pointed out-of-season shoes. Her eyes were chocolate brown and she had a bony attractiveness about her that made her seem almost arrogant, not what Celia was expecting but she could've been in the company of worse individuals. The woman answered with a slow discordant tone.

"Yes, may I help you?"

"Thank you. My name is Celia Rose and I've traveled here from Charleston, South Carolina. I'm looking for some information on a member of this community. Her name is Christina Davis."

"And just what do you want to know about Ms. Davis?"

"And you are?" Celia stretched out her hand for a proper greeting.

The elder woman took it and squeezed lightly.

"My name is Mrs. Carter, and I'm in charge of the programs here at Mills-town Church of God." She turned to the women behind her who were intently listening to the present conversation. They nodded their heads in agreement. They were apparently Mrs. Carter's followers, which didn't surprise Celia at all. People from areas like these usually had groups of citizens that enforced order and other necessities. This group was more of a primitive posse, a stark contrast to the distinguished groups located in Charleston.

"Excuse me, ladies. We'll meet again tomorrow to discuss the uniforms for the usher board; in the meantime, please don't forget your quarterly dues for Sunday morning."

After the women had left, Mrs. Carter continued. "I'm a little curious as to why you have such an interest in a person from this area. You're clearly not from here," she said, noticing Celia's designer attire. Celia laughed a little. Her initial impression was that Mrs. Carter was a little bit like herself, by being blunt when it came to gathering information, especially about different people in their hometown. "No, I'm not from here. And to be frank, Mrs. Carter, Ms. Davis is trying to get the men of my city in trouble." The woman didn't look surprised, so Celia continued. "And I need to know how to stop her. I can pay you to cover any time you spend with me."

The elder woman's eyebrows rose. She'd spent enough time in this town to know when someone was playing a role and when they were being sincere. This woman was obviously distressed over her son's descent into darkness and she wanted to help. Mrs. Carter linked her arm in Celia's and guided her to the front steps of the tiny church.

"Mrs. Rose, my sincerest apologies for your inconvenience. That young she-devil caused a world of trouble down here before her mama sent her away to cause harm in your beautiful city."

"Oh my word. She was sent away?"

"Yes, she was and to wind up in a prestigious place like Charleston. Did no one warn you of her taking residence there?"

"No, I'm afraid there wasn't any notification Charleston was harboring a harlot. I've done nothing but try to protect the integrity and social structure of our fair city, none of which I can do now as we have been literally infested with scandal on our streets."

"Oh Lord. That is awful," Mrs. Carter said, touching the fake pearls around her neck.

"As you well know, South Carolina does not harbor whores and loose women. We are a conservative state with high morals and values. Women like Ms. Davis don't need to travel up and down the road giving it away to every man there is." She touched Mrs. Carter's hand and eyed her intently.

"We need to protect our eligible bachelors from the advances of wanton women." She was referring to her son, but Mrs. Carter didn't need to know that little bit of information. She tensed as an image of Christina came into her mind, an image of an innocent and lovely young woman. But it had all been a part of her performance. She'd been setting her family up from the very beginning, and her Michael was the top prize.

The elder woman nodded. "I completely agree. The young man she got in trouble is someone I saw grow from a little boy. He was blind-sided by her tempting spirit and fell victim to the nest of Satan between her legs."

"That is just terrible," Celia said.

"He is now married with a child on the way, but he will always be known for messing with an ill-gotten young woman, causing reputations to be soiled."

Celia's search for the truth was finally in her grasp. She would now suspend any further research into Christina's past as Mrs. Carter proved to be a viable source of information, leading her in the right direction. She had the woman in the palm of her hand. All she had to do now was seal the deal.

"The reputation of these men must be saved, Mrs. Carter. We must see to it that the rest of the men in this town as well as in mine do not get mixed up with these kinds of women."

"What do you have in mind, Mrs. Rose?"

Celia smiled. "I just need a tad bit of information, especially when, where, and who she was involved with here."

"And just what do you intend to do with this information? The young man's reputation was stained, and I'm sure his family doesn't need any more terrible news. Christina, on the other hand, is a different story. That young lady needs a lesson in the vows of chastity."

A wicked gleam entered her gaze. "Let's just say when I'm through she'll never harm another man or his family ever again."

The elder woman smiled. "Well, Mrs. Rose, I certainly hope you're going to stay awhile. We have a lot to talk about."

What were the chances of her bumping into people who knew Christina and her secrets? The timing was perfect, and Celia definitely deserved a pat on the back for her efforts in exposing Christina. There was also the fact that other people knew what was going on and chose to include the girl in Charleston's most important event of the season. All parties involved would certainly need to be cautioned about the harboring of whores in the community. For her part, she was glad to be in charge of exposing the sinful woman in their midst so that nothing like this ever happened again.

Still, what she had learned made little sense, as she pondered her options on the ride back to South Carolina. The Wrights had to have known what was going on, along with others in the lady's society. She had proof from the horse's mouth and wagered they knew the particulars of Christina's dalliances in Virginia too. Celia called Maude for her bath and carefully selected her ensemble for the evening. She would have stayed in the house a bit longer but the anticipation of revealing what she knew gave renewed excitement to her life. With her talent, she could open a business that dealt with exposing the secret lives of the people of Charleston. For a fee, of course.

"Wife of mine or not, she has to be brought down to reality."

Celia froze upon hearing the familiar voice. Once the car had pulled into the driveway she immediately went upstairs to change into a new wardrobe, and wasn't expecting company. Lover or otherwise.

"Mrs. Rose don't want to be disturbed, sir," she heard Maude say.

"She's going to hear me, by God. She can't ruin people's lives and get away with it. Celia!"

She didn't think James was going to be anywhere near the area. These days he was holed up somewhere in a townhouse, doing business as usual. Her heartbeat quickened as she exited the room and headed down the staircase. Well, he certainly knew how to make an entrance, by yelling at her servants and making a spectacle out of himself. He could've at least knocked on the door instead of barging in like a raging bull. Still, when she saw him at the bottom of the stairs he was as handsome as ever, especially since they'd been apart these past few months. She didn't realize just how much she'd missed him until now.

"Truly I didn't ruin anyone's life, James. Now you on the other hand have ruined an entire family. Care to guess whose?" she said sweetly.

"This is not about our family, Celia. Residing for two months in a townhouse in the middle of the city put me in position to learn a few things. For instance, my wife cares more for judging and ruining the lives of other people than looking at herself in the mirror."

"Playing the martyr, dear, doesn't suit you at all. Besides, our community deserves to know the women they're inviting into their homes."

"Then why don't you reveal your secrets, Celia? I'm sure the community would want to know about the goings on in your life as well."

"Don't you dare bring me into this! I've built the social status of Charleston from the ballroom parties to each charity event. I belong here. Others are simply blessed to walk into the same room that I'm in."

"You're not even listening to yourself. What happened to you? What happened to the woman I fell in love with?"

"You know, I asked myself the same question about you."

James shook his head. This conversation was going nowhere and there was no use in trying to correct her when this was what she'd been doing all along. He turned around and left, the door slamming behind him. He'd been completely blind to his wife's antics all this time, ignoring her rants whenever he came home, preferring to do business in his office. He stayed away more times than he really needed, using the excuse that he preferred to be hands on with the business when he could've hired help. Was this really his fault? He shook his head again. There were some things that he could take responsibility for, but ultimately Celia's decisions were her own, and those decisions he couldn't possibly take credit for.

Within the next hour, Celia planned to make two unannounced visits and one would be to Bessie Washington's house. James coming over almost distracted her from the task at hand. She wished he could understand the need to protect their family, but he hadn't been around long enough to share a meal with them, so his opinions didn't really matter. She was the one that kept their family together despite his constant absence and solitude even when he was around. The emotional loss she felt of a husband not being there for his family was nothing compared to what was going to happen if she didn't straighten this mess out with Michael.

"I know your little secret, Christina," she said, entering the house.

They heard the screen door slam as Celia made her way past Bessie and planted herself in the living room with one hand on her hip.

"What on earth is going on, Celia? Haven't you had enough of harassing my niece?"

"Your niece has been dallying with my son and I intend to put a stop to it by any means necessary," she said, pointing a bony finger at Bessie. "I told you I'd figure it out and now that I have everyone will know what your niece truly is."

Christina, hearing the commotion, slowly got out of bed and placed Isaac in the bassinet. She tried to keep her composure as she entered the living room, being careful not to wake him. It took her a while to rock him to sleep this time, and she didn't want to disrupt the schedule she'd put him on.

"What is going on here?" When she walked into the room she hadn't expected Celia Rose to be standing there. Her usual well-kept manner was replaced by a wild-eyed tigress that looked ready to pounce at any moment. There was a confident smug expression plastered across Celia's face, and Christina immediately became suspicious as to why she was there. "Mrs. Rose, what are you doing here?"

"There she is! Just the person I want to see."

"We've said all we needed to say to one another. Why are you here?"

"Just to tell you I've already informed my son that you manipulated a young man in your town into sleeping with you and then tried to trap him by getting pregnant."

"What? That's not true." The woman was clearly insane. She wondered where she got that information and from whom. "You know nothing of my life."

Celia ignored Christina's denial and kept up with her accusations. "And now you're trying to do the same thing with my son. I received the whole story from a Mrs. Carter in your little town. Does her name ring a bell?"

Christina gasped, her mouth forming a surprised oval shape. Lord help her. She'd been dreading this ever since she moved to Charleston. "How could that be, Celia?" she heard Auntie interject.

"Mills-town is a long way from here, unless you already had someone working for you to find out just where to go."

"She's lying, Auntie." Christina finally found her voice. The shock of what the woman had just said had left her mute for a couple of seconds. "Unless Mrs. Carter is the ghost of Mills-town past, no, I'm not lying. I believe the awful lies being told to my son from your niece are far worse than anything told to me."

"How could you be so sure she was telling the truth, Celia? I don't recall Mrs. Carter being a fan of anyone in our family, and she wasn't exactly the one to rely on for gossip when I lived there either."

Bessie's explanation only seemed to worsen the situation as Celia suddenly doubled over in hysterics. The woman's actions screamed hospital care, and they were left with trying to figure out what she planned to do with the information she had recently acquired.

Celia finally stopped laughing and straightened her posture. "I'm happy to announce she told me everything about your niece from her extensive history as the town trouble maker to giving Lewis Harris a horrible reputation. What a busy little whore you've been, Christina."

"What I did in my past has no bearing on today." Christina felt close to tears and had to sit down as the impact of what she'd just heard hit her hard.

"I beg to disagree. Young well-bred ladies are taught to conduct themselves in a manner that reflects the family name. You obviously didn't care about embarrassing your mother and your uncles."

"Celia, you've gone too far." Auntie walked closer to stand beside Christina. "You know nothing about what happened. How dare you try to accuse my niece of anything? This isn't a courtroom."

"Oh, but it should be, because I would make a wonderful judge and jury." She turned towards Christina. "You got pregnant by your cousin. And now everyone will know, including my son."

"He already knows about Isaac, so your plan isn't going to work, Mrs. Rose," she replied.

"On the contrary he only knows about the baby, but he doesn't know the rest of the story."

Christina's eyes shut as she recalled their last conversation before going to that hole-in-the-wall club. She had tried to tell him the whole story then, but he had walked out. She swallowed hard. At that moment she knew the ammunition against her had been served on a silver platter to Celia, and right now the woman looked ready to shoot.

"I never thought someone could be so vindictive or cruel. You must really think I'm a threat to your family to go to these extremes. You're a monster."

"No, Christina. You never saw me as a possible threat. But you really should have. Do you think I just give parties and consort with the wealthier side of Charleston society?" She stepped closer to where Christina was seating. "Not only do I watch out for my family's best interest, but also this town's which is why everyone will have a clear reading of what's going on very soon."

Christina missed the threat, but Bessie didn't. She stepped closer to the woman staring menacingly at her niece. "Celia, what are you talking about? What on earth have you done?" She would never have described Celia Rose as evil, but now she knew the word existed exclusively for her. The woman spawned straight from hell.

"If you want to throw threats against someone, Celia, why don't you throw them against someone who can handle it? I'm sure my relationship with Joseph has been on the gossip rounds a time or two."

"Ah, yes the elusive Joseph and Bessie Washington living in sin did make for interesting conversation, come to think of it. But then again your whole family has led quite a scandalous existence, haven't they?"

"Careful, Celia," Bessie said, her voice taking on a dark sinister tone. "You are moving into very dangerous territory. Don't you for once think I won't have you thrown out of here on your ass before I let you speak badly about my family," she patted Christina's arm. "Christina and Michael want to be with one another, and maybe you need to settle with the fact that it may happen whether you like it or not."

"The hell I will," Celia said, her face deepening to a red crimson.

Bessie nodded. "I know that may not be a part of your plan, but from the way those two have acted around one another these past months, anyone with good vision can see they have a real connection. If you go against that, Celia, you stand to lose a lot more than you bargained for."

That point seemed to irritate Celia further.

"That may be true, Bessie, since your niece has tempted my son past the point of thinking straight. But, like I've said before, everyone will see what I've written soon enough." She cast both of them a deviant smile.

"Listen to yourself, Celia. You're taking things out on a young girl who has done nothing to hurt you or Michael." Auntie paused before asking, "And what writing are you speaking of?"

"I did what any normal mother would do to try to save her son. Her story was printed in the paper earlier this afternoon and by tomorrow everyone will know of your trashy niece." She gestured in Christina's direction.

No one saw the slap that came next. Christina had her head in her hands when she heard the pop. Aunt Bessie had quietly inched her way closer to Celia. Before she knew it a stinging slap had connected to her left cheek.

"Get out of my house. And the next time you call someone trash, look in the mirror. I'm sure Mr. Rose would love to know just how much you like pruning trees in the dead of winter."

Celia half ran and half walked to the front door. She reached for the doorknob and turned around to face the two ladies now huddled together on the couch.

"Read your paper. I'm sure it'll tell you everything." She slammed the door behind her.

Christina sprang from her seated position to her room and started packing. The sun was still high enough and wouldn't set for some time, which would provide just enough daylight for Isaac and her to make their way back to Virginia. She wasn't taking any chances, and she knew Celia's threats were real enough that waiting around for the inevitable was simply out of the question.

"Christina, what are you doing?" Bessie watched her niece move from one room to the next, gathering her things as well as Isaac's. After a while, she sat down on the edge of Christina's bed willing herself to say something that would lessen the seriousness of the situation. Every time she looked up, Christina was muttering to herself, reciting what needed to be collected as she threw her belongings in the suitcase.

Her gaze finally met Bessie's.

"I'm leaving, Auntie," she said between sobs. "It's too late to stop what Celia has already put in place. I wouldn't know where to start even if I had the means to stop her. I can't take this anymore."

"What do you mean? You can't just pack up and leave with Isaac." Bessie glanced over at the packed suitcase. "I love having my family around and I can't just let them go, not this soon. Not like this. There's no reason you can't stay and meet this thing head on. I'll be by your side, and Joseph will be also."

"Did you hear what she said, Auntie? How are people supposed to look at me once they see what she's done? That woman is pure evil and whatever is in that paper I don't want to stay around to read."

"Slow down. I'm sure she was here just to blow off steam." For Bessie it was a matter of keeping her family together. She knew she was grasping at straws with that statement, but she needed something to say that would slow her niece down.

Christina looked at her in disbelief. "When have you known Celia to just let off steam?"

"Good point. I just think if you leave now, you'd be playing right into her hands."

"Celia had an agenda this whole time and she saw it through to the end." Christina finished closing her bag and buckled it tight. She heard the door to the kitchen slam and knew that Joseph had just come in. "But what about Isaac? You can't just take my nephew with you on that long road. Who is going to hold him?"

Christina shook her head. Maybe leaving with Isaac was a risk at the moment but she had to go before everyone found out about her. She could feel the nauseating sickness rise from her stomach and released a long breath. "I have to go, Auntie."

"What's going on Bessie, Chrissy?" Joseph asked as he walked into the room. There was an awkward silence that followed his entrance into the room. The wood from the fireplace crackled as Joseph waited for someone to speak, while Isaac's baby gibberish was left to fill the space of unanswered dialogue. She picked him up while searching for the right words to say.

"I didn't expect to leave so soon, and I know I should think more clearly about this, but there really isn't time."

"What are you talking about, Chrissy?"

Instead of having Christina explain, Bessie turned towards him and rubbed his forearm. "Celia has decided that Christina and Michael are unfit to be together. And she put Christina's past in the paper for everyone to see."

"Hell," Joseph replied, dropping his head. "What kind of mess is this?" His attention turned towards the packed suitcases surrounding the bed. "This mean you're leavin?"

"I have to go, Joseph. For the sake of Isaac and me, we can't stay here any longer." Without saying another word Christina gave Bessie and Joseph a quick hug, and headed out the door with Isaac. She had half expected her aunt and Joseph to come after her and stop her from getting into the car. Thankfully, they didn't. They stood on the porch steps holding one another like two parents watching their child going away from home for the first time. They were almost like her parents for they were two people who had cared about her and Isaac tremendously for the past year. She put her hand over her mouth to suppress the sobs that threatened to escape. Going back to Virginia was one of the hardest things she had to do, but it was her only option. So why did she feel the need to turn the car around and drive back to the place that had been her only home for the past year?

She had to see Michael before she went back to Virginia and hopefully he hadn't heard anything yet about what was going on.

Chapter 20

Michael finished reading the rest of the paper he was seething with anger, not at the story itself, but at the audacity of the person who wrote it. He slammed the paper on top of the desk and contemplated going to visit her before he finished with his finances. Michael knew something was going on that morning. He normally had his house-keeper pick up the paper before he sat down to a hot cup of coffee. However, this was Saturday. He let his house help take weekends off to be with their families. Someone else had put the paper on his desk this morning and he knew who that person was. He decided to wait. If she wanted to be this hateful and vindictive he would find a way to deal with her, ensuring no more hurt and embarrassment would go to Christina or anyone else involved. He just had to figure out how to limit the damage.

Michael frowned at the knock that shook him from his thoughts. Damn! He really wasn't in the mood for visitors today unless it happened to be Christina. His heart suddenly picked up a steady beat with the thought of her being on the other side of the door, while his footsteps quickened their pace. The excitement quickly vanished when his former mistress was revealed wearing an angry look that made him want to slam the door in her face.

"How could you prance around town with that jezebel?" she said as she strode past him.

"Patrice, you of all people shouldn't be calling others names. Have you looked at your own profession lately?"

He watched her expression turn from lust to shock to pure frustration. The woman really did have emotional issues that had never surfaced until now. Before, her usual outbursts were accompanied by sweet words meant to stroke his ego and get him into bed; now they were a continuous cry for attention. He was getting more annoyed with her antics every time she was in his presence.

"Answer me, damn it. How could you have picked her over me?" she asked, with a panicky sound in her voice.

"In case you didn't know already, I'm in love with Christina."

His response should've sent her hand reaching to slap his handsome face, but all she could think of was another word he'd never used with her before. "Love her? Not once did you even portray a single ounce of feeling for me the way you're doing with that girl."

"She's different. What can I say?"

"Oh yes. She's different alright," Patrice said with a laugh. "Why is that? What makes her so different than any other girl here in Charleston? Is it because she's from Virginia? Or do you just have a knack for falling for girls who seem unavailable?"

With each question she asked, Michael became more agitated until his face was scarlet with anger. "What is that supposed to mean?"

"It means your little love interest has more of a mess up her sleeve than you realize."

"And all of this coming from someone whose lovers spans the eastern seaboard."

She stepped closer to him. He was so good looking she wondered if he had any idea she wanted to be in his bed at this exact moment. "You didn't seem to mind those lovers when you were with me," Patrice said, coming to stand directly in front of him with her hands on her hips.

Michael looked at her. She was changing her emotionally erratic mind again. He would never figure Patrice out and decided that it really wasn't worth trying. Why had he wasted such valuable time on a woman like this? She looked pathetic standing in front of him and questioning him about his life. She reminded him of his mother, who was demanding, nosy, and always wanting to be the author and finisher of someone's life, namely his. Well, he'd had enough of those types of women and it was time he let at least one of them know exactly what he thought. But before he could tell her she pulled his head towards hers and planted an undesirable wet kiss against his lips. Her arms immediately went around his neck to get him into what her mouth was trying to accomplish. The kiss was meant to acknowledge her need of him as she tried her usual seduction of his mouth. She suckled his lower lip and slipped the tip of her tongue inside. But it felt like kissing a stone tablet, cold and unfeeling. Michael wasn't at all into the kiss or the female trying to rouse him. He tried to peel her arms from around his neck but she held a tight grip and desperately tried to hold on.

"Michael, I have to talk to you…"

He pushed Patrice away immediately but not before Christina saw the display.

"I'm sorry I didn't knock." She turned around and ran from the room.

"Christina! Christina, come back!"

Patrice grabbed his arm to keep him from going after her. It was bothersome to think Michael cared for the girl this much. Neglect and fear were creeping into her mind. This was a new feeling and she didn't like it. "Let her go. You don't need the likes of her."

That statement earned her a glare and he shook her hand from his arm. "Shut up, Patrice. What I don't need is a tramp like you."

It wasn't what he said, but how he said it. "What?"

He had never spoken to her like that before. Maybe on occasion he'd been annoyed with her lack of propriety towards their relationship but this was something different altogether. This was a different Michael. "She's not even suitable to be in this house."

He didn't yield to the insult, and he let her know once and for all their relationship was finally over. "She's going to be my wife, so hell yes she's suitable. You on the other hand are not." He opened the door Christina had just run through. "Get out of my house."

A deafening screech sounded throughout the house as Patrice's anger finally exploded. "Rot in hell, Michael Rose! When that girl figures out who you really are she'll go running for the hills like the rest of them." The last of her tirade echoed as the door slammed behind her.

Michael didn't linger to watch her exit. He hurriedly wrote another version of the story, rushed over and handed it to the editor with a stern expression. It didn't take the man long to know he meant business. After Michael explained what was to be printed; he gave him a firm handshake before he left.

He was in a desperate race against time as the car pulled to a screeching halt in front of Bessie Washington's home. Christina would be wondering why he hadn't responded sooner, but his biggest fear was that she believed he didn't want her because of her past. As angry as he was at the fact that another man had hurt her to the point where she barely trusted anyone, he still believed the love they felt for one another would counter that. There was one thing that bothered him deeply. He had broken her heart once before by not responding well to Isaac's existence. Would she claim this time that his response was again delayed? He wouldn't make the same mistake twice with this news. If he could just talk to her then she would know that he didn't care about her past; only their future together was important. Michael all but ran from his car, leaving the door open, and leaped onto the front porch.

"Christina, Christina! I'm not going anywhere until you come outside and talk to me."

The house was quiet. The sound of laughter from a week ago was clearly absent. He knew someone had to be around somewhere as he descended the small steps to look around the back yard.

"Hello, Michael."

He forgot his manners and took the steps two at a time, stopping a hair's breadth from Bessie's face. "Hi, Ms. Bessie. I didn't mean to disturb you but I need to speak with Christina."

"She's not here. She left for Virginia."

"She's gone back home?"

"Yes, on account of your mother having the paper print that awful story for everyone to see."

"I've already taken care of that, ma'am. I had the paper print another story stating that what my mother reported was false. She may know one of the writers, but I know the owner."

"That was very kind of you, but I'm afraid it's too late." Her voice was despondent; Michael noticed the sad mixture of unhappiness and loss. This was the woman who took Christina in and loved her as if she were her own daughter. She couldn't deny the way she felt even if she tried.

He put his head down and started walking back to his car. All of his efforts were for nothing. She had left without saying goodbye and he didn't get to tell her of his plans to wed her. He suddenly felt he was part of the reason she left so suddenly. This wasn't supposed to happen. "I should've been here for her, fighting for her. I messed up big time."

"No, no, this was not your fault," she quickly assured him. "I guess I can take part of the blame as well."

"How's that possible?" he asked.

"If I had stepped in when I noticed there was tension between Christina and your mother maybe none of this would've happened. My protective instincts kicked in a little too late."

She sat on the top steps and folded her hands in her lap. The very thought of her niece having a devastating secret revealed by a malicious person turned her stomach. Why hadn't she seen this coming? Or was she just too preoccupied in finding the perfect match for Christina.

"I wasn't aware that my mother had such a vendetta against her," he replied solemnly.

"No one could've predicted this would happen, Michael. Your mother's actions do not reflect how you feel about Christina. We all know that."

Michael shook his head. "Then why do I feel guilty, like I've just let the one person I care about down?"

Christina had to have been gone well over an hour yet he still felt something could be done in rectifying this whole ordeal. He wouldn't let her get away that easily, not without telling her how he felt.

His brows shot up as an idea formed in his mind. "Ms. Washington where in Virginia might Christina reside?"

"It's a place called Henry County, about thirty minutes from downtown Richmond. It's where I grew up."

"If I drove there, would you ride with me?"

There was a brief silence before a smile spread slowly across Bessie's face. She nodded. "Maybe if she knew how you felt she would change her mind." Bessie stood from her seated position. They needed to make plans for their upcoming trip, and it couldn't be done by brooding in the front yard over what had already taken place.

"We'd best get going if we're going to get Christina back here." Her smile made him feel at ease as he walked back to the house.

"We're going to need a plan of action before we hop in the car."

Michael escorted Bessie into the house. They both were on a mission to get the person they loved back to Charleston where she belonged.

An invitation for lunch was waiting for her when she arrived home. It was just what Celia needed after her long trip back from Virginia. She dressed for the occasion, preferring to wear the new hunter green shoes and matching purse she had bought last month. The women will be green with envy, Celia thought with amusement. She stood there for several moments admiring her figure until the bedroom door opened revealing a quiet skittish maid.

"Curtis waitin' outside for you, Ma'am."

"Thank you, Maude."

Celia had almost forgotten that Curtis was downstairs waiting with the car running she was so preoccupied with her appearance. She stood there for several more minutes putting on the final touches of her makeup and admiring her figure before closing the bedroom door. Celia wished that damn invite could've come sooner. And it wasn't just that she needed an audience to deliver the news about Bessie Washington's niece; she needed to let them know their president Margaret knew about the girl also. How could she not?

This was the perfect opportunity to expose Margaret's unsuitable president-like qualities, and to reveal that she, Celia, would be best suited for the job as president of the Ladies Society. It just made sense, as she was the one with the most connections out of everyone in the group. Celia had worked hard to make her social soirees the most coveted events in Charleston. She had wanted to bring her daughters along with her but they had flatly refused her request, stating they had been bossed around by her enough.

She wondered if this meeting would in fact lead to a changing of the presidency within the club. Did they want her to be in charge of everything including the social events? Of course they did. Why would they hand out an invitation to a luncheon that wasn't already scheduled on the calendar? She suddenly was giddy with excitement.

All the people she could invite or not invite coupled with the parties she would plan on a moment's notice were literally within her grasp.

As the Wright's home came into view she was delighted with the outcome but was curious how her name entered the conversation of being in charge. They no doubt value my experience and skills, Celia said to herself as she walked through the black wrought iron gates. The Wright's city home was gorgeous, with its front and rear balconies, grand staircase, formal ballroom, and marble steps leading to the front door. They were one of the well-respected colored families in Charleston, and probably the only colored family who owned a city home with marble steps. Celia secretly envied Margaret. She would've given anything for the extensive travel list Margaret could easily boast about during their meetings, but didn't. She hated living in one place year round, preferring to travel whenever she could. She was just limited to the east coast because of her husband's strict budget control over her finances. The only thing she wasn't too crazy about was being a missionary. She didn't understand why Margaret and her husband wanted to be missionaries, always obligated to people, and being around all those poor people. Celia cringed at the thought. But still to see another part of the world, Celia always wished it were she and not Margaret on the arm of that buffoon husband of hers. He had more money than her husband, a fact again she was envious of.

She stood on the veranda and rang the doorbell. It took some time for someone to come to the door and she was just about to scold the butler for keeping her waiting, but when it opened Margaret was on the other side looking dazzling in a periwinkle long sleeve dress. Damn, I should've worn that color.

"Hello, Celia. Come in."

"I'm surprised you're opening the door, Margaret. Where's your hired help? Surely you can afford the assistance," she said sarcastically as they made their way past the large eat-in kitchen to the massive living area.

They were all seated in an arranged circle of chairs with Margaret placing herself in the center. There was a polite sound of laughter until she entered the room, followed by a seemingly forced quietness, which Celia thought was odd since she'd spent several years planning and coordinating with the same people. They held themselves stiff against their chairs and looked at her with stern expressions. Only Mrs. Lewis was at ease, but that was because she had probably downed a few corn whiskey shots before coming in, as was her custom before every meeting. While the ladies remained in their current state of reticence, Celia decided to vocalize her gratitude for being at the luncheon. Besides, this would be her opening speech in accepting the title as their president and she wanted to make a good first impression.

"Hello, everyone. I can't tell you how good it is to be home. Virginia weather is a stark contrast to our beautiful Charleston and…"

"Please sit, Celia, as we have much to discuss," Margaret interjected as she met Celia's astonished gaze with a stern look of her own.

Celia took the seat facing the group of women and waited for their response, smiling as she normally did when given a boost to her ego or reward for her diligent hard work.

"Celia Rose, you have disrespected the club and the core values with which it was founded."

The room suddenly felt like it was getting smaller or was that just her imagination, as every face honed in on her presence.

Celia tried keeping her emotions in check, giving a nervous laugh before saying, "Excuse me? The invitation said luncheon with the ladies. I don't understand what's going on. Please explain this accusation." She watched the faces of the women for any positive expressions and didn't receive any. Everyone sat stone-faced, looking in her direction. Suddenly she realized there wasn't going to be a new position for her, nor the usual meeting she normally came to. This felt like an interrogation brought by Margaret's band of fashionably dressed women and she was the prime suspect.

"We are not here to degrade or humiliate young ladies, Celia. We are here to teach them and direct them in the correct path."

This was about Christina Davis. That little bitch! She gritted her teeth and contemplated denying her involvement in the whole mess. But she went on the defensive. If they wanted to know what happened all she had to do was tell them her perspective. Surely they would understand a mother's instincts about the women her son dated.

"I didn't degrade anyone. If you're speaking of Christina Davis I did what any concerned mother would do out of love for her son."

"That is not what we portray here. Your actions are not what this society does to any young woman of this community or elsewhere."

"I may have gotten a little carried away but it was all out of love. I hope you can understand it."

"If your heart is like this, I question your feelings towards the members of this group and what we do for others."

"I would never disrespect the fine women of this club in any way shape or form," Celia said, trying to defend herself.

"But you would humiliate those that aren't part of this club. Women who one day could become members, isn't that right?"

"You don't understand," Celia said. "I was trying to keep my son from going down a wrong path. Any one of you would have done the same."

"Your actions have prompted this counsel to terminate your membership indefinitely. You will no longer be welcomed in the ladies society of Charleston."

"Wait! What do you mean?"

"Not only was I at the social gathering when your initial feelings were made known about the girl, but I read that horrific post in the paper that you paid someone to write for you. Bessie Washington also informed me of your little visit to her house. What do you have to say for yourself?"

"I did this organization a service when I exposed that wench to everyone," Celia replied, her voice taking on a different tone now. She couldn't believe these women would take the side of nobody against her. The events of that girl's life shouldn't even be a part of this meeting. What was going on here?

There were several murmurs of disapproval and shaking of heads. They were going against her and she suddenly felt backed into a corner with no way out.

"No, Celia. You embarrassed yourself as well as this group of well-respected women."

"I don't know what you mean." She felt like a cornered mouse with the cats ready to strike.

"What if we were to expose your trysts over the past several months? If we were to really open past occurrences I'm sure everyone would be quite interested in the goings on at your home, Celia."

"I've done nothing that would make you speak such lies about me." Did they know about her lover? Did James mention what he saw that day to one of their husbands? That son-of-a-bitch! Maybe coming here wasn't the best idea after all.

Mrs. Wright spoke to the group. "Let us not forget where we've come from, ladies. We too have made mistakes in our past and if it hadn't been for the generation before us to guide us in the right direction, who knows what roads we may have taken."

The ladies' approval echoed throughout the room as she continued. "We cannot judge the mistakes of others because we are not perfect people ourselves."

Celia tried searching for the right words to say to the women, but she couldn't assemble a single rebuttal that would convince them she was remorseful.

"We don't want to alienate these young women from our group, no matter where life takes them. We must help and support them however we can." She turned back to Celia. "You are dismissed from this council, Mrs. Rose. We wish you luck in your future endeavors."

"What?" They couldn't let her go! Every fiber of her being wanted to scream out in protest. How could they do this? She was Celia Rose. She was the one that threw the illustrious parties and eloquent dinners. They just couldn't throw her out! "No, you can't do this, Margaret, Mrs. Schuler, Alice, please."

She looked around for understanding but received none. They were staring at her with cold unsympathetic faces just before one by one they retreated from their seats. She felt as if she were an insignificant statue pleading for attention in the middle of the room.

"I did it for all of us. Don't you see?"

Celia was groveling now, something she'd never done in her life. Her knees touched the seat of one of the empty chairs and slid to the floor. "We see that you don't have the best interests of this council or other potentially good young women who may lead this council one day in the future," Mrs. Wright countered.

"Please don't."

"Mr. Leroy will see you to your vehicle. Good day, Mrs. Rose."

They left her there on her knees, begging for acceptance from empty chairs.

Chapter 21

Christina didn't know the ride home would have a stronger effect on her than if she had decided to stay in Charleston. The trip gave her time to think about days spent with Michael and the friends she had made, which deepened her saddened state even further. She gripped the wheel tightly as images of his lips against hers sent a quivering sensation coursing through her veins. By the time she noticed the familiar landscape, the car was rolling along the dusty dirt roads of her hometown.

Nothing seemed to have changed. Except her. She was a mother and recognized there was more to her life than before. As the car pulled into the front yard, her younger brothers and sisters realized who was behind the wheel and ran to greet her. Their yells and screams almost prevented her from hearing her older brother's playful greeting.

Russell stood on the porch with his hands in his pockets and a wide grin on his face. "Well, look who decided to come home. I missed you, little sister."

"I missed you too, Russ."

It took him two strides to get to her, followed by a bone crushing bear hug, which lifted Christina clear off her feet.

"Have you gotten taller?" she asked, laughing and trying to catch her breath.

"Nope, just more muscular from Mama feeding me those collard greens with boiled eggs mashed in. Where are you hiding my nephew?"

Christina pulled Isaac from the car floor, uncovering his sleeping form for her brother to see.

"Wow, I'm an uncle," he said, as Christina handed Isaac to him. "And a damn fine one, I might add."

Christina was glad to see her brother but knew she couldn't delay seeing the rest of the family. During the ride home she went over what she'd say to her mother and hoped the conversation wouldn't produce a yelling match as it had so many times before. "Where's Mama, Russ?"

"She's inside the house getting dinner ready. Mama's gonna be real surprised you showed up."

"Yeah, I know. I wasn't supposed to be here for another month or so."

"I'm glad you're here right now. After you left things got real strange around here. You wouldn't have liked the scene that was in the front yard."

"What do you mean?"

"Butch Curtis came to the door and asked for your hand in marriage."

Christina wasn't surprised by that statement only annoyed as she breathed in exhaling slowly. The man was still trying to mess with her.

"What happened?"

"After mama told him no he tried to force his way in while talking crazy. He said he could destroy our family cause he did it once before."

Christina shook her head. Butch Curtis was stirring something up and she knew it now piqued her brother's curiosity.

"So I hit em with a one-two punch knocking him on his ass and told him to get the hell out of here."

"Good, but that won't stop him. We need to find out what happened ten years ago Russell."

"We will lil sis but first things first. What brings you back? Don't tell me you want Lewis Harris! I gave him a nice shiner after you left."

"No, I don't want Lewis Harris. And thank you for sticking up for me."

She looked through the screen door. Mama hadn't appeared yet and she was beginning to wonder if she was deliberately staying in the house.

"I've grown up, Russ. Charleston gave me the time to mature and finally figure out what I want in my life."

"And what's that?"

"I want to raise my baby. Isaac is a blessing and he belongs with me." Russell looked at his nephew. The baby was the image of his grandfather and could easily pass for a brother as he too had some of his father's features. "Mama won't be happy about that."

"We're just going to have to talk and hopefully she'll see it my way."

Her mother's voice rang through the house as the screen door swung open.

"Russell, who are you talking to," she asked before her eyes settled on her oldest daughter. "Christina? You're home?" She walked slowly down the steps with outstretched arms that enveloped her daughter. They held one another tightly until finally her mother broke the connection with a kiss to the cheek.

"Yes, Mama, I'm home. Are you happy to see me?" Christina asked, searching her mother's face for acceptance.

"I thought you were coming home next month. I don't have a room prepared for you and your cousin is out of town, so the baby will have to stay here before she comes back."

"I'm here to talk to you, Mama. And no one is taking my baby. Isaac is going to stay with me."

Her mother's face produced a long frown before she said, "Come in the house. Russ, gather your brothers and sisters for dinner in a few minutes. Let me have a talk with your sister first."

"Yes, Ma'am," he replied before giving Christina a proud smile of support and handing her the sleeping Isaac.

"Give me my grandbaby," she demanded, taking Isaac from her. "I need to hold him for a while before your cousin takes him." She said this undoubtedly, which infuriated Christina. This conversation wasn't starting out so well. Her mother wasn't listening to her, and she needed to make her understand that things were going to change from here. She couldn't do that by yelling, so she took deep breaths while walking into the house after her.

They settled in the kitchen on either side of the table. Christina watched her mother kiss Isaac's forehead again and again, thankful he hadn't awakened yet.

"Mama, I'm going to raise my baby and tell everyone he's mine."

"Now Christina, we've already discussed this. The baby will go to one of your older cousins until he's of a certain age, or until you get married."

"Mama, Isaac is my child. He's not my cousin's or anyone else's. If you can't accept that then we'll live somewhere else."

Her mother looked at her with a wide-eyed expression. "Think of your younger brothers and sisters."

"Mama, think of me. All this time you made me feel like it was my fault, that I did something wrong. Yes, I made a mistake. But you cannot ask me to give away my child, whom I have grown to love. I cannot and I will not."

"But Chrissy…"

"No buts, Mama. I have to introduce Isaac to a man who didn't want him or me in his life. How do you think that's going make him feel? He's just a little boy."

"You can keep him from all of that unnecessary pain if you just let me take him to your cousin's."

"Absolutely not."

"Christina, I don't think you realize the responsibility of a child and what it takes."

She knew her mother still had the idea that she was protecting her, but during her time in South Carolina something had happened. She became a mother and was ready to take on the full responsibility of her child. She just needed her mother to understand that this wasn't just about her, but Isaac as well.

"I'm going to go now." Christina took Isaac from her mother's arms and headed to the door.

"Where are you going?"

"I'll be staying down the road with Aunt Beatrice for the time being."

"But your home is here, Christina."

"Where was all this when I was begging you to let me stay in Virginia?"

"Chrissy, please stop blaming me for something that had to happen. Your reputation and the family name were at stake. Do you think I honestly wanted to send my daughter to another state?"

"To protect the family name, yes, I do." She opened the door. "But what you don't realize, Mama, is that you put me and my feelings aside in order to do that."

"Chrissy, stop. Your home is here. It's always been here. Please don't leave."

"My home is wherever Isaac is."

Christina got back in the car. She felt elated. It wasn't all of what she really wanted to tell her mother, but it was a start. She was now a mother herself and wanted the best atmosphere for her and Isaac.

Aunt Beatrice's house was three minutes away, a quaint two-story home set against a wooded area. The front yard was packed with what looked like the rest of her family, and she was welcomed with open arms when she got out of the car. Aunt Beatrice stood on the front porch and walked down when she recognized her niece.

"Oh Chrissy, I'm so glad you're here."

"Aunt Beatrice, would it be alright if I stayed for a while until I get on my feet?"

"Yes, it would be fine. Your uncle and I are the only ones here so you'll have plenty of space to move around. Have you eaten yet?"

"No, I haven't. I could use a bite of your famous corn muffins."

"Wonderful! Now bring that baby in here and let us see him."

Christina went through the kitchen just in time to see Uncle Bill come in after them. "I heard you were in town, niece. Have you come to stay with me?"

"Hi Uncle Bill, how are you?"

"Not well Chrissy. It's been bothering me real bad the way I treated you before you left and if you can forgive me it would make me a very happy man." Bill was showing a great deal of compassion, a side of which she'd never seen coming from him.

"Forgive?" Christina said, surprised her uncle would be asking such a thing. She'd already forgiven him but was just waiting for his acknowledgement.

"I've already forgiven you. My time in Charleston offered a lot of forgiveness not only for the people who hurt me, but for myself."

"That's good to know, Chrissy. I was hoping you'd say that. Things haven't been the same without you around here."

While Christina searched for the words to respond to that bit of surprising news, Bill stepped forward and gathered her in his arms for a hug, which caught her off guard. "I believe I owe you that," he said, finally letting her go long enough for the shock to wear off and to catch her breath.

"Thank you, I needed that."

"I did too, and I'm not afraid to admit I was wrong in this whole thing. You cannot know the many times I've beaten myself up for treating you that way. Your father would've had my hide if he was here right now, and your mother has cursed me out more times than I care to admit. I never would have done what I did had I known it would cause bad blood between us." Having presented his apologetic side, Bill walked over to look at Isaac, who was still asleep in Aunt Beatrice's arms.

"Well, he looks just like his Grandpa Abraham," he said as he observed Isaac's features, rubbing the young child's head.

"I couldn't say who he looks like more," Beatrice replied, giving Isaac a thorough once-over. "Possibly Abraham, but it's really too early to tell. Plus he has to be awake long enough for me to get a proper look at him."

"I can tell you who he doesn't look like," Bill said angrily.

"Bill, don't start. Please!"

"I'm not startin anything—"

Christina didn't wait for her aunt and uncle to finish, but retreated into one of the guest rooms upstairs. The day's events were finally catching up to her and she needed rest before anything else was brought up. Aunt Beatrice would bring Isaac to the room when they were done discussing who in the family he resembled the most, which she didn't mind in the least. Christina was thankful her family overlooked what had happened and loved Isaac in spite of where he came from. It was a good enough ending to a long dramatic day.

༄

Christina's homecoming over the next couple of days was pleasant in one way and vague in another. Her mother hadn't shown her face at Aunt Beatrice house, not even to see Isaac although she did ask her about him from time to time. Uncle Jerry even appeared during the day to wrestle up some groundhogs from the nearby vegetable garden before sitting with her and Isaac. Aunt Vera, on the other hand, cried every time she held her nephew, doting on him and stating on more than one occasion that he looked like Uncle Carl instead of his grandfather Abraham. She missed everyone. But what she really needed was for her mother to be here, supporting her.

During the day, Christina was dragged to a few get-togethers and other social functions by her friend Roxanne. She was glad for the company. It kept her mind occupied so she couldn't think about Michael too often, which she had been doing every moment since returning home. The gossip about her leaving for South Carolina had dwindled over the year, as everyone found new people to talk about. Her mother had let it be known she had been living happily with her aunt Bessie, learning new cultures and etiquette all this time, and was only in Virginia for a short while. Her mother, Auntie and Roxanne had formed a triple team against the naysayers. They provided a protective barrier between Christina and the outside world so that every question asked was met with a logical response, so well done that no one questioned its authenticity.

Christina went along with their fabricated story, because it was easier than elaborating on what some already knew. But naturally, questions were asked about South Carolina and the appealing island she had been living on. Christina was hardly able to hide her sad feelings about leaving when she described the natural beauty that had surrounded her there. "The ocean was so close you could see the blue water clear through the trees. It was absolutely beautiful."

She sighed.

Just a few days back home in Virginia and she already missed South Carolina. How was it conceivable that Charleston had become her home in just one year? Why, she had spent her whole life in Virginia, walking amongst its colonial homes, playing on the cobblestone streets of Cary Town, watching the small boats on the James River, and feeding the geese at Byrd Park. But these places no longer mattered. Virginia was no longer her home. She missed waking up to the smell of the salty sea air mixed with marshland just beyond Aunt Bessie's house. The ocean's sound would never stop roaring in her ear, and she would always remember the smell of the Sweet Jessamine flowers growing profusely outside her bedroom window. Would she ever stop thinking about the hanging moss trees or the Crate Myrtles that lined the gravel road leading to Aunt Bessie's home? Would she soon stop hearing in her mind the music she and Michael danced to that first night he kissed her?

Aunt Beatrice had planned a welcome home party for the weekend to include not only her family but Lewis's, too, so everyone could be introduced to baby Isaac. Christina agreed. This moment was long overdue and she was prepared for it. During the day people were coming in and out helping with the decorations and cooking. She made sure to stay out of the way, feeding Isaac when needed and taking small naps with him when possible. Aunt Beatrice peeked in the room to check on her. "Lewis won't be coming, Christina. That bastard is too chicken shit to come and see his son."

That bit of news wasn't shocking. "Auntie, it's okay."

"It's not okay, Chrissy. He's the father and he knows it. He could at least show his face."

She watched as Aunt Beatrice picked up Isaac, rocking him back and forth. "If it were up to me, I'd drag him down here by his balls and make him see the mistake he's making."

"Auntie it is fine. Everything will be alright."

Beatrice shook her head. "Isaac deserves better than that. You both do."

Christina watched as her aunt breathed out her frustration and took Isaac downstairs to the others. She wasn't at all shocked by Lewis' absence. Clearly he hadn't grown up in the year she'd been gone. She suspected his grandmother had something to do with his decision not to come. Christina went to the window and looked out over the yard at everyone as they arrived for the party. As long as Isaac had people who cared about him she would be fine.

Coming downstairs, she met Aunt Beatrice in the kitchen, finding that dinner was in its final preparations. Auntie was stylish in an all blue dress with matching pearl earrings and necklace. She was barking orders at the men, making sure everything was in its correct place while taking pies out of the woodstove. The men were carrying chairs in for the guests upon her orders and didn't seem to mind her bossiness as they complied with each direction she gave. Auntie had invited several of her friends, along with Roxanne and Porsha. All sat in the living room area sipping lemonade. Christina was thankful she had her friends with her, as questions from some of the women could be exhausting at times.

"You must miss South Carolina, Christina," one of the women remarked. "I know I definitely would. It's such a gorgeous place to be, especially in the fall."

"My family hadn't seen Isaac yet and they couldn't come down to visit, so I decided to come here."

"Your young man must not be too thrilled with that, the baby being away from him and all," Mrs. Gilbert commented.

Christina looked at Roxanne for an explanation, wondering how they knew about Michael, but her friend shrugged her shoulders as if to say they came up with this all on their own. She tried to hide her surprise that Mrs. Gilbert could know anything about her relationship with Michael, especially his connection with Isaac.

Aunt Beatrice chimed in at that moment. "I'm sure Michael has a deep affection for the baby, given how his relationship with Christina has developed. It takes a strong man to raise another man's child, especially when that other man has no backbone and can't even be considered a man himself. Am I right?"

"Oh yes. I completely agree with you, Beatrice," Mrs. Gilbert replied steadfastly.

Christina was pleased that Mrs. Gilbert didn't ask her to elaborate about her relationship, and was grateful Aunt Beatrice knew how to intervene at the precise moment when such a question arose. She couldn't be angry with the woman for being so inquisitive, only angry with herself for not cutting the discussion off before it got that far. She had wasted so much energy trying to avoid such questions that when they were finally asked she didn't have a rebuttal. She felt foolish and quickly changed her approach from eluding questions to facing them head on.

"Forgive me, Christina, but Mrs. Gilbert wasn't given the full story of your relationship with Michael and as you know with all stories, they are prone to becoming misinformed gossip at times."

Christina wanted to laugh at Aunt Beatrice's clear sarcasm but thought better of it. There was a brief silence before she spoke again, clearing her throat as she tried to work out in her mind what to say. They had obviously been busy in fabricating this part of her story and she needed to add to its validity, partial truth of course, at least for the time being. "Yes, of course ..." She tried to find the right words. "Michael was a blessing in disguise. I'm lucky he came into my life at that particular time."

"I can't imagine having another man raising my child other than the father," said Mrs. Gilbert. The comment made some shift uncomfortably in their seats.

"Well, it happens to many of us, Charlene. Just ask your sister. I'm sure she could tell you the juicy details of raising another man's child," Aunt Beatrice replied.

Christina smiled to herself. Frances, Mrs. Gilbert's sister, was married with ten children; however, her first two were by a man she met at the rail yards. If Mrs. Gilbert wanted to bring her indiscretions into the conversation then Auntie was going to make sure the sister's name would be brought in as well. Mrs. Gilbert seemed to get the hint because she switched the subject quickly.

"How is that beautiful baby boy, Christina?"

"Isaac is doing well. The Virginia climate is much the same as South Carolina's except during the summer. His adjustment hasn't been difficult."

"That's good to hear. Virginia weather is quite unpredictable at times and I know you don't want him catching a cold."

"He's doing better than I thought he would. Plus he has his aunts and uncles to spoil him whenever possible."

"That's no surprise, since he was born away from your family here," Mrs. Gilbert said. "I'm sure everyone is eager to get to know him and catch up on your stay in Charleston."

"Yes Charleston is a beautiful place. I recommend traveling there to anyone who is able to go."

She wondered what would happen when they found out she wouldn't be going back to Charleston. No one knew that she and Isaac wouldn't be returning and that they planned to stay in Mills-town. Christina sat on the sofa waiting for the next words to come out of her mouth. She would tell the women of her stay in Charleston and revel in the details of each blessed moment on James Island. She just hoped the tears could be held back long enough for the story to reach its conclusion. Aunt Beatrice and her mother were the only people that knew she was home to raise Isaac herself.

She hadn't told them the full story about Michael, preferring to wait to delve into that sometime later when she had settled in fully. She was anticipating disappointment from both of them, given her history with falling in love. No one knew the real gravity of her sadness. It was like reopening a closed wound, only this time she was sure it could've been prevented had she just ignored Michael's advances. How long would she keep thinking about him? Her head was trying to convince her heart not to miss him for long, but her heart wasn't convinced.

Several women turned towards a knock at the front door while Aunt Beatrice removed her apron on the way to answer it. Mrs. Gilbert smiled apologetically at Christina. "That would probably be Mrs. Carter. I saw her at church the other day and she told me she'd try and stop by to see you and Isaac. It would seem she kept her promise."

Christina heard Roxanne groan beside her and frowned. Why would Mrs. Carter come to see her and Isaac? The way she treated her before she left hadn't been forgotten and she didn't want to be cordial to someone who made it a point to try and destroy a person's reputation just because they could. She wasn't about to let this woman destroy her homecoming and mentally prepared herself for a very bad confrontation. If Mrs. Carter wanted to be disrespectful she'd be dealing with someone who no longer avoided confrontation than the little girl that left a year ago. Just as she was preparing herself for Mrs. Carter's entrance, Aunt Beatrice came to the living room with a twinkle in her eye and a wide grin plastered on her face.

And then the image of him, still etched in her mind, came to life. The soft white cotton shirt pressed against his tight mocha chest, the wide shoulders, the thick muscle arms, as if he needed any further attention to his virile body. He stood there tall, broad, infinitely male, and staring at her with the same intensity in his eyes she was giving back to him. Those warm brown eyes made her nervous with their directness, as they started at her head and moved over her body so slowly she thought he was intentionally trying to make her uncomfortable. Christina was jolted from the stare between them when Aunt Beatrice announced his arrival.

"Well, I'll be blessed!" Aunt Beatrice exclaimed. "He couldn't wait for you to go back to Charleston now could he, Christina?"

Christina kept her gaze on Michael as she stood up from the couch. Why was he here? Did he come to see if what his mother uncovered about her was true? All of the women were smiling except for Christina whose mouth had an oval shape that wouldn't move. Aunt Beatrice walked him to the center of the room to let everyone have a better look at him.

"Christina? Honey?"

She turned slowly toward her aunt and had to search for words to reply, as the male figure standing beside her aunt all but took the words out of her mouth.

"Everyone, I'd like you to meet Michael Rose."

Without skipping a beat, he put on a charming smile. "It's a pleasure to meet all of you."

"What a pleasant surprise, Michael. We weren't expecting you. As you can see, even Christina is in shock!"

Michael tore his eyes away from her and turned on his most captivating smile. "It was a spur-of-the-moment decision. But you're quite right. It was most inconsiderate of me to barge in on your gathering."

Beatrice scoffed at the idea of Michael apologizing for interrupting their dinner. "Nonsense! Right, ladies? Young man, you are most certainly welcome in our home at any time." The women were so taken by him they weren't about to say no as they smiled and nodded their agreement.

"Ladies, we can settle outside in the back yard. I'm sure these two would like some time alone together." One by one they exited the room, leaving Christina and Michael by themselves.

The air seemed tense as Michael shifted from one foot to the other while looking at Christina. Hell, it infuriated him every time he thought of that damn moment when she walked in on him and Patrice. After kicking Patrice out, finally, Michael realized that Christina had come by to explain her side of the story. He wanted to apologize before she spoke.

"Before you start…."

"I'm sorry, Christina," he cut in, determined to apologize first. "I should've kicked Patrice out of my life long before I met you."

That gave her pause. But she quickly recovered, determined to know what he was doing in her hometown. "What are you doing here, Michael?"

"I needed to see you to tell you that Patrice and I are not together, and I don't agree with what my mother did."

"I saw you kissing Patrice, and I thought you were avoiding me again like it was my fault."

"I admit my actions have led you to believe I wasn't sincere in my feelings towards you, but I had to tell my mother she could no longer hurt you. I went to your aunt's house later on but you were gone. I'm sorry if that gave you the wrong impression."

She sat down on the arm of the chair. "Well, it did."

He reached out and stroked the side of her face, sending shivers up and down her spine. "Why did you leave me?"

"You seemed preoccupied with Patrice, and I thought you agreed with your mother's side of the story, so I decided to return home."

He sat down and brought her hands to his lips. The feeling it brought almost made her cry; she missed this type of intimacy with him.

"I love you, Christina. Patrice means nothing to me. She was only there to question why I had feelings for you, which I explained to her was none of her business."

"The kiss did look a bit forceful now that I think about it," she admitted.

"Nothing is going to make me leave you."

She shook her head. "It doesn't matter. I can't go back to Charleston, not after what happened. They have attacked me in the town paper."

"I've already taken care of that. No one will write about you ever again."

"What did you do?"

"Let's just say the person that agreed to write the column has agreed to report honest news from now on. There's an apologetic letter stating that what was written about you was false."

Christina sighed. He really went above and beyond for her in more ways than one.

"I'm sorry for jumping to the wrong conclusion."

"I'm sorry for giving you the wrong impression."

"So what do we do now?"

"I left your Aunt Bessie and Joseph over at your mother's house before I came here."

"Aunt Bessie is here?"

"Yes. She insisted on coming to offer me support in case things didn't turn out the way we planned."

"The way you planned? You mean you and Auntie had a strategy in mind before coming down here?"

"Yes, we did," he said with a half-smile. "But I would've planned with anyone to get down here to see you."

Christina gazed at him lovingly for going to such lengths, not only to salvage her reputation but also driving to Virginia to see her again. It was what she needed to see and hear, and she thanked her lucky stars there was a man who wanted to be with her that much. Amazingly he considered her son as well, which was an added blessing.

"It's getting late in the evening. Maybe we can talk about this tomorrow."

"I still need to meet your mother tonight," he said with a grin. She was trying to delay the inevitable.

"You might leave me after you meet her."

"Not a chance," he said, gently stroking the side of her cheek.

༺༻

The house was alive with music and people by the time Christina and Michael walked through the door. Uncle Jerry was playing his favorite guitar while Uncle Carl was singing along to the music, making up words. Aunt Bessie and Joseph were holding their stomachs laughing at Uncle Carl, while the kids were running from room to room before dashing through the screen door to the outside. The scene was all too familiar to her, and she glanced at Michael to make sure he wasn't appalled at what he saw. He was smiling at the scene before him and nodded to Christina reassuringly before she addressed her mother. "Mama, I want you to meet someone," Christina said. "This is

Michael Rose, a young man I met in Charleston."

Her aunts and uncles were seated at the kitchen table, engaged in full conversation before she announced their arrival. The group discussion immediately went quiet as all observed Michael from head to toe. "Good evening, Mrs. Davis. Christina has told me so much about you."

"She hasn't told me a thing about you. Come have a seat. Christina, there's some lemonade in the ice box. You can make your gentleman here a cold drink."

They were all still staring, which made Michael uncomfortable. He needed to break the silence and thought there was nothing like the truth to start a conversation. It had to be better than the quiet that was in the room now.

"My name is Michael Rose. I met Christina in Charleston, South Carolina. I'm in love with your daughter, Mrs. Davis, and would like to court her."

Mary Davis was a statue after this declaration, while everyone else started talking at once.

"So you're sweet on my niece, are you?"

"Too pretty if you ask me."

"Did you knock her up or something?"

"You wanna fight me, soldier?"

"I need a drink."

Michael didn't know who to respond to first and was sure he had made the last statement several times inside his head.

"As you can see, you'll have to speak with her uncles first to get their approval. Her father has been gone for some time now and they had a hand in raising her."

"How many uncles does she have?"

"She has ten uncles in Virginia and three great uncles in North Carolina. But the ones here will do just fine. I'll send a message to the rest of them within the next week or so to come and meet you. They'll want a good look at you."

"Thank you, ma'am."

She chuckled a little. "Don't thank me just yet. Wait till you meet them. Then we'll see if you wanna thank me. Christina, why don't you come with me to see your grandmother. She'll want to know what all the commotion is over here."

Twenty minutes later Michael was seated at the kitchen table surrounded by frowning men with questioning looks. Michael thought they were more like vultures waiting to devour their next meal. He cleared his throat.

"I don't believe I know any of your names."

Each one looked at the other and introduced themselves one by one. Carl was seated wearing old-fashioned jean overalls, except for the crisp white dress shirt underneath. Jerry was dressed in a plaid shirt for the evening, with blue pants laden in so much dust that when he patted his legs particles drifted in the air. He was the eldest uncle out of the rowdy bunch and appeared tremendously angry over the fact Michael was interested in his niece. And Bill, also known as the town radio station, was in a khaki work uniform, with a toothpick sticking loosely out of his mouth.

The angry scowls and irate disposition he was being given was a clear indication this uncle would be hard to win over. The other two uncles decided they needed a little more time to scrutinize Mr. Rose and declined the offer of his hand until further notice. They weren't considered close relatives, choosing to live further down the road in King William, only contacting their sister Mary when they were in town. Michael shook the hands offered, receiving a tight grip in return. He leaned forward against the table and placed his elbow on the thick wood. Behind him the small window creaked in defiance against the wind outside. While Michael was glad to be in the company of Christina's family, he was also cautious. The way she was treated before was a heavy burden as expressed by everyone's distrustful look towards him.

After introductions were complete one of the uncles spoke up. "What you do for a livin', Mr. Rose?"

Michael looked over at Jerry who had an old acoustic guitar hanging across his hip, strumming the six-string absentmindedly with his knuckles. Jerry looked like he just stepped off a traveling rail car full of dust and soot, for he was dark skinned, with coal black hair and black eyes. He had been around since Christina was a young girl, and was more than just an uncle to her; he was her best friend and a confidant. "I work with my father in whole foods," Michael said with a grin. "I handle the finances and employees and he keeps the business running as smooth as possible with customers."

"And how is that gonna benefit our Chrissy?" Jerry asked, his brows coming together in a frown. "Chrissy ain't dependin on no man for no money, when she can have her own."

"Beggin your pardon, sir, but I'm not here to tell Christina what she can and cannot have. I'm here to love her the way she needs to be loved."

"What about Issac? You know she got herself in the family way before she met you. How you feelin' 'bout him, huh?"

"Isaac is a blessing to me. I would have him in my life as my son, even if I'd never met Christina. I love her, and it's as simple as that."

Michael's audience looked at one another. Then Jerry's sudden change in expression alerted Michael.

"Is she in trouble again?" Jerry asked seriously, his gaze going from Carl to Bill then back to Michael. "It must be something for you to follow her all the way from South Carolina."

Michael followed Jerry's gaze and knew these men were concerned about Christina's well- being.

"I got an idea why he's here, and it's more than what he sayin'," Jerry said.

"So do I," Carl said, frowning. "I'll wait to talk to you 'bout it myself, since we have a house full of men who want to talk to you all at once. It's best if we talk in private."

"Why not now, Carly?" Jerry asked angrily.

"What do you want with our niece, young fella?" Bill asked, clearly annoyed with Jerry's scrutinizing tone of voice.

"I love her, sir. I fell in love with Christina when I first met her."

"Then why did she come back to Virginia?"

"That was partially my fault. My mother had something to do with that."

"Are you a mama's boy?" Uncle Jerry chuckled before being hushed by Bill and Carl.

Michael waited until he stopped his hysterics before answering. The normal composed stature he usually portrayed was being tested as the postponing of his and Christina's reunion was finally starting to annoy him. Carl must've sensed his aggravation and started to recall how Vera's family was wary of him when they first met, pointing at Jerry in remembrance of those times. Jerry acknowledged Carl's viewpoint. "I guess I betta get back to the questions then."

"Yes," Carl said tightly. He watched as Jerry shook the young man's hand with an apology.

"I'm sorry you came down here to listen to my fussin'. I can't bear to see my Chrissy hurtin' by anyone, and I hope you understand that."

"I know this must look suspicious to you all, but I'm here for a genuine reason, I can assure you. Christina knows my feelings for her are real." Michael took this cue to further explain his feelings and why he was there.

"I'm willing to do whatever it takes to be with Christina and Isaac." All of the men looked at one another and nodded. Michael sensed they were impressed by his boldness to come down to their town to ask for their niece's hand. It showed more than just his love; it showed courage.

"Any man willing to come all this way deserves an answer. Jerry, go get Christina and Mary over here to answer this man."

"Aw hell, Bill, why I got to be the one?" "Cause you Chrissy's favorite."

"Damn right I am," Jerry said, heading out the door.

When Christina and her mother came back she stood next to Jerry and watched the conversations around her. The atmosphere had changed just that quickly from intense to a bit more relax. She wondered what caused the drastic changed.

"Are you glad your young man is here, Chrissy?"

"Yes, Uncle Jerry, I'm really happy."

"That's a big charge for a young man to take care of a young'un and all."

Christina looked at him while he shuffled his feet, then her brow raised. "You think he's not right for me?"

Jerry grinned at her. "No one will ever be good enough for you, Chrissy."

She laughed. "If this is your way of telling me something, I'd like to hear it coming from you."

He slipped his arm around her shoulders and hugged her to him. They stayed there in comforted silence, the answer of his acceptance being obvious between them giving a calm declaration. The current atmosphere gave her hope, and she searched for Michael until she saw him sitting next to Uncle Carl talking and laughing. As though sensing her eyes on him, Michael turned and smiled but kept their conversation going until she couldn't take being ignored much longer. "What's going on?" she asked, searching their faces for an answer.

Christina watched as Michael made his way through the crowded kitchen to her.

"You and this young man need to get some things straight," Carl said, folding his hands on his lap.

Michael took that as his cue. "Christina, do you think you could be happy with me?"

"I think I could." She noticed her family hadn't moved to allow them any privacy, and she knew answering his questions was just as important to them as it was to her.

"Could you be happy with me and Isaac?"

"Yes. You and Isaac are my family now. I couldn't be happier with anyone else."

They all heard a slap and jumped.

"Good, cause if it's one thing we don't like is our Camilla Jean unhappy," Jerry said.

"Who's Camilla Jean?" Michael whispered.

Christina laughed and shook her head. Michael would not only have to start getting used to the family, but the many names Uncle Jerry had for each one of them.

"Is that all, young man, cause you look like you want to say a little more?" Carl asked, still waiting for Michael to reveal his true intentions other than courting his niece.

"Yes, I'd like something more and if Christina could give it to me now it would make me the happiest man on this earth."

"Ima, get my knife. Mary, you listenin' to this shit?" Jerry asked, reaching to retrieve something from his pockets.

Mary quickly reached for his hands. "Yes, Jerry, please now let him answer."

Michael continued, determined not to let anything else distract him. "Christina, after everything is settled, would you do me the honor of becoming my wife?"

She heard a barrage of comments come in again.

"What?"

"Boy, have you lost your mind?"

"You ain't takin my niece!"

"Mary, help me get my knife. I'm gone cut him."

All except Uncle Carl, to whom he'd mentioned his plan, had expressed their disapproval.

"I would like to court you for a while. We'll do things right first before we start to plan."

Everyone started putting in their comments again as she heard more knee slaps and cursing. Uncle Jerry was the biggest offender of them all, changing his opinion in a matter of seconds and adjusting his pants pocket. He had to be told several times to sit down. My family, Christina thought. He wants to marry into a crazy, unconventional and sometimes irrational family. The man must truly be in love with me.

"Are you alright, Christina?" Michael asked with a concerned expression on his face.

"Yes, I'm fine. Uncle Bill, Uncle Jerry, please let me answer." She gave him her full attention. Her heart was beating fast inside her chest.

"Michael, are you sure about this?"

"Yes, I'm sure. I've never felt this way about anyone in my life."

She nodded her acceptance of his answer. "I need to speak to my family. Can you give me a minute?"

"Yes, take all the time you need," he said, drawing her hand to his lips. "Mrs. Davis, may I use your restroom?"

"Sure. The bathroom is outside to your left and make sure you look in the hole first for critters. Yesterday Jerry got bit somethin' awful on his rear end."

Michael's brows rose in question about what she meant by critters in a hole. They waited until he closed the door.

"I don't like this man travelling all the way from Charleston, South Carolina to court our Chrissy. Something ain't right with that picture show," Bill said.

"Bill, you were the one making fun of Chrissy before she left; now all of a sudden it's our Chrissy. You got some nerve," Mary exclaimed, chastising her brother.

"I know. I was wrong for that. I'm glad she ain't with that no good Lew Harris."

"I'm glad you finally admitted it."

Christina looked at her mother. The evening's events were playing out alright, but she wanted to know what her mother thought of everything. Her opinion meant more than anyone in the room and she didn't think she could go through with the courtship if her mother didn't agree.

"Mama, what do you think?"

"It seems like the young man is quite smitten with you."

"Yes, he is. Michael is a wonderful man."

"Do you feel the same way about him?"

Christina walked towards her and kneeled down. "Yes, I do. I'm in love with him and have been for quite some time."

"If your father had felt like that towards me years ago I would've never had those issues with him. I loved your father so much."

Christina held her hands. "I know you did, Mama."

"I don't want you to end up like me, Chrissy, heartbroken and alone." She didn't know what to say to that and started to rub her hands in comfort. The tears came next as they fell and settled like small pools of water on her lap. She was crying not only for herself, but for her mother's pain as well. Mary Davis worked hard for her children's benefit, asking nothing in return, and yet her heart remained broken all these years. She deserved everything good in life; Christina just wished she could give it to her.

"I want you to have a good life, Chrissy. I realize what I did may have been a mistake, and I should never have sent you away like I did. You're my baby and I'm sorry." They hugged each other tightly, letting go of past hurt and pain shared by both. Christina's tears spilled onto her mother's shoulder while her arms wrapped around her waist. She realized her mother had been her biggest supporter even when she was going through difficult growing pains in her life. "It's okay, Mama. It's okay."

They stayed in that embrace until Michael came back. Her mother released her from her arms and wiped the tears from her eyes. "Young man, you have my blessing to court my daughter. One of my brothers will give his answer in place of my late husband. Bill?"

Uncle Bill stepped closer to Michael and stared for a couple of seconds before shaking his hand. "Young man you have my permission. Treat my niece with care, you understand?"

"Yes, sir, I will."

"Well now that's settled, where are you staying, Mr. Rose?"

"I'm not sure. I didn't think that far ahead before coming up here."

"Jerry, let Mr. Rose stay with you. Michael and Christina's courtship can maintain respectable distance from your end of the street."

"Ah hell, Mary, I don't know this whippa snappa. He might steal my groundhogs."

"He seems nice, so give him a chance. And those groundhogs haven't been cooked or cleaned yet, Jerry. It'll be alright."

"Well, I hope he likes to wash from a basin and can hold his self on the shitter. Those critters are somethin' awful this time of year."

Mama patted his hand. "He'll be fine."

Uncle Jerry shook his head. "His ass gone hurt if he don't look down in that whole."

Christina walked outside with Michael close behind her. The night sky seemed calm with a few stars peeking from the heavens. A perfect ending to an otherwise exciting afternoon. "So where do we start?" she asked.

He placed his arms around her waist. "We can start by first giving me a proper introduction to Isaac. I'll need to meet my future son first and foremost."

"How did I get so lucky to meet you, Mr. Rose?"

"I think I'm the lucky one here. I came away with a family to love me just as much as I love them. I'm the luckiest man alive." He leaned in for a kiss, wanting to taste the sweetness of her lips before they departed for the evening.

The screen porch flew open. "You gonna be a dead hog if you don't get your hands off my niece. Mary, he bein nasty!" Uncle Jerry hollered as he came down the steps to stand in front of them.

Jumping back from one another and laughing, they knew their touches would have to wait till they could steal some time during their courtship.

"Now how am I gonna babysit two horny grown-ups?"

Christina watched as Uncle Jerry ushered Michael down the road. She knew her family would make sure they did things right before the wedding. And she had the feeling life was going to get much better from here on.

Chapter 22

James Island was abuzz with the news of Michael Rose and Christina Davis' nuptials. The procession of cars that followed one another into the area gave every indication folks were excited to see the long-time bachelor finally settling down as they pulled into a finely decorated landscape of white and coral roses. The gazebo placed in the center of the courtyard was surrounded by white flowing fabric with candlelit pieces at its base and a seven-piece orchestra to the left. The sitting area in front of the gazebo was a sea of white chairs with coral and baby blue fabric, as the guests mingled with one another before the ceremony was to begin.

This journey to South Carolina marked a new beginning for Christina, unlike the first, which was uncertain and had very few expectations. The family was excited and more than willing to lend a helping hand. However, when they finally reached James Island the decorations and food preparations had already been taken care of by several attentive butlers and maids. This was just fine with the family, as they quickly made use of the house accommodations, including the liquor. The men settled in the study, where they saluted the soon-to-be married couple with glasses of brandy, while the women gathered in one of the upstairs suites. They were each trying to make sure Christina's dress was assembled in all the right places and the veil was placed on the back of the hair bun at the nape of her neck.

"Christina, I'm truly jealous," Roxanne said. "Not only do you have a very handsome husband but you have the most gorgeous wedding dress I've ever seen."

Christina beamed. "Thank you, Roxy."

"Trust me, honey, he won't care at all about that once he sees your—

"That's enough, Vera," Mary exclaimed, eyeing her sister-in-law.

Only a handful of family members had made the seven-hour trip for the wedding. Uncle Jerry had to be told several times he couldn't go fishing in his new tailor made suit, and Bill kept questioning just how much money Michael's family had because no black person could ever afford the mansion they were currently staying in. They were all here, including her grandmother, who was the first person in the car leaving Virginia that morning. Apparently she needed a real vacation for the year. Christina got up from the chair and peeked outside to the courtyard. She spotted Michael whispering to the preacher while his groomsmen were straightening their ties for the ceremony.

Their courtship had lasted a very long six months. Michael stayed with Uncle Jerry and came every day to see her. It was like clockwork. Breakfast was always with the family; then at twelve o'clock Uncle Jerry's truck would pull up in front of Mama's yard. She could hear him on some occasions chastising Michael about respecting her virtue and the importance of family unity. He was definitely serious about his chaperone duties, and he always insisted they stand apart to keep the gossip at bay. Michael stole a couple kisses here and there, but only when Uncle Jerry started talking about Patsy, which drew his attention elsewhere.

As the ceremony started, Christina felt like the happiest woman on earth. She was content with her life now, knowing that she was blessed with a wonderful man by her side. Their vows were spoken to each other with promises of love and commitment, honor, and unselfishness. During the reception Michael wrapped his arms possessively around her and kissed the top of her forehead.

"And how are you, Mrs. Rose?"

"I'm doing quite well, Mr. Rose."

"You know I never got to escort you to your coming out party." He chuckled, remembering the first time he danced with her at the social luncheon.

"Those dance lessons were right on time don't you think?"

Christina laughed. "Before those lessons, I recall stepping on your feet so many times you stopped dancing in the middle of the song."

"That was because I wanted to hold you in front of all those men vying for your attention."

She swatted his arm playfully. "It was because you didn't want me trampling your feet. I meant to ask you if they were okay, but you didn't seem to mind."

"Oh, I did mind. Especially when I saw you dance with Mr. Wright. Poor man, I knew from the wincing expression his feet were taking a beating as well."

She punched him playfully again and gazed into his eyes. "You held me quite tightly then too, sir."

"Like I'm doing now," he murmured.

"Yes, like you're doing right now."

Michael looked around at the smiling faces of his guests and thought this was the perfect time to exit the room while everyone was preoccupied.

"You know, Mrs. Rose, we can retire early if you wish."

She lightly touched his collared shirt. The thought of his hands on her body made her heartbeat quicken its pace. "I don't think our guests would mind if we went in a bit early."

He took her hand and led her towards the staircase. They made their excuses for leaving, receiving hugs and kisses and well wishes from their guests. The bedroom upstairs was decorated with small candles on the window sill and dresser. Red and pink rose petals covered the massive bed with a trail leading from the hallway to the bedroom. She felt his kisses on her neck as they walked into the room.

"What have I done to deserve a wonderful man like you?"

"I think I should be the one to ask that particular question. I'll be the first to admit you changed my life in more ways than one," he continued as his arm came around her, one holding her waist, the other moving slowly upward towards her hair, releasing the pins that held the perfectly coiffed chignon in place. She saw the passion in his eyes and felt the faintness of his lips when he added, "For the rest of my life, I'll show you just what you mean to me."

"Michael, I…."

But his mouth had already claimed hers, and with his hand now pressing firmly against her back she was assuredly not going anywhere. Going slowly was a first for him but he wanted her to remember this evening for the rest of their lives and he knew she wanted the same. He kissed her deeply, his tongue caressing and enticing, conjuring every carnal desire she withheld.

Goodness, did he know how to kiss. Her arms were wrapping around his neck, gripping his shoulders when his tongue went on its assault of her mouth, demanding, plunging in and out, and giving her encouragement to explore his mouth in return. This new erotic sensation was something she'd never experienced before, a disruption to her senses that consumed every fiber of her being and left nothing to her imagination except the man in front of her.

Michael was enthralled with this woman, for he never had someone want to give as much affection as his new bride was currently giving. He suckled on her lower chin, and inhaled the fragrance from her neck, the sweet scent increasing his passion by the minute.

"Christina," he whispered, "I think my finesse is slowly fading."

"How is that possible?" she asked.

It took every ounce of strength he had to answer her. "I just want this night to be as memorable for you as it will be for me."

She could feel his tense muscles underneath the white shirt, and, slowly, undid each button to reveal more of his solid powerful frame. His chest rose intimately in sync against hers and she wanted to close her eyes and caress that very part of him which she'd already claimed.

"It will be, Michael," she whispered, "for both of us."

His gorgeous brown eyes changed from a light cinnamon color to almond brown, the telling signs of his passion growing with each darker shade. He lifted her effortlessly into his arms and carried her to bed. The feel of him, his intoxicating scent flaring against her nostrils, his heat enveloping her, lashed at her senses with infinite pleasure.

"Michael, I want more."

Christina was surprised at the brazenness in her own voice, and felt the vibration coursing through his body or was it her own trembling causing the sudden eruptions?

She was holding on to his neck entwining her fingers in the curly hair along his nape, so it wasn't complicated for him to undo the ties at the back of her wedding dress. He pulled the dress from her body with one swift tug while he held her with one arm, releasing a tidal wave within her soul that had her moaning into his mouth.

He laid her gently on the bed, careful not to crush her with his weight, but Christina didn't notice. The need to feel him inside of her grew by the minute. They discarded the rest of their clothing, never taking their eyes off one another, savoring the joy of finally being able to touch the most intimate parts of the other person.

Michael shifted his weight again, poised just above the opening to her womanhood before burying himself deeply inside her. Her whole body seemed to welcome his with fervor as she matched every stroke, rise, and fall of his body. The burst of fire that exploded from that moment was so intense, she felt elevated from her core, encircling him, pulsating against him, every caress matched by his own.

He'd taken his pleasure, but not without first giving her what she needed. The shuddering spasms seemed to last well past his climax, so much she'd left red nail marks on his upper arms. He kissed the center of her neck, unaware of his injuries, only arrogantly mindful of the blissfully happy woman beneath him.

When Christina finally was aware of her surroundings, she was being held with sweet tenderness while her head rested underneath his chin. He caressed her half exposed body atop the damp sheets that had just experienced there magnificent lovemaking.

"Do you think anyone cares we're gone?"

"If they did they're probably toasting our lovemaking even as we speak."

"I can't imagine your side of the family doing that; on my side, a different story."

"You'd be surprised at how forthright my family can be sometimes."

"I think I'm going to get used to them either way."

"Indeed you will."

They decided a nice bath would be pleasant before putting on their nightclothes just in case they were interrupted for the evening. The urge to make love again was proving overpowering as they each washed one another from head to toe until they were both sated and lying beneath the covers, wrapped in each other's arms.

"Knock knock. Someone wanted to see his parents before they turned in for the night."

Michael opened the door to find his mother-in-law standing with Isaac taking him from her arms. "You wanted to be with your old man, did you?"

"Yes, he did. He noticed you two were absent from the festivities still going on."

"People are still here?"

"Yes, indeed. Uncle Jerry is passed out downstairs and hugging a statue of a stone dog; Vera is giving sex advice to your sister; and everyone else is dancing the night away."

They all laughed. It seemed everyone was getting better acquainted with one another, with the exception of Uncle Jerry.

Michael placed Isaac between him and his mother on the bed. The little boy grabbed a fistful of sheet and tried to stuff it in his mouth, his squeals of laughter reverberating throughout the room.

"Where do you think you too will end up living?" Mary asked.

Michael looked at his son, his chocolate eyes twinkling like his mother's. "I think we can spend time in both places if that's okay with you, Mrs. Davis?"

"That would be perfectly fine. I wouldn't mind having my grand-baby around at all."

"And what do we tell Aunt Bessie?"

"I think she'll be as happy as I am right now," Michael said.

The next day they said their goodbyes to their families, each promising to visit as soon as possible. An hour later they were officially settled in Michael's home, the cool South Carolina breeze welcoming them to their new life together. Michael gathered Christina into his arms and kissed her. They sat side by side on the welcome bench of their new home with Isaac nestled happily between them. They were all eager to start a new life and future together as a family.

www.ingramcontent.com/pod-product-compliance
Lightning Source LLC
Chambersburg PA
CBHW071118170626
46809CB00002B/410